Praise f

T0012375

"This cozy con   nasty
crime, shady sus   g, and
lots of books!"   —RT Book Reviews

"Diverting entertainment. . . . An engaging story line, an
intrepid heroine. . . . Good for lovers of intrigue."
—*Richmond Times-Dispatch*

"Lorna Barrett never fails to offer a suspenseful cozy mystery. . . . Entertaining, highly enjoyable."
—Cozy Mystery Book Reviews

"Fans of Carolyn Hart and Denise Swanson, rejoice! . . .
This first-rate cozy artfully blends crime, cuisine, and even
bookselling in a cheerful, witty, well-plotted puzzler."
—Julia Spencer-Fleming, *New York Times* bestselling author of
Through the Evil Days

"A mystery bookstore in a sleepy New England town, a cat
named Miss Marple, a nasty murder, and a determined
heroine. . . . Delightful. . . . Everything a cozy lover could
want and more. Bravo!"
—Leann Sweeney, national bestselling author of
The Cat, the Vagabond and the Victim

"Lorna Barrett's new cozy creation . . . has it all: wonderful
old books, quirky characters, a clever mystery, and a cat
named Miss Marple!"
—Roberta Isleib, author of *Asking for Murder*

"Tightly plotted and paced to keep you turning the pages,
this series is indeed getting better with each book."
—Gumshoe Review

"Charming. . . . An engaging whodunit."

—*Publishers Weekly*

"[A] delightful, and often funny, mystery series about a town that lives and dies by the love of books."

—Kings River Life Magazine

Berkley Prime Crime titles by Lorna Barrett

MURDER IS BINDING
BOOKMARKED FOR DEATH
BOOKPLATE SPECIAL
CHAPTER & HEARSE
SENTENCED TO DEATH
MURDER ON THE HALF SHELF
NOT THE KILLING TYPE
BOOK CLUBBED
A FATAL CHAPTER
TITLE WAVE
A JUST CLAUSE
POISONED PAGES
A KILLER EDITION
HANDBOOK FOR HOMICIDE

Anthologies

MURDER IN THREE VOLUMES

HANDBOOK FOR HOMICIDE

Lorna Barrett

BERKLEY PRIME CRIME
New York

BERKLEY PRIME CRIME
Published by Berkley
An imprint of Penguin Random House LLC
penguinrandomhouse.com

Copyright © 2020 by Penguin Random House LLC
Excerpt from *A Deadly Deletion* by Lorna Barrett copyright © 2021 by
Penguin Random House LLC

Penguin Random House supports copyright. Copyright fuels creativity, encourages
diverse voices, promotes free speech, and creates a vibrant culture. Thank you for buying
an authorized edition of this book and for complying with copyright laws by not
reproducing, scanning, or distributing any part of it in any form without permission.
You are supporting writers and allowing Penguin Random House to continue to
publish books for every reader.

BERKLEY and the BERKLEY & B colophon are registered trademarks and
BERKLEY PRIME CRIME is a trademark of Penguin Random House LLC.

ISBN: 9781984802767

Berkley Prime Crime hardcover edition / July 2020
Berkley Prime Crime mass-market edition / June 2021

Printed in the United States of America
3   5   7   9   10   8   6   4   2

This is a work of fiction. Names, characters, places, and incidents either are the product
of the author's imagination or are used fictitiously, and any resemblance to actual persons,
living or dead, business establishments, events, or locales is entirely coincidental.

PUBLISHER'S NOTE: The recipes contained in this book are to be followed exactly
as written. The publisher is not responsible for your specific health or allergy needs that
may require medical supervision. The publisher is not responsible for any adverse reactions
to the recipes contained in this book.

If you purchased this book without a cover, you should be aware that this book is stolen
property. It was reported as "unsold and destroyed" to the publisher, and neither the author
nor the publisher has received any payment for this "stripped book."

For Frank and his enduring patience

CAST OF CHARACTERS

Tricia Miles, owner of Haven't Got a Clue vintage mystery bookstore

Angelica Miles, Tricia's older sister, owner of the Cookery and the Booked for Lunch café, and half owner of the Sheer Comfort Inn. Her alter ego is Nigela Ricita, the mysterious developer who has been pumping money and jobs into the village of Stoneham.

Pixie Poe, Tricia's assistant manager at Haven't Got a Clue

Mr. Everett, Tricia's employee at Haven't Got a Clue

Antonio Barbero, the public face of Nigela Ricita Associates; Angelica's son

Ginny Wilson-Barbero, Tricia's former assistant; wife of Antonio Barbero

Grace Harris-Everett, Mr. Everett's wife

Grant Baker, chief of the Stoneham Police Department

Marshall Cambridge, owner of the Armchair Tourist and Tricia's friend with benefits

Russ Smith, owner of the *Stoneham Weekly News*; president of the Stoneham Chamber of Commerce

Nikki Brimfield, ex-wife of Russ Smith; owner of the Patisserie bakery

Roger Sykes, new manager of the Patisserie

Hank Curtis, leader of a homeless encampment

Joe King, ex-sailor, now homeless

Susan Morris, murder victim

Kimberly Herbert, daughter of Susan Morris

Terry McDonald, owner of All Heroes comic-book store

Donna North, cake decorator and candymaker; owner of the Sweet As Can Be chocolate store

HANDBOOK
FOR HOMICIDE

ONE

It had been a quiet ride back from Logan International Airport on that beautiful mid-September morning. Tricia Miles glanced across the seat to take in her chauffeur. She and Marshall Cambridge, her more-or-less significant other, had gotten off an Aer Lingus red-eye flight to Boston some four hours before. She hadn't slept a wink, and the drudgery of going through customs, collecting their luggage, and then retrieving Marshall's car from the long-term parking lot had left her feeling sluggish and drained. All she wanted to do was go home, pet her cat, and sleep.

She'd known the trip wasn't going to be a vacation. Of course, she enjoyed the Emerald Isle's countryside, meeting the people, and the food and drink, but she also had to depend on the other members of the tour—and most of them elderly—for company. It was a working vacation for Marshall, who'd teamed up with Milford Travel to lead the tour. As expected, he spent more time playing fixer for everything that could go wrong—from lost luggage to motion-sick passengers on the bus that transported the group from Dublin to Belfast and back again.

As she gazed at the scenery that zoomed past the passenger-side window, Tricia wondered if she was ready to analyze how she felt about the tour—and, truthfully, her relationship with

Marshall. She'd been avoiding the latter for the past few months. He was a great conversationalist and a man of the world with many wonderful attributes. He was kind to animals, old people, and especially to her. But she wasn't sure she loved him. She hadn't mentioned the L-word, and in the months since they'd started dating, neither had he.

That was actually okay with her, but it seemed to be a topic many people in the village of Stoneham, New Hampshire, where they both lived and worked, wanted to talk about. People like Pixie Poe, the assistant manager at her vintage mystery bookstore, Haven't Got a Clue. People whom she ran into at the local eateries and the coffee shop, and even when out walking her sister's bichon frise, Sarge. Everybody seemed more interested in her relationship with Marshall than she was. Why didn't that raise a red flag?

Because she liked him. Because he wasn't demanding. Because . . . she was pretty sure that this relationship wasn't going to last much longer. Why? There seemed to be a definite lack of passion—on both their parts. That wasn't something she wanted to talk about with family, friends, acquaintances, or, especially, near strangers.

Marshall turned off Route 101 and steered toward Stoneham. For some reason, Tricia thought they'd arrive back in the village a lot earlier in the day, but the digital clock on the Mercedes dashboard said it was almost eleven. Her jet-lagged internal clock told her it was early evening, and her stomach growled to let her know it was ready for sustenance. Her fridge was empty, so she'd either have to hit her sister's retro café, Booked for Lunch, for her midday meal, or open a can of soup, which at that moment seemed like a lot of work. She'd pick the former, but earlier than she and Angelica usually met. She didn't think she could hold out until two o'clock. And after a week of wonderful food that wasn't always healthy, she decided what she really wanted was just a cup of chowder and half a ham-and-cheese sandwich.

"Want to stop for a bite?" Marshall asked, as though reading her mind.

"No, thanks. I'm okay."

He gave her a skeptical glance before turning his gaze back to the road. He'd obviously heard her stomach protest about its empty state.

Familiar landmarks flashed past, and Marshall slowed as they entered the village, making a left-hand turn into the municipal parking lot. He found a spot under a lamppost and pulled his key from the ignition. "Home again, home again."

Tricia offered him a wan smile. "It's almost like we never left."

They got out of the car, and Marshall opened the trunk and retrieved their luggage. They'd both traveled light—just one suitcase each—and Tricia extended the handle on hers and waited until he'd done likewise, then they set off toward their respective homes.

"I had a good time," Marshall said conversationally as they headed down the sun-drenched sidewalk.

"Yes. It was very pleasant," Tricia agreed.

They walked in silence for a few paces.

"We should do it again sometime—but without the crowd," Marshall suggested.

"That would be nice."

No passion. Not a speck of passion.

They passed the Have a Heart romance bookshop, but Tricia's gaze didn't stray toward the big display window, where, no doubt, its proprietress was standing at the cash desk. Tricia and Joyce Widman hadn't spoken to each other since June. That was okay. And she fought the temptation to look inside the Patisserie, Stoneham's only bakery, too. Not that its owner, Nikki Brimfield, would be in attendance. She'd found a manager and blown off the village of her birth, leaving her soon-to-be ex-husband and toddler son behind while hoping to win a big, televised baking competition in Los Angeles. Rumor had it that she'd also shacked up with TV chef Larry Andrews. Fine. They deserved each other.

They passed the Cookery, Tricia's sister's cookbook and

gadget shop, but it was only the manager, June, behind the register. She waved, and Tricia gave her a smile in return. Then they paused in front of Haven't Got a Clue.

"This is it," Marshall said.

"Yes."

He leaned forward and gave her a light kiss on the lips. "Until later?" he asked hopefully.

"I'll give you a call," she promised.

He reached for her hand, squeezed it, and gave her a wistful smile. "Until then."

He gave her another brief kiss, which she was sure was witnessed by her staff, and she turned and opened the door. The little bell jingled merrily as she entered.

"Welcome home!" Pixie squealed with delight, rounded the cash desk, and threw her arms around Tricia. "Did you have a good time? Are you tired? Did you like the food? Did you take a lot of pictures?"

"Slow down," Tricia said, and laughed.

Pixie stood back. "I just made a fresh pot of coffee. Sit down, have some, and tell me all about your trip."

Tricia let out a pained laugh. "I've been sitting for the past two hours."

"Well, then stand and tell me all about it."

"I'd much rather hear about what's been going on here while I've been away," Tricia said, glancing around her store to see that all was well. Her gray long-haired cat, Miss Marple, had apparently been dozing on the big square coffee table in the reader's nook, but she sat at attention and gave a hearty "*Brrrrpt!*" in greeting.

Tricia hurried over to her cat, picked her up, and kissed the top of her head. "Boy, did I miss you." Miss Marple instantly began to purr, and Tricia rubbed her ears, which sent the purrs into overdrive.

"Mr. Everett brought her back this morning," Pixie said.

"Was she any trouble?"

"Not a bit. He took the cash to the bank, but he should be back soon to give you a full report." Pixie's smile faded, which Tricia was quick to notice.

"Hey, your interview with the cable news crew finally hit the airwaves."

"When was that?" Tricia asked.

"About a week after you went on your trip."

"Oh, then I've missed it."

"The cable company ran it every few hours for a couple of days. It must have been a slow news week," Pixie said.

It sure had been. Tricia had recorded the interview nearly a month before. The station had done a series of success stories based on businesses in southern New Hampshire. They'd been desperate to interview the reclusive Nigela Ricita, who'd brought prosperity back to the village, but had to settle on speaking with Antonio Barbero, her general manager. Next up, they contacted Tricia's sister, Angelica, and Tricia had come four or five more rungs down the ladder of success. They'd featured the store as well as Tricia's prized collection of vintage mysteries.

"For about three days, every time I logged in to get my email, the clip would be playing. I'll bet half the state has seen it."

"Everyone but me."

"Rats. I should've taken a video of it from my phone. But don't worry, I'm sure if you Google it, you'll find a link to the report."

"I'll give it a try. Did we see an uptick in business?"

"I'd say a ten percent blip on the weekends. Not bad for this time of year."

"Excellent. Did anything else happen while I was gone?"

"Um, not really," Pixie hedged.

"But?" Tricia coaxed.

"We did have one teeny problem," Pixie said, and squeezed her right thumb and forefinger together as though in reassurance.

"And that was?" Tricia asked, suddenly feeling very tired.

"Um, someone tried to break into the store."

"What? When?" Tricia demanded, setting her cat back down on the coffee table.

"Last weekend. But don't worry: the alarm went off and scared off whoever it was. The security company called me, but I let the cops come and waited until they had a look."

"Was anything damaged?"

"The back door, but I had it fixed and put in a new dead bolt, just in case." She reached into her slacks' pocket and pulled out a single key. "You can add this to your ring. I already gave one to Mr. E and Angelica."

"How did she react about the attempted break-in?" And why hadn't Angelica mentioned it to her in a text or email or when they'd spoken hours earlier when she had returned to the States?

"She thanked me over and over again for taking care of everything. Nothing was taken, and, as a safety measure, I switched the light in the alley from motion detection to having it shine all night once the store is closed."

"Thank you for that."

Pixie waved a hand in dismissal. "It was nothing. Just part of my job. Since just about everybody in town knew you were on vacation and the store was empty, Angelica and I both wondered if someone decided to try to rob the place knowing there was no one in the building."

"Maybe," Tricia agreed. Was she going to feel safe knowing someone had tried to breach her defenses while she'd been away? But then, she had a lock at the bottom of the stairs that led to her loft apartment, and another sturdy dead bolt on the door at the top of the stairs that led directly into her home.

Pixie turned toward the cash desk and retrieved a folded piece of paper. "I've got a copy of the police report. You can look it over when you get the chance."

"Thank you." Tricia opened the paper and saw the typed page of notes on thermal paper—the kind police cruisers have. She would scan a copy and try to make the print darker. She noted Officer Cynthia Pearson had been the one to arrive on the scene after the attempted break-in. She was still on probation after the debacle three months before and had obviously been transferred to the graveyard shift.

"Now, why don't we have that cup of coffee?" Pixie suggested. But before she could move toward the beverage station, the door opened and a couple of women entered the store. "Welcome to Haven't Got a Clue," Pixie said with what sounded like glee. "I'm Pixie. Let me know if you need any help or want suggestions on a new-to-you mystery series you might like to try."

Tricia refolded the report and pocketed it, then grabbed her suitcase, pulled it across the store, and stuffed it into the dumbwaiter, sending it up to the third floor. She stared at the contraption. It could be a possible security breach. The little elevator could probably accommodate a person—if they weren't claustrophobic. There was no lock on the doors to the device that opened to the second and third floors of the building. She'd have to remedy that—and soon. Should she call her contractor, Jim Stark, or was this something Marshall could handle? He seemed pretty handy, but would he be willing to do the job on such short notice—and especially when suffering from jet lag?

She'd have to think about it.

The customers made their choices, and Tricia returned to the front of the store to bag their purchases while Pixie rang up the sale. They bid the women good-bye, and Tricia noticed that the trash bin was full of packing material.

"I meant to empty that right after the mail came," Pixie said, and made a grab for it.

"I can do it."

"No, get that cup of coffee. You deserve it," Pixie encouraged.

Yes, Tricia did. So, while Pixie took the bin to the back of the building and unlocked to the door to the alley, Tricia pulled out one of the ceramic cups reserved for her and her staff and poured the coffee, doctoring it with just a little milk. Pixie had obviously stopped at either the Patisserie or the Coffee Bean and had bought some of Mr. Everett's favorite thumbprint cookies, and she placed a couple on a paper napkin, then took it and the cup to the reader's nook. But before she could sit down to enjoy her treat, the back door opened, and Pixie stood there for a long moment.

"Uh, Tricia. Could you come outside for a minute?"

Tricia heaved a sigh. Now what? She wrapped the cookies in the napkin and placed a magazine over the top so as not to tempt Miss Marple, who was sitting in Sphinx fashion, and headed for the back of the shop.

As she neared her friend and employee, she noted that Pixie's face had paled, which was something of a feat, considering how much makeup she habitually wore. "Is something wrong?"

"Um, maybe. I kind of want your opinion on something."

Tricia took the lead and exited the store. As soon as her foot hit the first step to the alley, her nose was assaulted with an overpowering odor. "What is that?" she asked.

Pixie didn't answer and instead said, "Um . . . I was about to toss the trash into the dumpster when I saw . . ."

Maybe it was the jet lag, but Tricia didn't immediately catch her drift. Had someone tossed a dead rat or a raccoon into the store's dumpster?

Tricia trundled down the stairs and looked into the grimy metal container. The smell was unpleasant, and she was about to turn away, when she noticed the shoe. But it wasn't just a scuffed-up penny loafer; it was a scuffed-up penny loafer that enveloped a sock-covered foot.

Stoneham's police chief, Grant Baker, turned his stern gaze on Tricia. "How long did it take after your return home before you found your latest stiff?"

"Hey," Pixie protested. "Have some respect. That's a dead lady you're talking about."

Baker ignored her and continued to stare at Tricia. Mr. Everett had returned from the bank and stood a discreet distance from the trio, looking quite upset, but Tricia had to attend to Baker before she could reassure her friend and employee.

"For once, it wasn't me who found a corpse. It was Pixie," Tricia said, feeling just a little irritated.

Baker turned his attention to Pixie. "And?"

"Well, I was taking out the trash when I smelled that awful smell," she said rather sheepishly.

"And did you know what it was?"

"Yeah. I've smelled that stink before."

"And what was the occasion?" Baker asked, his tone just a tad threatening.

"When I was an EMT. More than once we were called out to a crime scene only to find a sti—" She stopped herself. "A deceased person." She shook her head. "That poor lady. Stuffed in a dumpster."

"How do you know she didn't just crawl in there and die?" Baker demanded. "And how do you know it's a woman?"

"It was obviously a woman's shoe," Tricia said flatly.

She looked out the back door, where a couple of officers were unwinding a roll of yellow crime scene tape.

"Do you have any idea who the deceased is?"

Tricia shook her head and glanced at Pixie, who seemed to squirm. Baker's gaze swiveled her way, too.

"Um, maybe."

Baker raised an eyebrow.

"I kind of recognized the shoe," she admitted.

"And why was that?" Baker asked.

"Because . . . because it used to be mine."

"Really?" Tricia asked, surprised.

"I think the dead person might be Susan Morris."

Baker frowned. Tricia didn't recognize the name.

"Why was she wearing your shoes?" the chief asked.

"Because I gave 'em to her. Susan and me were kind of acquaintances."

"What does 'kind of' mean?" Baker pressed.

"I would see her at the laundromat in Milford sometimes—this was before me and Fred got our house here in the village—and we talked."

"What else do you know about her?" Baker asked, and Tricia found herself leaning in to listen.

"She lived in her car."

"She what?" Tricia asked, taken aback.

"It was no big deal—at least, not to Susan."

"Why would she have to live in her car?" Tricia asked.

"Because she couldn't afford an apartment. But she did okay. She paid her car insurance, had a PO box for her mail, and stowed everything she needed in her car."

Tricia thought of all the stuff she owned—or, rather, how much it owned her—and couldn't imagine a life without a clean bed, food in the fridge, and a real roof over her head. "How could she survive living like that?"

Pixie shrugged, as though the question didn't have much merit. "It's just what you do when you're broke. I lived in my car for six months between stints in the big house," she admitted.

Tricia cringed inwardly. Pixie had a criminal record longer than both of her arms. Did she really need to remind Baker of that when she'd just found a dead body? Her crimes were not violent in nature. The former lady of the night was no doubt going to be in Baker's sights as the prime suspect in the death. That's just the way cops roll. Tricia looked in Baker's direction. He didn't seem surprised by Pixie's revelation.

"Did you know this woman lived in her car?" Tricia asked Baker.

"Yeah, but we tried to keep her out of the village once the sun set. It sets a bad example. We don't want others taking up residence just anywhere. I'd even asked the board of selectmen to enact a policy, but it hasn't come up for a vote yet."

"Did you do anything to help her? Perhaps suggest she try to get help from Social Services?"

"That's not my job."

"Well, maybe it ought to be. Then perhaps a homeless person wouldn't have ended up dead behind my store." Tricia turned back to Pixie. "Tell me, how did this poor woman stay . . . fresh?"

"She had a membership at the gym in Milford. You can do most of your business there. Of course, she also had a bucket in her car for—"

Baker cleared his throat. "When was the last time you saw the deceased?"

"Obviously less than an hour ago."

"I mean alive," Baker said flatly.

"See or talk to?" Pixie asked.

"Both."

Pixie looked thoughtful. "Lately I've seen her walking around the village during the day. She'd wave to me from the sidewalk and I'd wave back. Talk to? Maybe a month or so ago."

"And exactly where was that?"

Pixie's eyes narrowed, and when she spoke next, her voice was flat. "The grocery store in Milford. It was in the produce section. In front of the heads of lettuce."

"Pixie . . ." Tricia warned.

Pixie blinked innocently—that is, until she caught sight of Baker's annoyed expression and lowered her gaze.

"I wonder if Ms. Morris's death might have anything to do with the attempted break-in of my store over the weekend," Tricia speculated aloud.

Baker turned his ire on her. "No."

"How can you say that?"

"Just because you read a lot of mysteries—"

"And police procedurals," Tricia broke in.

"—doesn't mean you know what you're talking about when it comes to real crime."

Tricia folded her arms across her chest. When it came to solving crimes, so far her record was unblemished. Still, she refrained from pointing that out. Since she'd ended her relationship with the chief several years before, the two of them hadn't exactly been friends. Oh, he could be friendly—if he thought she had information he might need—but those times seemed to be coming with less frequency.

"How long do you think it will be before the medical examiner comes to remove the body?" Tricia asked.

"It depends on how busy she is and what other cases her office is handling."

Tricia sighed. Bad as she felt for poor Susan Morris, the idea of her body further decaying from the heat of the day in the grimy old dumpster was going to be unpleasant for everyone, including the poor officers who were assigned to the scene—although, looking out the back door, she noted that two of them now wore masks. They'd come prepared and had no doubt dabbed a little Vicks VapoRub on them to help cover the odor.

"Since the crime scene isn't technically in my store, can we continue doing business?"

"That's rather cold of you, isn't it, Tricia?" Baker asked, his eyes narrowing.

Tricia sighed. "I didn't know the woman. I've been away for two weeks and I'm jet-lagged. I haven't had a decent meal in over twenty hours. I'd like nothing more than to—" Tricia's ringtone sounded. She retrieved her phone from her slacks pocket and checked the number. Angelica. She ignored it. "You haven't answered my question, Chief."

Baker frowned. "I suppose so. But keep this back door shut and locked. I don't want any gawkers interfering with our investigation—and that includes the two of you," he said none too kindly.

Tricia's phone pinged. A text message from Angelica. *What's going on behind your store?*

Tricia ignored it. "Thank you." She gestured toward the back exit, and the chief left the building. Tricia closed and locked the door, noting that there were several flies making circuits around the store. Mr. Everett was at the ready with a fly swatter and began to chase after them, with Miss Marple joining in the game and following him around the shop.

"I guess it's a good thing business has been slow today," Pixie said at last.

Tricia nodded.

Pixie sighed. "Poor Susan. She could never seem to catch a break."

"Did she have any family?"

Pixie nodded. "A daughter."

"And she let her mother live in a car?" Tricia asked, aghast.

Pixie shrugged. "Maybe she didn't know. And not everybody cares about their family like you and Angelica do—especially letting people like me and Mr. E into your lives."

That was true. Tricia's own mother was a prime example.

"Speaking of Angelica, I've ignored a call and a text. I'd better get back to her before she comes charging ov—" But Tricia didn't get to finish the sentence, because her sister actually did charge through the door. Perhaps *charge* wasn't the word: *hobbled* was more accurate because of the crutches that supported her.

"Tricia! Why are you ignoring me?" she called, distraught.

"No 'Hello, welcome home'?" Then the sight of the crutches sank in and she saw Angelica's right foot encased in a bulky boot. "What happened to your foot?"

But Angelica didn't answer and tottered over to stand in front of her sister, dumped one of her crutches, threw her free arm around Tricia, and pulled her into an awkward hug. "Welcome home." She pulled back. "Now, what's going on? June texted me and said there were police cruisers behind your door, as well as crime tape. Don't tell me you've found yet another body?"

"*I* didn't."

Pixie waved a hand, looking sheepish. "Um, this time it was me."

TWO

The Brookview Inn's private dining room's elegant décor and the soft but cheerful classical music issuing from cunningly concealed speakers worked its magic, and for the first time in what seemed like days, Tricia actually felt herself relax . . . just a little. She brushed past the brocade-upholstered wingback chair to gaze out the room's window, which overlooked the inn's grassy frontage. Already a few leaves had fallen. It would be winter before she knew it.

Tricia had planned to retreat to her apartment, eat something simple, and maybe take a nap, but Chief Baker insisted that she stick around her shop until Susan Morris's body had been removed from the premises. By then it was nearly three o'clock, and she was dismayed to find that the county's tech team had emptied everything from the big, rusty dumpster. They'd been dressed in protective hooded bunny-suit coveralls and respirators—enough gear to protect them from the plague. Tricia only hoped that by the time she came back to her store they would have returned everything they deemed actual garbage back inside the dumpster for the trash men to pick up the next day.

Angelica had stuck around, too, taking up residence in the reader's nook, but the sisters hadn't had much time to catch up on things. Once she was cleared to leave, Tricia retrieved her car and drove the two of them to the Brookview for an early supper.

The Brookview's kitchen was officially closed until the dinner hour, but no one said no to Angelica. The fact that she owned the place, albeit not all that widely known, had a lot to do with it. Her son, Antonio Barbero, who managed the inn, had personally led his mother and Tricia to the private dining room and promised that their standard order of martinis would be delivered momentarily. Of course, not many people knew about their relationship, either—and that was just the way Angelica wanted it.

Tricia stood by the opened window that overlooked the inn's neat front garden. It still looked pretty, even though the official first day of fall was only days away. A movement to her right caused her to turn. Angelica sat on one of the upholstered wingback chairs with her right leg elevated on a small stool that didn't match the décor, probably something Antonio had found and had left in the room to accommodate his mother. Tricia noticed her sister's worried gaze upon her.

"I met her, you know."

Tricia blinked. "What?"

"Susan Morris. I met her at the day spa when we were hiring." She meant her latest business venture—this under her own name and not the Nigela Ricita Associates umbrella, which Antonio helped manage.

"What job was she interested in?"

"Anything she could get. She had no cosmetology experience, but she knew we'd have laundry and need cleaning services, but Randy had already contracted for those jobs. In retrospect, I guess maybe she was looking for a free place to shower." Tricia had already told her about Susan's living arrangement.

"Maybe," Tricia said as her gaze fell to her shoes—shoes she'd put on at the hotel in Dublin what seemed like way too many hours before.

"You're awfully quiet," Angelica said.

"I feel like . . . like I should be more upset about that poor woman's death. She probably died right outside my shop, and I asked Grant if we could continue doing business for the day. He told me I was cold."

"You look tired. Really tired. And why not? How long has it been since you've slept?"

"A day . . . probably longer. I don't think I could even calculate it."

"Once you've had something to eat, I'll take you home and tuck you in. Well, I would if I could. Up and down the stairs once a day is about all I can manage right now. In fact, I'm not supposed to do stairs if I can help it."

"With everything going on at the shop, you haven't told me what happened to your foot."

Angelica lowered her head and her voice. "Bunion surgery."

"Surgery?" Tricia repeated, just a little shrilly. It all made sense. Angelica had been caught wearing sneakers more than once during the summer, and she'd begun to wear shorter heels. Since the sisters had been reunited some six years before, Angelica usually towered over Tricia because of her footwear.

"Why didn't you tell me? You know I would have canceled my trip to Ireland to take care of you."

"That's exactly why I didn't tell you. I wanted you to have fun and relax."

"You were hoping I'd have a wonderful time with Marshall and maybe get engaged?" Tricia asked accusingly.

"I don't know about that. I mean, if you did, who would I spend happy hour with?"

Tricia managed a smile.

"You need to decompress from your trip. And, honestly, Antonio and Ginny have been so helpful. And June has been a dear, too."

"Did you swear Pixie and Mr. Everett to secrecy, too?"

"Of course. And they've been angels. Mr. Everett has been taking Sarge for walks, and Grace came over with a lovely bouquet and a casserole, too. And I've got a little knee scooter so I can stand for a while and not put pressure on my foot, so I'm good to go. Antonio even brought over a transport chair from the Brookview, although Sofia has had more fun playing with it than I've actually used it."

"How long are you liable to be laid up?"

"Well, that's a good question. Anywhere from six weeks to six months."

"Six months?" Tricia repeated in disbelief.

"The surgical part is six to eight weeks, but the swelling might not go down for four to six months. And before that, I'll be scheduled for the other foot. And worse—worst of all—I won't be able to wear heels until probably next summer."

"If you ask me, heels are what got you into this situation."

"But my stilettos make me look—and more importantly, feel—beautiful. Now I'll be ugly and have to wear flats."

"Hey, *I* wear flats," Tricia protested, "and I resent being called ugly!"

"I didn't say you were ugly. But one can't show off one's shapely legs in flats."

"Start wearing slacks," Tricia advised. "When do you ditch that boot?"

"If I'm lucky, in a week. But then I will have to wear a brace."

"Slacks!" Tricia sang.

"I got my stitches out yesterday. Do you want to have a look?"

Tricia stifled a groan. Why was it that surgery patients always seemed to want to show off their scars? "Why not?" she said, and helped Angelica take off the boot and remove the compression anklet. Angelica's foot was still swollen, but not as badly as Tricia had imagined. The puckered skin from the incision was only about two inches long. Tricia wasn't grossed out. She'd read about far more graphic, sometimes horrific injuries in some of the books she carried in her own store.

"It looks like it's healing nicely."

"I'm supposed to start physical therapy soon. Any chance you could take me? I'd hate to keep imposing on Mr. Everett and everyone else."

But imposing on Tricia was okay? Then again, what were sisters for?

"I'm sure I can be away from my store for an hour or so."

"Oh, good. The surgeon ran me through it, and . . . um, I know some people have an aversion when it comes to feet, but I'm not sure I'm going to be able to reach down and do the exercises myself. I looked at a video online, and you need to grasp your foot with both hands."

"Could you settle your foot on your opposite knee and do it?"

"I guess," Angelica said, not sounding at all sure.

Tricia sighed. "I suppose I could learn."

"Oh, you are the best sister in the world."

Yes, she was.

Angelica guided Tricia through the process of rewrapping her foot and securing the boot, and then Tricia took out the bottle of hand sanitizer she kept in her purse, rubbing a dollop around her hands and fingers. She could tell from Angelica's expression that she wanted to talk about something that had nothing to do with bunions or Susan Morris's death.

"Why don't you tell me all about your vacation," Angelica urged.

Tricia wasn't sure she wanted to discuss that subject but was saved when a knock on the door caused the sisters to look up, and Antonio reentered with a round tray with two martinis. Since the restaurant was between shifts, he'd probably made the drinks himself. He was a pretty good bartender, so she had no worries the martinis would be too weak or too strong.

Antonio set white cocktail napkins embossed with the inn's name on the table between the chairs, then set down the glasses. "The sous-chef can whip you up just about anything you'd like," he said, his slight Italian accent acting as a soothing balm.

"What would you like?" Angelica asked Tricia.

Tricia thought about the poor woman in the kitchen, who was trying to get everything ready for the dinner service. She probably didn't relish the idea of cooking a couple of meals when she needed to put together her *mise en place*. "I'm really not very hungry. How about some salad greens with a little protein . . . maybe a hard-boiled egg?"

"Are you sure?" Antonio asked.

"And maybe a roll?"

He gave her a reassuring smile before turning to Angelica. "And you, Mama?"

"I'll have the same, thank you."

Antonio nodded. "I will be back soon." He turned and left the room, closing the door behind him.

Tricia reached for her glass, took a sip, and sank back in her chair, kicking off her shoes. "I needed this."

"I'll bet," Angelica said and picked up her glass. She took a sip. "You were just about to tell me all about your trip to Ireland."

No, she wasn't, but Tricia supposed her sister wasn't going to let go of the topic.

"It's a beautiful country. Very green."

"I could have learned that from a postcard," Angelica deadpanned.

"It probably wouldn't have reached you for another two weeks."

Angelica waited.

Tricia sat up straighter and took another sip. "The tour was very successful. Everybody seemed to have a wonderful time. There was a lot of singing on the bus. Several couples joined up for dinners and such, and we were all on a first-name basis long before we landed in Boston, with many people vowing to keep in touch." It wouldn't happen, but she had appreciated the camaraderie—especially since it felt like she'd been traveling as a single and not with Marshall. And that was the problem. Of course, she'd predicted it would happen. But Marshall so wanted her to be a part of his big, new adventure, and she'd felt the need to escape

Stoneham and her rather humdrum life, if only for a fort-night. But did she really want to tell Angelica all that?

"Was there time for romance?" Angelica asked, her eyes widening in anticipation.

Tricia's glare just might have scorched. "No."

Angelica frowned. "Did you bring back any souvenirs?"

"Just for Sofia." Sofia was Antonio's toddler daughter. "Why? Did you want a bottle of Irish whiskey? I can get you one of those at the liquor store if you'd like."

Angelica sighed. "No. I prefer gin or wine and you know it." She frowned before going back to her previous topic. "So you and Marshall didn't make any plans for the future?"

"Like what?"

"I don't know . . . perhaps talk about an upcoming trip."

"I don't think we'll be doing that."

"Making plans or maybe changing your living arrange-ments?" she asked hopefully.

"Neither."

"Are you angry with him?"

"No," Tricia admitted. "I knew when I agreed to accom-pany him to Ireland what it would be like. I only hoped I'd be wrong."

"And you weren't."

"It's difficult being right all the time," Tricia admitted with a wry smile.

Angelica frowned. "Are you two through?"

"I honestly don't know. But I wouldn't mind a little breath-ing room, and I wouldn't be surprised if Marshall felt the same way. He's already got a lot of plans for the future that don't include being in Stoneham."

"Do you think he'd sell the Armchair Tourist and move away from here?"

"He likes to travel—a lot more than I do." Tricia sipped her martini. "Can't we talk about something else? Like why you didn't mention to me that someone tried to break into my store while I was gone?"

Angelica eased farther back in the chair. "With every-thing that's been going on, I almost forgot about it. I tried to talk to Chief Baker, but you know he won't give me the time of day. I was able to speak to one of the officers at the station, though, and he said no other businesses along Main Street had reported anything suspicious."

Tricia frowned. "Then it sounds like Haven't Got a Clue was singled out."

"But why?" Angelica asked.

"I have no idea." Tricia pondered that thought for a while. What could she possibly have that anyone could want? She had some rather nice jewelry, some of it gold, but nothing of any great value. She had a TV and computers in her home and the store's office, but so did every other business in the village.

"On a more cheerful note," Angelica began, "the cable company ran the story on you and your store."

"So Pixie said. Was it any good?"

"Marvelous! You're so poised in front of a camera. You could've been a news anchor."

Tricia doubted that, but she had done a lot of public speaking during her days as head of a big nonprofit agency in Manhattan. "I'll have to do an Internet search to find the clip."

"I would have recorded it for you, but I never knew when it would air."

Tricia frowned. The cable news channel had a habit of recycling its content on the hour. Angelica had probably just been too busy to think about that, and Tricia decided not to bring the fact to her attention. Instead, the sisters sipped their drinks.

"I don't suppose you want to talk about the dead woman Pixie found in your dumpster," Angelica suggested.

Tricia did her best not to roll her eyes. "That's another topic I'm not all that interested in discussing."

"But you need to in case they find out the worst happened."

"You mean that she was murdered?"

Angelica nodded.

"That hasn't been established. As Susan Morris was a woman of limited means, she might have just been dumpster diving, looking for something to eat or salvage, and got stuck in the trash, unable to extricate herself." At least, that's what Tricia hoped had happened.

"And if she was murdered?" Angelica asked.

Tricia drained her glass. That conclusion hadn't escaped her.

"Then Pixie might have a lot to worry about."

After weeks of heavy meals, Tricia thoroughly enjoyed her light repast, although Angelica did indulge in a fat slice of German chocolate cake after her salad. "Everybody knows chocolate is good for healing surgical wounds," she'd said straight-faced. Tricia held her tongue.

The sisters returned to Main Street, and after Tricia made sure Angelica had made it safely up the stairs to her apartment, she headed back to Haven't Got a Clue. It was later than she realized when she walked back through the door—past five o'clock—and the store would be closing in less than forty-five minutes. Now that Tricia had returned from her so-called vacation, Mr. Everett had gone back to his regular hours. They'd changed, since Pixie was no longer working Saturdays. He worked the same number of hours, but now he helped Tricia take care of the store on the weekends while Pixie indulged her creative side, crafting fancy acrylic nail designs, and did a Saturday shift at Angelica's Booked for Beauty Day Spa.

Pixie stood behind the cash desk with a paperback edition of *Murder After Hours* spread out before her, but her expression was rather blank, as though she hadn't been absorbing what she'd been reading.

"Pixie?" Tricia asked.

Pixie seemed to shake herself. "Oh, you're back. I didn't hear the bell."

"Is everything okay?"

Pixie let out a weary sigh. "I . . . uh . . . I'm worried about what Chief Baker is going to do."

Tricia had an inkling of where this conversation was likely to go. "And?"

"What if he decides to arrest me for Susan's death?" The poor woman sounded panicked.

"Did you kill her?"

"Of course not. But just Google the phrase 'chronic recidivist.' What it won't tell you is how many ex-cons have been railroaded back to prison for stuff they didn't do."

Tricia's gut tightened. "Why would you think Chief Baker would accuse you—and I mean besides the fact that you've previously served jail time?"

"After you left, I got to thinking about how both of us reacted to Susan's death. I mean, neither of us was exactly rending our clothes in grief."

She had that right. "I never met the woman, and I have a classic case of jet lag," Tricia said defensively.

"Yeah, but I don't have that kind of alibi."

"I'm sure you don't need an alibi. It's obvious that Susan had been dead for a while. And nobody in their right mind would dump a body at their place of work."

"Yeah, but cops—and especially district attorneys—don't put that kind of thought into things. They like cases wrapped up fast and neat—and often don't care if they've got the right person."

There were plenty of examples of that in fact and in mystery fiction.

"I should've played dumb. I should've pretended I was more upset," Pixie said.

"Why weren't you upset?" Tricia asked.

Pixie shrugged. "I guess I kind of figured that something bad would eventually happen to Susan. Not that she hadn't figured out how to be safe living like she did, but because she was so nice, so trusting. People take advantage of a person like that."

Plenty of people had taken advantage of Pixie's good nature.

"I hate to say it, but we'll just have to wait and see. And

it goes without saying that I—and Angelica and the rest of our little family—will have your back."

Pixie's smile was tight. "Thanks, Tricia. I never had anybody willing to stick up for me the way you and Angelica have."

Tricia offered her friend a wan smile. "You've had a long day," she said kindly.

"Shorter than yours," Pixie pointed out.

That was true. "It seems like the store is pretty dead—no pun intended—so why don't we close up for the day? Go home to Fred. Put your feet up and have an adult beverage—or maybe three or four."

"That sounds like heaven about now." Pixie looked down at her book. "And maybe I should take a lesson from Dame Christie's Miss Marple and start asking questions around the village—you know, about Susan. I've got to find out what the chief knows about her—if only to protect myself."

"I don't think that's a good idea. He might think you're trying to interfere with the investigation."

"Then how about you? You've solved more than your fair share of murders."

"We don't know that Susan Morris was murdered," Tricia insisted.

"Not until the autopsy comes back," Pixie muttered.

"I think it's prudent for you to show as little interest in the investigation as possible."

"Then will you ask some questions on my behalf?" Pixie asked.

"Of course. I have a personal stake in what happened to the poor woman. She either died in my dumpster or was put in there."

"Thanks, Tricia. You'll find out the truth. You always do."

Not always. And sometimes the truth was more fleeting than time itself.

THREE

After being awake for more than twenty-four hours, Tricia slept like the dead. In fact, it was only Miss Marple pawing at her nose that finally interrupted her much-needed slumber. The clock said it was almost eight, and Tricia realized she'd slept for more than twelve hours. The good news was that rest had done her good and she felt like she needed to get back into her regular routine. The bad news came when she stepped on her scale and realized she had gained at least five pounds while on the trip. She'd packed loose, comfortable clothing so the gain hadn't been so noticeable. And she hadn't overindulged—at least, not much. It was a lack of exercise that had caused the gain, she told herself after getting dressed.

Tricia paused at the bottom of her stairs, looking at the shiny new lock on the store's back door, a feeling of unease crawling through her. She'd almost forgotten about the attempted break-in. But it had happened days before, and the new fortifications had so far held. Unless something else happened, she wasn't going to dwell on it.

Much.

But she also decided she needed to fortify the dumbwaiter and address it that day for sure.

Grabbing her jacket, Tricia left her home and business and headed out the front door for her daily brisk walk.

Not a lot had changed during Tricia's two-week absence. The summer flowers along Main Street had been switched from pastel petunias to yellow, gold, and orange chrysanthemums. There was a delightful chill in the air, and she and the others she saw and met along the way were wearing light jackets, sweats, or sweaters. And as she passed the Sweet As Can Be candy shop, she noticed a sign in the window that said NOW HIRING.

Tricia had met the shop's owner, Donna North, some three months before while training for the Great Booktown Bake-Off. Donna had taught her the basics of cake decorating, and it was with Angelica's help that Donna had achieved a long-held dream of opening her confectionery just the month before. Tricia knew Donna had hired at least one part-time person to work the counter while she made her hand-dipped candies in the commercial kitchen in the back. Had she lost that person so soon?

The lights were on in the shop, and Tricia saw Donna stocking one of the refrigerated cases. She knocked on the door, and the weary-looking proprietress looked up. Tricia waved, and Donna shut the case's sliding glass door and approached the shop's entrance.

"Back from your trip to Ireland?" Donna inquired as Tricia entered and inhaled the intoxicating aroma of chocolate.

Did everybody know about her vacation?

"Yes, just yesterday."

"Then you must have missed the TV interview you did before you left."

"Yes, I did.

"Nobody recorded it for you?"

"Not that I know of."

"That's too bad. It was good. You and your store came off looking great."

"I'm pleased to hear it."

"What brings you to Sweet As Can Be so early in the day?"

"I saw your sign in the window."

Donna gave a mirthless laugh. "Are you looking for work?"

"Not a chance. What happened to your helper?"

"She's dead," Donna said flatly, and her eyes glistened. "I heard it on the radio."

For a moment Tricia didn't understand—and then she remembered the events of the day before. "Susan Morris worked for you?"

Donna nodded. "I don't know how I'll replace her. She picked up the job so fast, and the customers all loved her."

"I didn't even know Susan worked for you."

"Did you know her?"

"No. But my assistant manager, Pixie, was an acquaintance."

"What's worse is the news report said they're treating her death as a possible homicide."

Tricia's heart sank. Once Pixie heard that, her paranoia was sure to escalate. "I'm so sorry."

"I heard that someone in the village had died, and when Susan didn't show up for work yesterday, I tried calling her. She was no slacker. I even thought about going to her home to see if she was sick or something, but when I looked at her job application, I saw she'd listed her address as a PO box."

Just as Pixie had said. Was it Tricia's place to tell Donna the truth?

"I also heard she was found behind your store." Donna's tone was filled with disapproval.

"That's true," Tricia admitted.

"And that this isn't the first time you've found a dead person."

"I didn't find her," Tricia was quick to point out, but didn't elaborate.

"I guess it doesn't matter," Donna said sadly. "I liked Susan. She was smart, she was funny, she was . . ."

"Homeless," Tricia said.

Donna blinked. "What?"

"She lived in her car."

"That can't be," Donna said, bewildered.

"I'm afraid it was."

"Why didn't she say so? Why didn't she ask for help?"

Tricia shrugged. "Apparently she was fine with it."

"How could anybody be fine with living in a car?" Donna asked, distressed.

"I guess it happens a lot more than most of us think."

Donna shook her head.

"What will you do until you hire someone?" Tricia asked.

"My sister said she could lend me a hand for a few days. She helped me set up the store and knows the routine. Sometimes she works for me on weekends, but she's got a regular job and can't help until Saturday. I've got a couple of big orders to fill before then. I don't know how I'll make out."

"Have you called one of the temp agencies in Nashua?"

"No, but that's a good idea. Thanks." Donna let out a weary sigh. "Did you have a nice time on your vacation?"

Tricia saw no reason to dump more pain on the poor woman and simply answered, "Yes."

"I haven't been on a vacation in years, and now, since I opened the shop, it'll be even longer," Donna lamented. "But once this place is a success, I'm going someplace spectacular. I'm going to Vegas."

Tricia stifled a laugh. "I hear it's nice."

"Casinos; big, flashy shows; and all-you-can-eat buffets—that's what I want to experience."

"I hope the opportunity comes up soon."

"Meanwhile, we're here in boring old Stoneham."

"Not as boring as you might think. Did you know there was an attempted break-in at my store last weekend?" Tricia asked.

Donna's expression darkened. "No. I take it they didn't get in."

"The security system kicked in and apparently frightened them off."

"I don't have one. Maybe I should get one installed."

"It wouldn't hurt."

Donna's frown deepened. "With all the expenses I've already got, I don't know how I can afford one."

"Could you afford to replace your equipment if it was vandalized?"

Donna looked doubtful. "My insurance might pay for it, but I've got the bare minimum."

The women were silent for a long moment before Donna spoke again. "Can I help you with anything else?" she asked hopefully.

Tricia wondered what she could do to lighten Donna's mood. She should buy something. Then again, she thought about that extra five pounds she was carrying, plus her sister being homebound for weeks with no way to get in even a few hundred steps a day as exercise. But Donna looked disconsolate, and Tricia forced a wan smile. She indicated the display case filled with heavenly truffles, bonbons, caramel corn, peanut brittle, and more that stood between them.

"How about selling me two one-pound boxes of those wonderful chocolate-covered creams?"

After returning to Haven't Got a Clue, Tricia hung up her coat and decided to set up the beverage station for the day, placing one of the boxes of chocolates out for her staff and customers to enjoy. She snuck just one piece for herself— maple cream—and bet that Donna had made it with the best New Hampshire syrup, which was produced locally.

The coffee was brewing when Pixie showed up for work just a wee bit late, wearing a black suit, black pumps, and an ebony pillbox hat with a veil that dipped just below her eyes. Her expression was just as somber.

"Good mourning?" Tricia asked.

"Not so much," Pixie replied.

Tricia didn't feel up to explaining her little joke and felt bad for even making it. Pixie looked disconsolate. "Would you like me to hang up your hat?"

Pixie's eyes rolled upward, and she sighed. "I guess this

getup is a little over-the-top, but it pretty much reflects my mood."

"It's very pretty," Tricia said. "I especially like that little cluster of pearls on the bow, but it does seem a little—"

"Morbid?" Pixie asked.

"Formal," Tricia corrected. "I've just made a fresh pot of coffee. Why don't you pour yourself a cup?"

Pixie removed the pearl-tipped hatpin and took off her chapeau. "I'll hang this up first."

Tricia watched as Pixie slunk to the back of the store, donned her name badge, then returned to the shop's front to pour coffee for both of them.

"I bought some chocolates from Sweet As Can Be. Why don't you have a few? Maybe they'll cheer you up," Tricia suggested.

"It might take the whole box, but thanks. And thanks for getting the coffee ready." Pixie glanced at the clock. "Oh, goodness—I'm ten minutes late for work!" she cried.

"It's all right." Tricia waved a hand around the empty store. "As you can see, we're not exactly inundated with customers."

"I'm sorry, Tricia. It's just that—"

"I know what it's like to have Chief Baker's judgmental gaze fixed upon one." She'd seen it far too many times.

Pixie's gaze dipped to the chocolates and she chose one of the creams, bit it in half, and chewed. Pistachio, from the look of it. She paused before taking another bite. "Yeah. As I was walking home from work last night, the chief intercepted me right on Main Street. He popped out of the police station like he'd been waiting for me and invited me to his office for a little chat," Pixie said unhappily.

Tricia's hackles rose. "Oh?"

"Except it wasn't all that short, and I kept asking if I needed a lawyer."

"Oh, Pixie—why didn't you call me?"

"He said if I had nothing to hide, I didn't need an attorney, and as I wasn't being arrested—yet—I didn't need to call anyone."

"He actually said 'yet'?"

"Well, no. But that's what he meant." Pixie chose another cream.

"What did he want?"

"He kept hammering over and over again the same questions—How long had I known Susan? Where was I on Tuesday?—and he wanted an hour-by-hour description." Pixie popped the entire chocolate in her mouth and chewed rapidly.

"So you have an alibi, right?" Tricia asked.

Pixie's expression darkened and she swallowed. "Do you really think I need one?"

"Apparently the chief does."

Pixie straightened. "Yes, I do have an alibi—several in fact. I was here at the shop all day; then Fred picked me up at closing and we went to the Bookshelf Diner for dinner, where I had a burger, onion rings, and a chocolate shake. I struck up a conversation with Gina, the waitress, so she can pin me to the place and time. After that, we went home. We stopped to speak to our neighbor, Ed, who gave us some of the last of his grape tomatoes. Then we watched TV for a while and went to bed. When the paper came at seven fifteen in the morning, I was there to take it from the delivery guy. I walked to work, for everyone to see, and got here early. Along the way I ran into Mr. E, who was walking Sarge, so he can vouch for me, too."

"I'm sorry, Pixie. I don't doubt for a moment that you're telling the truth."

"Well, the chief can confirm with everybody I interacted with—if he cares to do so."

Tricia didn't blame Pixie for having her doubts about law enforcement. But she also had faith that Baker was just doing his job. Okay, maybe she crossed her fingers that he was just trying to ensure he fulfilled his duty to interview everyone who knew the dead woman.

"With all that went on yesterday, I don't suppose the chief shared his news with you," Pixie said.

"News?" Tricia asked. For some reason her abdominal

muscles tightened, and she wasn't sure she wanted her coffee after all.

"Yeah, Chiefy and his girl are going to tie the knot."

Tricia blinked in surprise. It wasn't like Pixie to share gossip, so she had to be really irked at Baker. "When did this happen?"

"While you were on vacation."

It probably shouldn't have come as a shock. Baker and his lady friend had been seeing each other for more than a year. The man had had quite a problem making a commitment when he was dating Tricia, but it looked like he'd changed his mind. Either that or his girlfriend—and Tricia had never learned the woman's name—wasn't as picky as Tricia had been when it came to pinning the man down.

"Well," Tricia said, managing to keep her voice level, "I wish them all the luck in the world."

Luck? Oops! She'd meant happiness . . . hadn't she?

"It's not going to be a long engagement, either," Pixie added.

Tricia blinked. "Oh?"

Pixie nodded. "They've already booked the Brookview Inn for their reception."

Tricia's eyes widened. Why hadn't Angelica mentioned this little piece of information when they had lunch the previous day? Was she trying to spare Tricia's feelings, or was she concerned that too much had happened upon Tricia's arrival home and didn't want to dump yet another brick on her shoulders?

Brick? Why should she even care what Grant Baker did in his spare time? His private life was none of her business.

Pixie reached for another chocolate, again popping the entire thing in her mouth and washing it down with a gulp of coffee. "With everything that happened yesterday, I forgot to mention that I visited a rummage sale over the weekend and bought some stock. There are a couple of boxes in the office downstairs. I also wrote out an inventory. It's on the computer. You might want to check it out to see if you agree with my suggested prices. I left a receipt by the phone."

Tricia hadn't even visited her office since returning home. "Thanks, Pixie. You're a doll."

Pixie actually blushed. "Oh, and it's Thursday. Don't forget, you've got lunch with Ginny at Booked for Lunch at one."

"Thank you for reminding me. I'd completely forgotten about it. I've got to get back into my routine."

"It'll happen soon enough," Pixie said.

The bell over the door rang—their first customer of the day. Pixie's demeanor immediately changed for the better as she straightened and smiled brightly. "Welcome to Haven't Got a Clue. I'm Pixie. Have you visited us before?" she asked the woman dressed in a heavy denim jacket, which seemed like overkill for the early fall weather.

"Yes, thanks. But I could sure use some suggestions on new authors."

"New, old, we've got 'em both," Pixie said. "Dead authors, live authors. Do you like cat mysteries? They're popular these days. Or perhaps supernatural? Witches are hot, too . . ."

Tricia slipped away, heading for the basement office, where she sat down at her desk. First, she Googled bunion surgery, not surprised to see it agreed with what Angelica had told her the day before. Tricia bit her lip and wondered about Angelica's dog. The little guy needed to be let out at night. Since she lived next door, it made sense that she should volunteer for that duty. Angelica had fed Miss Marple a few times when Tricia had changed plans and spent the night elsewhere or gone on a business trip. She would offer to do so the next time they spoke.

That decided, next she inspected the boxes of books Pixie had mentioned and was soon absorbed by the task. There were several surprises, and several were a bit musty. She would treat them before adding them to the shelves on the floor above.

Eventually, her stomach growled and she glanced at her

watch, surprised to see it was ten minutes to one. Pixie should have hollered down the stairs to her and taken her lunch hour fifty minutes before.

Tricia dashed up the stairs and found Pixie behind the combination display case/cash desk, reading. "Why didn't you call me? You've missed your lunch."

Pixie waved a hand in dismissal. "I'm not hungry. I figured I'd go when you got back from your lunch with Ginny."

Those lunches were usually less than an hour.

"Are you sure?"

"Yep. You'd better hurry and get ready," Pixie said.

Eight minutes later Tricia was out the door and crossing the street for Booked for Lunch.

She entered the little café and took a seat in the booth that Molly, the waitress, had reserved for her and Ginny. She'd already poured two glasses of water and removed the RESERVED sign as Tricia settled her purse at her side.

Tricia needn't have hurried. As usual, Ginny was late. It seemed to Tricia that these regular Thursday lunches were stolen time away from Ginny's job as the events planner for Angelica's company, Nigela Ricita Associates. It gave her a twinge of guilt, but Ginny did deserve a break from her job, and Tricia knew Angelica wouldn't begrudge her a midday meal.

Tricia didn't have to wait more than a few minutes before Ginny eased into the other side of the booth. "Sorry I'm late."

Tricia smiled. "Not by too much. "

"Hey, that was some interview you did on TV."

"So I've been told. I've yet to see it. I keep forgetting to Google it."

"You should. It's great PR for Haven't Got a Clue and the whole village."

Tricia felt a swell of pride course through her but didn't want to push for details. "What's on your plate today?" Tricia asked.

Ginny's eyes were bright with enthusiasm. "My team and I spent the morning brainstorming ideas for the upcoming holiday season. They are the most amazing people—so smart, so talented. I can't wait to share with the boss all our ideas for the entire Nigela Ricita empire."

Angelica empire.

Molly approached their table. After almost a year on the job, she knew Ginny was on a tight schedule. "What'll you ladies have today?"

"A BLT for me," Ginny said.

"And I'll have the soup of the day and half a turkey sandwich on whole wheat—with the works," Tricia added.

"It's broccoli cheddar," Molly warned, knowing it wasn't one of Tricia's favorites, "but Tommy has some vegetable beef he can heat up if you'd prefer."

"Yes, vegetable beef sounds like a delicious choice, thank you."

Molly jotted it down on her pad and made a hasty retreat.

"So, how was your vacation?" Ginny asked eagerly, as though starved for the mere thought of getting away from it all.

"It was . . . okay," Tricia admitted.

Ginny frowned. "That doesn't sound good."

Tricia shrugged. "I knew before we left that it wasn't going to be a pleasure trip for Marshall—and he was determined to make the tour a success for Milford Travel."

"And where did that leave you?" Ginny asked with more than a bit of disapproval in her tone.

"I was a tourist who got to see just how beautiful Ireland is—and how generous and welcoming the population at large is, too."

"Did you have *any* fun?" Ginny asked.

Tricia hesitated before answering. "The other people on the tour were friendly and everybody had a wonderful time."

"Everybody but *you*?" Ginny pressed.

"I enjoyed the people, the places, and the food."

"But not your time with Marshall."

"He was pretty much unavailable," Tricia said, and sighed.

"That doesn't sound good."

"It was what it was. I bought a lot of books, all new-to-me

authors, and I brought back a present for Sofia. I'm sorry, but she's the only one who'll get one."

"And I'm sure she'll love it when you give it to her on Sunday when we're all together for dinner."

Tricia managed a smile. She'd missed two of their family dinners because of the trip and looked forward to the weekend. Sometimes Marshall attended the gatherings, but it was never a given. He said he didn't feel like he blended in. Maybe if he attended more of them, he would. Maybe she'd invite him again . . . and maybe she wouldn't.

Ginny sipped her glass of water, looking pensive.

"Is something wrong?" Tricia asked.

Ginny let out a long breath, her head drooping. "Just a little discord on the home front." She leaned in closer. "Antonio's been hinting that he'd like us to have another baby . . . but I'm just not sure."

"Why is that?" Tricia asked.

Ginny let out a sigh. "I love my job. I love my daughter. I don't think I could handle two kids and work."

"But Antonio is a great hands-on dad."

"Yes, he is—when he can be. He's also a father with a terribly demanding job."

"You could take a couple of years off."

"I could," Ginny admitted, "but I don't want to. I don't want to sound ungrateful, Tricia, but when I worked for you, I wasn't really challenged. I loved working at Haven't Got a Clue, but at that time I never had an inkling that I was capable of so much more."

Tricia found it hard to look Ginny in the eye. Back then, she hadn't been willing to give up the kind of responsibility she allowed Pixie to have. Was it because Ginny was so much younger than Tricia's current assistant manager? Heck, she'd called them both assistants, and it was Pixie who balked at being a true manager because she knew Tricia couldn't quite handle relinquishing that role.

A wave of guilt washed over Tricia. "I'm sorry about that."

Ginny waved a hand in dismissal. "I admit it: I wasn't

that interested. I didn't see retail as a career. But at that time there weren't many options here in Stoneham. When Nigela Ricita Associates came to the village, everything changed."

"For the better?" Tricia asked.

Ginny nodded. "I probably wouldn't have met Antonio if I hadn't been working at the Happy Domestic. All our lives would be different—and I don't think for the better."

"You're absolutely right," Tricia said, forcing cheerfulness when what she really felt was even more guilt.

Molly arrived with their lunches, setting them down on the table. "Let me know if you need anything else."

"Sure thing," Ginny quipped, and plucked half of her sandwich from the heavy china plate.

Tricia picked up her spoon and plunged it into the soup, coming up with a piece of potato that still bore its skin. She changed the subject.

"Did anything else interesting happen while I was gone?"

"The Brookview Inn is in a bit of a tizzy, what with planning a last-minute wedding."

"Oh, yeah? Who's getting married?' Tricia asked.

Ginny picked up a potato chip from her plate. "I thought someone would have told you already."

"Told me what?"

"That Chief Baker is getting married."

"Oh, that?" Tricia said, trying to sound like she really wasn't interested in that piece of news. "Pixie mentioned it, but she didn't have many details." Okay, that was a fib, but Ginny might have more information to share, and Tricia sure as heck wasn't going to discourage her from talking about it.

Ginny picked up one of her potato chips and chomped on it. "I guess they're in a hurry to get married—at least, that's what I heard."

Grant Baker in a hurry to get married? Now Tricia had heard everything.

Well, not really.

"I don't suppose you heard anything about their plans," Tricia mentioned offhandedly.

"Oh, sure. Antonio told me all about it. I guess it's going to be quite the affair."

"Oh?" Tricia asked innocently, taking a sip of her water.

"Well, of course. The chief's bride-to-be is the former governor's daughter."

Tricia nearly spewed the mouthful of H_2O with which she'd been bathing her gums. "What?" she asked, almost choking.

"Oh, yeah. I thought you knew."

"I knew Grant had been dating someone; I just never heard who."

"She's a lawyer who works pro bono for high-profile cases. I guess she's filthy rich."

How had that fact eluded Tricia for so long?

"That's . . . that's so nice," she said, and managed what she hoped was a sweet smile.

Ginny wasn't fooled. "I'll bet she's a bitch."

"Ginny!"

"Well, what power does she have over the chief that he chose her when he couldn't see what a prize he had in you?" she said, sounding hurt.

Tricia gave her niece-in-law a fond smile. "Some things just aren't meant to be."

"I want you to be just as happy as I am, Tricia."

Did that mean happily mated? And hadn't Ginny spoken just minutes before about her uncertainty when it came to her and her husband's views on expanding their family?

"It was me who walked away from that relationship," Tricia reminded Ginny.

"Well, if he hadn't dragged his feet and turned on you every time a dead body showed up around town—"

"My, this soup smells good," Tricia said, cutting Ginny off and picked up her spoon, desperate to change the subject, and then began an in-depth description of the books Pixie had acquired while Tricia had been out of the country. Ginny played along but hurriedly ate her lunch. She had more important things to attend to, and Tricia could almost sense Ginny's anticipation to get back to work. She loved her daughter and she loved her job. Tricia didn't envy the choices Ginny might be forced to make in the future.

And then there was Tricia. It seemed that she had all the freedom in the world and yet nothing the least bit challenging on the horizon.

Then she thought again of Pixie and the fear she'd seen in her eyes that morning.

Perhaps a more drama-free life was best in the long run.

But not nearly as interesting.

FOUR

The weather was fine, but the customers were few and far between. That gave Tricia and Pixie time to sort through the books for shelving and those that needed treatment. Pixie took care of the former, while Tricia attended to the latter. She used several methods to deodorize books, ranging from kitty litter to baking soda to dryer sheets. One or a combination of all three usually did the trick. Once the books were placed in a sealed box, Tricia returned to the sales floor to rejoin her assistant manager.

Although it was Mr. Everett's day off, he popped into Haven't Got a Clue that afternoon after taking Sarge for a walk. "That little dog is a joy to spend time with," he said, brandishing one of his rare smiles.

"That he is," Tricia agreed. "Would you like a cup of coffee?"

"Oh, no. I just stopped in to say hello."

"And we're glad you did," Pixie said. Her melancholy from earlier in the day seemed to have diminished.

"Ms. Miles, I meant to tell you how much Grace and I enjoyed the interview you did for the cable news channel," Mr. Everett said. "You did Haven't Got a Clue proud."

Tricia felt a blush rising. Was everybody in the village going to mention it?

"Thank you," she said, and quickly changed the subject. "Now that you're here, Mr. Everett, I wonder if I might impose upon you for a favor?"

"I'll do whatever I can. What do you need?"

Tricia explained what she wanted to be done on the dumbwaiter, and Mr. Everett was only too happy to oblige. He left immediately for the big hardware store on Route 101, and within an hour was back with several bolts and set to work to affix them to the dumbwaiter doors. "I bought enough to retrofit your sister's doors as well. We can't have your homes unsecured. Not in these troubled times," he said.

While he worked on the floors above, Tricia noticed that Pixie's gloomy mood reappeared during the afternoon, leaving a rather solemn pall throughout Haven't Got a Clue. That is, except when customers entered the store. Then, like a dedicated thespian, she came alive, talking and laughing, and finding the exact book that any avid reader was sure to love. It was a gift, but once the door had closed behind the shopper, Pixie's mood plunged, and she looked as though she'd lost her best friend. She was worried, and with reason, about what the future might hold, and Tricia felt helpless to reassure her.

Once he'd finished his work, Mr. Everett left them with a cheery "See you tomorrow" and headed next door to the Cookery to take Sarge on yet another walk, and the rest of the afternoon dragged. Eventually the hands on the clock pointed toward six o'clock.

"There's no point in staying open another minute," Tricia said after Pixie had tidied the store and cleaned the beverage station to perfection. "Why don't you head on home?"

"You're too good to me, Tricia."

Tricia shook her head. "Not nearly enough. And tomorrow, why don't you wear your pretty yellow floral dress."

Pixie shook her head. "It's too summery."

"Nonsense. You could wear your white sweater with it."

"After Labor Day?" Pixie asked.

Tricia raised an eyebrow in response.

"Okay. I guess I could," Pixie said, sounding defeated.

"Great. Now, go home to your husband and have a wonderful evening."

"Okay." It sounded more like she'd be facing a firing squad.

Pixie retrieved her hat, grabbed her purse, and gave a halfhearted wave before heading out the door.

Tricia sighed but then moved to lower the blinds, turn off the lights, change the OPEN sign to CLOSED, grab the second box of chocolates she'd purchased earlier in the day, and then lock the door. In just a few steps, she opened the door to the Cookery and stepped inside. June was tidying up, getting ready to leave for the day.

"Hey, Tricia. Did you have a good vacation?" Angelica's store manager asked.

"Great. Just great." If another person asked her about her vacation, Tricia was sure she was going to scream. Even though people were trying to be polite, she was getting tired of talking—or even thinking—about the vacation she hadn't really enjoyed.

"Angelica's upstairs, waiting for you. And you don't need to worry about Sarge. Mr. Everett came back for a third time today and took him for a comfort stroll. I'll lock up and see you tomorrow, huh?"

"Probably. Have a good evening, June."

"You, too."

Tricia headed for the back of the store, opened the door marked PRIVATE and locked it behind her before she headed up the stairs. Sarge heard her and began to bark. When Tricia entered the apartment, he went absolutely berserk with joy. "Calm down, calm down," she coaxed, and hurried to the kitchen island, where she set down the chocolates and opened the crystal biscuit jar on the counter, quickly tossing the dog one, but he was too wound up and kept jumping in the air as though on a trampoline.

"Sarge, hush!" Angelica ordered from her perch on one of the island's stools, her right foot elevated on another.

The dog quieted but still danced around Tricia's legs for another minute, demanding her attention.

"I'd say you were terribly missed," Angelica said, then nodded toward the counter. "What's with the candy?"

"Isn't one supposed to bring a gift to an invalid?"

"Just what I need when I have to lead a sedentary lifestyle for the next few weeks." Angelica shook her head but then said, "Thank you. You know where the drinks and glasses are," she directed.

Once Sarge had finally calmed down and accepted the biscuit, Tricia washed the slobber from her hands, dried them, and fetched the glass pitcher from the fridge, pouring the drinks.

"Thanks for sending Mr. Everett over to secure my dumbwaiter doors. It never occurred to me they could be a potential security breach. And the dear man wouldn't let me pay him for the hardware, and he's been so good about walking Sarge. We couldn't have asked for a better friend."

"I totally agree."

"When I'm back on my feet, no pun intended, I'm going to bake something special for him," Angelica declared.

"He'll like that," Tricia said, and passed one of the glasses to her sister. "Boy, am I ready for this," she said, and took a swig.

"Bad day?" Angelica asked, and again pointed to the fridge, where Tricia retrieved a bowl of Tommy's guacamole, removing the plastic wrap and setting it on the island. She grabbed a bag of tortilla chips sitting on the counter and poured some out into another bowl.

"It could have been better."

"Where do you want to sit?"

"It's still nice out. Let's go out on your balcony. We won't be able to do that for much longer."

Angelica nodded. "All too soon it'll be a skating rink. Can you bring out everything?"

"Sure," Tricia said, and snagged the drinks, setting them and the chips and dip on a tray.

They made their way across the apartment and Angelica opened the sliding glass doors, closing them again after she, Tricia, and Sarge stepped onto the balcony. They took their accustomed seats, Angelica settling her legs on the chaise, with Sarge jumping up to nestle beside her. Tricia kicked off her shoes.

"So, what spoiled your day?" Angelica asked.

"I wouldn't say spoiled, but . . . why didn't you tell me Grant Baker was engaged?"

"Oh, didn't I mention that?" Angelica asked, feigning innocence.

"You know perfectly well you didn't."

"Well, maybe because I knew it would spoil your day."

"It didn't spoil my day," Tricia reaffirmed. No, it was a combination of things that had rattled her. "I was just taken aback."

Angelica nodded. "It's always unsettling when a former lover—"

"Chooses someone other than you—or, in this case, me?"

"Well, I hadn't intended to put it so bluntly, but yes."

Tricia shrugged and took a larger sip of her drink.

"Have you heard from Marshall?" Angelica asked hopefully.

"No."

"Have you thought about calling him?"

"No."

"Oh, dear," Angelica said, and scowled before taking a sip of her drink.

"Please don't ask me about him anymore," Tricia implored.

"Ever?" Angelica asked, alarmed.

"No, but for at least today. We'll talk to each other when we're ready to talk."

The sisters didn't speak for a minute or so. Angelica dipped a chip into the guacamole while Tricia stared at the churchyard beyond the fence in the alley behind their buildings. It was Tricia who broke the quiet.

"So, what kind of reception is Grant having?"

"Do you really want to know?"

"I'm just curious. I love weddings—even if they aren't mine."

Angelica scowled. "I wasn't sure you ever wanted to get married again."

"I don't."

Angelica eyed her sister. "Doth thou protest too much?"

"No."

Angelica frowned and shrugged. "Well, it'll be a nice reception for fifty people. The Brookview is catering, of course, and the couple will provide their own cake— although goodness knows our own Joann Gibson is the best pastry chef in the area now that Nikki's flown the coop," she muttered. "The bride's colors will be harvest shades, and we'll be coordinating the linens to match."

"What's the entrée?"

"Surf and turf. And an open bar, of course."

"Nothing's too good for the former governor's daughter."

"Who told you that?" Angelica asked.

"Ginny. What's the woman's name?"

"Diana."

"Named after the princess?" Tricia asked tartly.

"Probably. She seemed very nice. She's younger than Chief Baker and a career woman."

"So Pixie said," Tricia noted, ignoring the mention of the fair Diana's age. "I hear she defends people for nothing," Tricia repeated.

"Why not? Apparently, she's filthy rich."

"And was that the attraction?" Tricia asked, knowing the lady attorney's bank account would far surpass that of the chief's.

"Tricia," Angelica chided, "it's not like you to be catty."

No, it wasn't. Still, Tricia plunged on.

"I suppose you've met her?" she said to deflect attention from her former remark.

"Um, I just happened to be at the Brookview when she came for a tour and put down a deposit."

"Why are they having their reception in Stoneham? Are they slumming?"

"Tricia," Angelica scolded once again. "The Brookview is a historic inn with an extensive pedigree. And don't forget, the property has had almost a complete makeover since Nigela Ricita Associates took over."

"Yeah, yeah," Tricia muttered and took another sip of her martini. She *was* feeling catty.

"We had a cancellation, and it was lucky we could accommodate them," Angelica explained. "Besides, the chief does work in the village. Maybe he wanted to contribute to our prosperity."

"Or maybe it was the only place they could find on such short notice," Tricia suggested.

"Be that as it may . . ." Angelica said testily, and took another sip of her drink.

"So, when's the wedding?"

"Four weeks from Saturday."

Tricia blinked. "So soon?"

"They've been an item for a while; why wait?"

Tricia pursed her lips, feeling like a sore loser. It had been she who'd cut things off with Baker when he wasn't willing to commit to her. Why she felt any emotion connected to the man—except, perhaps, annoyance—was beyond her.

"They're getting married by a judge—an old friend of her family, I guess," Angelica added.

"I suppose you've even seen her dress."

"Just a sketch. Do you want to hear more?" Angelica asked.

"I don't think so." Tricia shifted her gaze to the bowl of guacamole, selected a chip, dunked it in the dip, and ate it. "Not bad."

"Tommy thought of our appetizer, but Antonio sent over dinner from the Brookview. He's such a good kid," Angelica said and sighed, then gave herself a little shake. "How did your lunch with Ginny go?"

"Okay, but she doesn't exactly seem happy that Antonio wants another child," Tricia said.

"It's not news to me," Angelica replied.

"Ginny likes being a working mom."

"Well, of course. And why wouldn't she? I'm an excellent employer."

"And what do you want them to do?" Tricia asked.

"Of course, I'd love to have another grandbaby, but there's no way I'm going to insert myself into that conversation. They have to work that out for themselves."

Tricia said nothing, but she had to admit she was rather surprised by her sister's reaction. When it came to just about any other subject, Angelica felt free to offer her opinion—and sometimes forcefully.

Her sister scrutinized Tricia's face. "You look skeptical."

"Maybe," Tricia hedged.

Angelica shrugged. "I made a choice when it came to Antonio." Angelica had been visiting Italy when she fell in love with a dashing guy with a lethal love of motorcycles. He'd died before they could be married. "Letting him believe someone else was his mother was a bad choice, but at the time I was interested in protecting him from the perceived stigma of an unwed mother and myself from the same thing. Conditions have changed. They're different for career women now, too."

Tricia wondered if Susan Morris had ever considered herself a career woman. Pixie hadn't spoken much about the woman except for her most recent circumstances. Who had Susan been before she was reduced to living in her car? She had a daughter, presumably in her twenties or thirties. Why hadn't said daughter helped her mother? Susan's possessions still sat in the municipal parking lot, and Tricia wondered exactly what was inside the vehicle.

"What are you doing this evening?" she asked.

Angelica shrugged. "Going over some paperwork. I'd love to take a nice, hot bubble bath before retiring, but I'm not supposed to get the sutures wet. Why?"

"It's too bad you're not up to taking a walk to go look at Susan's car."

"Who says I'm not?"

"Doesn't your foot hurt?"

"Of course it hurts, but who says I have to walk? I've got the transport chair from the inn. All I have to do is sit in it and you can push me all around the village."

Did Angelica have an ulterior motive for getting the chair—say, as a way to visit some of her Main Street businesses without having to walk? But, unlike a wheelchair, a transport chair had to be pushed.

"Why do you want to look at Susan's car?" Angelica asked.

"To see how she lived."

"Poorly, I would imagine. And how are we going to get into a locked car?"

"How do you know it's locked?"

"I'm sure the police would have seen to that after they checked it out."

Tricia raised her gaze to the sky above. "What if I told you I knew how to open a locked car door?"

"And where did you learn that?"

"In a book."

"A mystery?"

"Of course."

"And you've tried it?"

Tricia nodded. "Of course, it's a little tricky, but it does work for some vehicles. And if it doesn't, you can buy metal probes online."

"Who would sell such a thing?"

"Walmart, for one."

"Are you kidding me?" Angelica asked, stunned.

Tricia shook her head.

"How do you know all this?"

Tricia shrugged. "It's my line of work."

"Breaking into cars?" Angelica asked, aghast.

"No, reading mysteries."

The sisters stared at each other for a long moment. "Well?" Tricia asked.

A slow grin spread across Angelica's face. "I wouldn't miss it for the world."

After retrieving the car lock opener, Tricia returned to Angelica's apartment. The sun set much earlier than it had just a month before, but it was still light when the sisters exited Angelica's place, leaving a sad-faced Sarge behind. Tricia had called Pixie, who couldn't remember the make of Susan's car, but she did recall the color and told Tricia to look for dark windows and shades covering them.

They didn't want to draw any attention to themselves. They were just two women out for a walk on a pleasant fall evening, with one in a transport chair. Nothing out of the ordinary at all.

"Act naturally," Tricia warned as the sisters made their way north up Main Street.

"A song by Buck Owens, covered by the Beatles. Ringo sang it," Angelica said.

"What? How do you know all that?"

"Grandmother listened to a country-western station. Don't you remember?"

Tricia did not.

"Oh, my goodness, all those songs about love gone wrong—all by men, of course, with their nasally, twangy voices. And it's not much better today. You have to listen for hours before you hear a song by a woman country singer. Just another bastion of misogyny."

"And where did you get all this insight?" Tricia asked.

"I get around," Angelica said coyly, glancing down at the chair Tricia pushed.

"What if someone sees us poking around Susan's car?" Tricia asked, her resolve suddenly shaky.

"I've always found it best to do these kinds of things in plain sight."

"What do you mean?"

"Mother was a stickler that we never eat cookies before dinner. I tested that theory hundreds of times. She'd be absorbed in something—like writing invitations to her frequent dinner parties or reading the newspaper—and I could sit there and devour cookie after cookie right in front of her and she never caught on, never said a word."

Of course, if Tricia had tried the same stunt, she would have been sent to bed without supper—or to her room to think about her transgression—and probably forgotten about for hours and hours on end. Angelica could have set the house on fire and never been reprimanded for it, whereas Tricia would have almost certainly been sent to boarding school in some far-flung place as a punishment.

A smattering of vehicles dotted the municipal parking lot. Once the shops along Main Street closed for the day, only the locals parked there and were relegated to the back of the lot. Susan's Toyota Camry sat among those cars and, thanks to Pixie's description, was easily picked out. Tricia parked the transport chair at the rear of the car and stepped closer to inspect the vehicle.

A sun screen across the windshield made an effective barrier that no doubt gave privacy and perhaps shielded the interior of the car from the sun in the summer and provided insulation in the winter. The car's other windows were tinted—possibly at the factory or perhaps enhanced by a third-party vendor.

"Are you sure you'll be able to open the locked door?" Angelica asked.

"Not at all. But Pixie's already mentioned doing some sleuthing on her own, and it's better if I do the deed. There's no way I want her to get into trouble. Chief Baker would probably look for any way to throw her back into the stir."

Angelica giggled. "I love it when you talk like a pulp fiction detective."

Tricia strode over to the passenger side of the car, away from any prying eyes on Main Street, and was grateful that several cars surrounded the vehicle to give her some privacy. Withdrawing the thin, long piece of plastic from the sleeve of her sweater, she looked around to see if anyone was watching before she inserted it between the window and the car's body near the locking mechanism. It was more difficult than she had anticipated. Despite the fact Tricia had had some practice with jimmying, popping the lock wasn't as easy as pie—but then, Tricia wasn't much of a pie eater, and larceny just wasn't part of her makeup, either. But after thirty or forty seconds of jiggling the plastic up and down, she was rewarded with the sound of the lock opening.

"Gee, you *are* a pro at this," Angelica quipped as Tricia opened the car door and scooted onto the passenger seat, which was pushed up as far as it would go, leaving barely any room for her legs, which she left hanging outside the car. She unlocked the rear door, and Angelica got up enough to open it before sitting back down again.

The air was stale but also permeated with the strong aroma of what smelled like a vanilla candle, thanks to the freshener that hung beneath the rearview mirror.

Angelica sniffed. "Not as bad as I anticipated." Ha! She wasn't inside the Camry.

Tricia jostled around so that she could look over the seat and into the back of the vehicle, which was a jumble of bedding, pillows, and duffel bags that looked like they'd been dumped—probably the result of Baker and his men examining the vehicle's contents. Susan didn't appear to have much in the way of creature comforts. And as Tricia rummaged through the detritus, she found a white cylindrical plastic container lined with a trash bag. She had an inkling that it was Susan's toilet. Pixie had said she used a bucket for her bodily needs, but it looked like Susan had upgraded her facilities since the last time she and Pixie had conversed on the subject. Tossing the unzipped sleeping bag aside, Tricia found a cooler behind the passenger seat and struggled to open it, wishing she hadn't when the stench of rotting food assaulted her.

"P-U," Angelica said, wrinkling her nose.

Tricia slammed the lid down, but the odor remained, despite the air freshener.

"I don't suppose anyone mentioned how long the poor woman had been dead before Pixie found her," Angelica said.

"Not long. She'd worked at Sweet As Can Be the day before, but it was a warm day, and those dumpsters can get as hot as an oven. She wasn't smelling like a rose by the time Pixie found her, and it sounded like she was quite fastidious."

The sisters looked around the cluttered car. There were no extraneous papers, no dirt on the driver's- or passenger-side floors, or even dust on the car's dashboard. Tricia dug through the clothes and found a small hand vacuum that could be plugged into the vehicle's cigarette-lighter socket. Yup, Susan had kept her car and herself clean.

"What is it you hope to find here?" Angelica asked. "Surely the police would have confiscated anything they thought might be material to their investigation."

Tricia nodded. What had she hoped to find?

Looking at Susan's possessions in disarray made Tricia wish there had been something she could have done to help her, perhaps find her a real home. There were too many women—and men—living on the edge, under the radar, and she found herself carefully folding the poor woman's clothes. Angelica pitched in, and in no time they'd filled the two duffels and zipped them shut. Tricia straightened the thin sponge-like mattress and, as best they could, they made Susan's bed. They really should empty that cooler, but that would make their presence even more obvious. Tricia turned her attention to the glove compartment. It, too, was an untidy mess. It must have acted as Susan's safe, for Tricia found several old birthday cards and a bank statement with her PO box address, but anything else of a personal nature had probably been removed by the police. She removed the contents, laying the papers on the back seat. Angelica looked through the cards.

"'Happy Birthday, Mother,'" she read and opened the inside. "It's signed 'Love, Kimberly.'" She snorted. "If Kimberly loved her mom so much, why did she let her live in a car?"

"What if she didn't know?" Tricia asked, echoing Pixie's thoughts.

Angelica let out a breath. "You're right. We should choose to believe the best of her. Do you know if Chief Baker has contacted her?"

Tricia shook her head. As she did, she caught sight of something wedged just beneath the compartment's opening. Leaning closer, she saw the post of a pierced earring protruding. It took a bit of effort to dislodge it, and Tricia took a moment to examine the scratched and tarnished silver stud.

"Ahem," said a male voice, causing Tricia to practically jump. She shoved the earring into her sweater pocket and turned.

"Grant, what are you doing here?"

"I might ask you the same thing," Chief Baker grumbled.

"I was just . . . looking around."

"In a dead woman's car?"

Tricia extricated herself from the vehicle. "Am I going to be charged with trespassing? Who'd press charges?"

"Me, for one."

"Don't be absurd," Angelica chided. "We're concerned citizens—and why shouldn't we be? The woman who owned this car was found dead behind Tricia's store."

"And don't think I've forgotten that," the cop grated.

"Now, children," Tricia chided. She turned to Baker. "What's this about Susan's death being treated as a homicide?"

"It's not a secret," Baker said. "The lady didn't jump in your dumpster and just die of suffocation. The autopsy came back with a one-word cause of death: strangulation."

Tricia swallowed. That wasn't what she wanted to hear. Instead she changed the subject. "I hear congratulations are in order."

"Why?" Baker asked, looking clueless.

"On your upcoming wedding."

"Oh, yeah. That."

"Well, I certainly hope you're more enthusiastic when you talk about it with your bride," Angelica chided.

"Naturally," Baker deadpanned.

"I wish you all the happiness in the world," Tricia said, trying to inject some semblance of sincerity into her voice and not entirely succeeding.

"Thanks. Now let's get back to why you're rummaging around in this car."

Tricia sighed. "How did you know we were here?"

"Someone called nine one one to report suspicious behavior, and lo and behold, I find you two."

Tricia was not enamored by his sarcasm.

"Folding clothes and tidying this vehicle is hardly suspicious," Angelica asserted.

"It is when the vehicle's owner has been murdered."

"Poor woman," Angelica said, shaking her head.

"Were you able to contact Susan's next of kin?" Tricia asked.

Baker nodded. "A daughter, Kimberly Radnor-Herbert. She was quite upset."

"Is she coming to Stoneham?" Angelica asked.

"I don't see why she would. The body was taken to Nashua."

"Yes, but her mother's entire estate is here in this parking lot," Tricia pointed out.

"Book value on this car is only a couple of grand, and its contents are worth far less," Baker countered.

"Is the daughter from out of state?" Angelica asked.

"Utica, New York." He turned to Tricia. "Just how did you get into this car? It was locked."

"Are you sure?" Tricia asked innocently, hoping he wouldn't see the strip of plastic on the passenger-side floor.

"My force isn't negligent in that regard."

"Well, then I'm sure you won't punish them too severely for this lapse," Angelica said. She turned to Tricia. "We'd better get going."

Tricia thought fast. "I think I dropped my phone inside the car," she announced. "Hang on." Then she bent over, hoping Baker wouldn't see her as she scrounged for the lock opener. Grasping it, she shoved it up the sleeve of her sweater and then grabbed her phone from her slacks pocket. "Got it," she said, and straightened. "You might want to dump poor Susan's cooler. It's really quite smelly."

"I don't need any suggestions from civilians."

"Well, if her daughter comes to pick up the car, she might think otherwise. If nothing else, it would be a courtesy."

Baker looked thoughtful. "I suppose you're right. Now, if you'll excuse me, I'll do that. I don't need help."

"Let's go," Angelica prodded. "Good night, Chief."

"Yes, good night, Grant."

Baker nodded. "Ladies."

"Oh, one more thing," Tricia said. "Have you gone over the report for my almost break-in last Saturday?"

"No."

"Do you intend to?"

"No."

"Well, why not?"

"I have staff that takes care of that."

"You couldn't take an interest for an old friend?" she asked.

"You're not *that* old."

Tricia's ire surged. She ground her teeth and backed the transport chair away from the car with a jerk.

"Hey," Angelica protested.

"Sorry," Tricia muttered, and the sisters headed back toward Main Street. When they returned to the sidewalk, Tricia turned to see Baker dump the cooler's contents into one of the lot's trash bins. His face collapsed into a mighty scowl, and she giggled.

Angelica snapped her fingers. "Let's get some distance between us and the chief. Did you retrieve the car opener thing?"

"Why do you think I can't bend my arm?"

"Too bad you didn't snag anything else."

"Oh, but I did."

"What?"

"It's just an earring—a silver anchor. It can't be a clue."

Angelica shrugged. "You're probably right. Is our evening of larceny over? I've got a ton of paperwork to attack."

"You're just disappointed we didn't find anything earth-shattering."

"Maybe so," Angelica admitted. "And now that our curiosity is sated, it's time to get back to our real lives. And you should try to stay out of the chief's way."

"I try to make it a point. What do you make of his disinterest in his own wedding?"

"A shotgun affair?" Angelica ventured.

"Is she that young?"

"Of course not. And this isn't his first wedding—or hers, either, for that matter." Angelica sighed. "Sadly, weddings just aren't as exciting the second time around."

Angelica had been married four times; she would know.

When they arrived at the Cookery, Angelica got up from the chair and shuffled into the store. Tricia stowed the chair in the back of the shop before seeing her sister up the stairs. Afterward, she took Sarge out for a comfort stop. Upon her return, she offered to come back before she went to bed, but Angelica shook her head. "Don't worry about Sarge. He's crate trained." Tricia knew it would be a long night for the little guy.

"Good night, dear Tricia. See you tomorrow at lunch—unless Marshall calls with an invitation, of course," Angelica said.

"I'll let you know," Tricia promised. "Love you."

"Love you more," Angelica said and closed and locked the apartment door behind her.

Tricia continued on to Haven't Got a Clue and let herself in, locking up for the night and setting the security system. As she mounted the steps to her loft apartment, she wondered if she had any silver polish.

FIVE

 Tricia hung up her sweater, dug into her pocket for the earring, and headed for the kitchen. In the cabinet under the sink, she found what she was looking for: a squat, plastic container of silver polish. She'd had it for quite a while and had used a good portion of it before her ill-fated cocktail party at the end of winter. She hadn't thought about it since but was glad to find it behind the box of dishwasher powder.

Grabbing a sheet of paper towel, Tricia took a seat at the breakfast bar, dabbed the provided sponge with some of the purple paste, and rubbed it against the small earring, wiping away the tarnish. Cleaning it gave her no better clue about the earring's origin or its owner. She polished it with the toweling and studied it. What she needed was a magnifying glass to see if there were any identifying marks on the back. Before she could go in search of one, her cell phone rang.

Tricia didn't recognize the number on the display, which was unusual. She didn't give her number out to many people. Haven't Got a Clue had its own number. She tapped the little icon and tentatively said, "Hello?"

"Tricia? It's Fiona Sample." Nikki Brimfield's mother. Talk about an unexpected caller. Six years before, Tricia had arranged for the estranged mother and daughter to reunite. She'd met the delightful author several times after that when she'd come to Stoneham from her home in Ontario, Canada, to visit her oldest daughter and her family, and on the Authors at Sea cruise the year before.

"Hi, Fiona. What's up?" Tricia asked, although she thought she had an idea what the woman might want to discuss.

"It's Nikki. I know there's been some bad blood between you two—and I honestly don't understand why, especially now that she's left Russ," Fiona began. Nikki had been married to Russ Smith, owner of the *Stoneham Weekly News* and the current president of the Stoneham Chamber of Commerce, for almost two years. Theirs had been a rocky relationship from the get-go. Tricia had dated Russ for a short period of time. He dumped her when the prospect of a job at a big-city newspaper seemed possible. When no offer appeared, he'd decided he'd made a mistake and wanted Tricia back. She'd cut her losses, but Russ had gone so far as to stalk her for a while. Somehow Nikki got it into her head that it was Tricia doing the stalking, and she'd ended their friendship.

"Anyway," Fiona continued. "I'm sure the gossip mills in Stoneham know that she's hired a manager for the Patisserie and flown to California to participate in the Divine Desserts Competition."

"That news has been making the rounds," Tricia admitted, abandoning the silver earring on the paper towel and pushing it aside.

"I'm very upset about the whole situation. Nikki's cell phone number is no longer in operation, and emails to her bounce. She hasn't called to give me her new number, and I don't know how to get in touch with her. And I really need to."

"Couldn't Russ give you Nikki's number?"

"He says she didn't give it to him, either."

"I understand Nikki left little Russell with his father," Tricia said.

"That's the problem. Russ doesn't want to be the sole caretaker of his son. He called me last night and wants me to take him. He says, with the paper and his volunteer job at the Chamber, he hasn't got the time to fully devote to his son and thinks the child would be better off with me."

"And what do you think?"

"That that bastard never loved that baby and is looking for any chance he can get to ditch him."

"How about you?"

"You know I love my grandson, but I've got a husband, two teenagers, a career, and a house to take care of. And I live in another country. I'm not sure what the legal ramifications would be for me or little Russell."

"That does complicate things."

"That boy belongs with his parents—at least one of them. Do you think you could talk some sense into Russ?"

Tricia gave a mirthless laugh. "No way. The last few times we've spoken, he's been extremely rude to me." Out of spite, Russ had run for Chamber president against Tricia and another. When the winner of the election died before even taking office, Russ—who'd garnered precisely four more votes than Tricia—was awarded the title. Not winning outright was something else he resented, and he'd done his best to try to destroy the organization out of pure malice.

"I'm sorry, Fiona. I don't see how I could be of any help."

"What about Russ's friends?"

"I'm not sure that he has any."

"How about the women in his office? Do you know them?"

"Not personally. I mean, I've dealt with them in the past and they've always been cordial, but we're not friends by any means."

"But could you speak to them and ask them to talk to Russ?"

Tricia sighed. She liked Fiona. She'd like to be of help.

"I guess I could try."

"Oh, thank you so much."

"How goes the writing business?" Tricia asked.

"Very well indeed. In fact, that's another reason I simply can't bring little Russell to live with us. I'm sure you heard my lawsuit against Zoë Carter's estate was settled out of court and I regained my rights to the Jess and Addie *Forever* series."

"Yes, I'm so happy for you." Zoë Carter had found the manuscripts in an old trunk and passed them off as her work and made millions of dollars. Tricia had brought that fact to light and had been deposed in the case.

"While waiting for the settlement, I wrote another book. It'll be out next summer, and I'm on deadline with another book in that series and have another two Bonnie Chesterfield books to write in the next year."

"That's fantastic!"

"Yes. And my publisher has big plans for a ten-city book tour and a big-budget marketing plan."

"I hope you'll have time to visit us here in Stoneham," Tricia said.

Fiona laughed. "Of course. I'd love to do a signing at Haven't Got a Clue. If it wasn't for you, my life would be very, very different. I'll never be able to thank you enough."

"You already have. And I hope to be able to read many, many more books in both your series."

Again Fiona laughed. "Well, I'm dedicating this latest one to you—and, of course, darling Miss Marple."

"Thank you. I'll be sure to tell every one of my customers about it."

"Well, if I'm going to meet my deadlines, I must get back to work," Fiona said. "Thank you so much for talking to Russ's employees."

Tricia winced. She'd almost forgotten the real reason for the call. "I'll let you know their reactions in a day or so."

"Thank you, Tricia. You're a saint."

A saint or a sucker? Tricia pretty much knew which of those descriptors applied to her.

After ending the call with Fiona, Tricia fed her cat, poured herself a glass of wine, picked up the earring, and headed for the reading nook in her bedroom. It was her favorite space in the renovated apartment, and she liked to end the day there reading a new-to-her title or rereading an old favorite.

Before changing into night attire, Tricia opened her jewelry box and tossed the earring inside before she settled in for a good read. No sooner did she stretch out her legs on the upholstered chaise than again the phone rang. This time she recognized the number. Had Angelica been right? Was she going to get a lunch or dinner invitation? "Marshall?"

"Tricia. Are we still speaking?"

Tricia frowned. "Why wouldn't we?"

"I don't know. We didn't have much to say on the ride home from the airport."

"I'm never very chatty when I'm suffering from jet lag." Tricia decided she'd better address the other elephant in the room. "I suppose you heard about Susan Morris being found in the dumpster behind my store."

"Everyone in the village is talking about it."

Of course.

"Word is she was strangled," he said.

"That's right," Tricia said matter-of-factly as Miss Marple sauntered into the room.

"So, what do you think happened?"

"I have no clue, but as Pixie found her, she's concerned she might be blamed for the murder."

"On what grounds?"

"That she knew the woman," Tricia said as her cat jumped onto the end of the chaise.

"So what? I knew her, too," Marshall said.

"You did?"

"Not well. She interviewed for the job of assistant manager of the Armchair Tourist earlier in the summer."

"Why didn't you hire her?"

"She wasn't up to speed with spreadsheets needed for inventory. Other than that, she was very knowledgeable about world travel."

"She was?" Tricia asked, watching as Miss Marple turned around twice before settling down.

"Apparently she served in the military, traveled the world, and got discharged as a lieutenant in the Navy."

Not only had Susan been a homeless woman—she'd been a homeless Navy vet, too? Suddenly the anchor earring made perfect sense.

"That poor woman."

"Is it true she lived in her car?"

"I'm afraid so. Angelica and I checked it out earlier this evening. But according to Pixie she seemed fine with the situation—or at least she'd learned to make the best of it."

"How sad."

"Sadder still that there are literally thousands like her—and many not as lucky."

"You call that lucky?" Marshall muttered.

Tricia sighed. "Not really."

They were quiet for a long moment before Marshall spoke again. "I called to see if you were free for lunch tomorrow."

"What did you have in mind?"

"Somewhere quiet—and away from Stoneham."

"I think I could make myself available."

"Great. Then shall I pick you up around eleven thirty?"

"That sounds fine."

"Okay, I'll see you then."

"Good night."

Tricia set her phone aside and picked up her book, removing the bookmark, and began reading where she'd left off. Unfortunately, after reading the first paragraph three times, she still hadn't garnered its meaning.

Setting the book aside, she got up and went back to her jewelry box and took out the earring she'd abandoned only minutes before. This time she returned to her kitchen and the crock where she kept pens and her magnifying glass.

How had the earring gotten scratched? Susan had probably worn the set for years, lost one, and then decided to hold on to the other as a keepsake. It might be something Susan's daughter would like to have, especially if she remembered her mother wearing the set. But how would Tricia get it to the woman? She didn't want to admit to Baker that she'd taken the earring out of Susan's car. Because she had Susan's daughter's name, perhaps she could find out the woman's address and mail it to her. She'd think about it.

Returning to her seat, Tricia found that her cat had appropriated her end of the chaise.

"Off," Tricia ordered.

Miss Marple turned her head and closed her eyes.

"I mean it."

Miss Marple stretched out and rolled onto her other side, turning her back on Tricia.

"You're being very naughty."

Still no reaction from the cat.

Tricia stood there for a long moment, then picked up her book. Despite the early hour, she would read in bed. It wasn't as comfortable, but she'd done it thousands of times before.

As soon as she settled against her piled-up pillows, Miss Marple jumped up to join her.

"Were you lonely?"

Miss Marple merely said, "Yow."

Tricia turned her attention to the page before her, but her thoughts went back to her conversation with Marshall. Susan had been a veteran and homeless, too. Could either of those facts have contributed to her death?

SIX

Tricia returned from her walk the next morning in plenty of time to begin the workday at ten. She found she enjoyed her exercise routine far more in the spring and the fall, when the temperatures were cooler and the latter season was just beginning.

She made the store's first pots of coffee of the day (regular and decaf) and was about to choose the morning's music when the bell over the door tinkled, announcing the arrival of Pixie, who'd taken Tricia's advice of the previous day and was wearing her pretty floral dress and the white sweater.

"Morning. Have you heard anything about Susan?" Pixie asked anxiously.

"Good morning. If you mean have they made an arrest for her murder, no, I haven't."

"Damn." Pixie flopped down on one of the upholstered chairs in the reader's nook, looking glum.

"But I did find out something about her that I found interesting."

"From who? Chief Baker?" Pixie asked anxiously.

"I did speak to him," Tricia admitted, "but the only news he was willing to share was that Susan's daughter was supposed to go to Nashua and make arrangements to retrieve her mother's body. He said she was from Utica, New York."

"I didn't know that," Pixie said.

"Did you know Susan served in the Navy?"

Pixie shook her head. "She never mentioned it. Although, come to think of it, she did say she visited doctors in Manchester. Isn't that where the VA hospital is?"

Tricia nodded. "What did she go there for?"

"She never said. Just that she had an appointment for some kind of medical problem."

"When was this?"

Pixie shrugged. "Months ago."

Tricia nodded. With that subject exhausted, she changed to a new one. "I've got a lunch date with Marshall. He's picking me up at eleven thirty."

"Oh, good," Pixie said, brightening.

It seemed everybody was rooting for the two of them to get together. Why didn't Tricia feel so hopeful about their relationship?

"Me and Mr. Everett can handle the store—and we can swap lunch hours."

"Thanks."

"Did you have a chance to bake anything for the customers last night?" Pixie asked.

Tricia shook her head. "I hadn't even thought about it. After dinner with Angelica, we—" She thought fast. "—we went for a walk."

"Was that when you ran into Chief Baker?"

"Uh, yes. You might say that. Afterward I came home and read for a while and then went to bed. Why?"

"I was just thinking it's been a while since you made any cookies, and—"

"I suppose I could get us something from across the street at the Coffee Bean."

"They didn't have any cookies when I stopped in to pick up a muffin. Have you had a chance to meet the new guy who's managing the Patisserie?" Pixie asked. "He seems kinda nice . . . unlike his AWOL boss."

"No, I haven't met him," Tricia said. She hadn't patronized the bakery in almost three months. Her decision was based on the fact that Nikki had been so incredibly unpleasant toward her. If Nikki hadn't given her mother or her husband her new phone number, surely she'd given it to her new manager. Shouldn't Russ have already thought of that as well? And if this new manager hadn't given it to Russ, he wasn't likely to give it to Tricia, either.

Nikki had burned a lot of bridges these past few years and had few friends left in Stoneham, her hometown. Tricia was also pretty sure Nikki would have given this new manager her opinion on Haven't Got a Clue's owner—or was Tricia giving Nikki too much credit on that account? She may not have even mentioned Tricia's name because she thought so little of her.

"Have you heard anything about this guy?" she asked Pixie.

"I've met him. While you were gone, I bought some cookies."

"Yes, I saw."

"I couldn't let the customers—and Mr. E—go without," Pixie said defensively. "And without you baking . . ."

"I hope you didn't pay for them yourself," Tricia said.

"Well . . ."

"Let me know what you spent, and I'll reimburse you."

"Aw, you don't have to do that."

"It's a store expense—a deduction."

Pixie shrugged. "Well, if you put it that way . . . but you need to know that they weren't all that great."

"Really?"

"Yeah."

"This manager," Tricia prodded.

Pixie frowned. She listened to gossip but didn't often repeat it.

"I only ask because I got a call from Nikki's mother yesterday. Nikki changed her number and hasn't given it to her or her soon-to-be ex. What if there was an emergency with little Russell? Surely this guy would have her number." And if he'd give her the number, she wouldn't have to ask the women at the *Stoneham Weekly News* to intervene. "Do you think he might be persuaded to give it to Nikki's mother, or at least convey a message to Nikki?"

"He might. He does have a son, although I think he's a lot older than Nikki's boy. Do you want me to go ask him?"

Tricia shook her head. "I'm the one who spoke with Fiona. It should be me who makes the request." She checked her phone and wrote Fiona's name and number down on a piece of paper. "I'll go have a chat with this guy. What's his name?"

"Roger. Roger Sykes."

"I'll go have a word with him—that is, if you don't mind holding the fort."

"That depends," Pixie said with a grin. "If you bring back any goodies, will they be edible?"

Stoneham's bakery seemed to have a lull in customers on that particular morning, for there was nobody in the shop, where the heavenly aromas of cakes, cookies, and bread mingled in the air.

"Can I help you?" asked the man in baker whites behind the counter. He looked to be in his mid-forties, with salt-and-pepper hair.

"Yes, I'd like to buy some thumbprint cookies."

He shook his head. "Fresh out, I'm afraid. But the oatmeal raisin are pretty darn good—and they're healthy for you, too."

"I'll take a dozen," Tricia said, and watched as the guy bagged her purchase.

"Are you the head baker?"

"Well, I'm managing the place until I can buy it. I've got a couple of helpers who come in early and work until after lunch."

"I'm Tricia Miles. I own the vintage mystery bookstore, Haven't Got a Clue, a few doors down."

The man raised an eyebrow. Nikki had obviously mentioned her name. "I'm Roger Sykes." He didn't offer his hand.

"Aside from the cookies, I wondered if you might have Nikki Brimfield's new phone number."

He shook his head as he plucked a piece of baker's tissue from the nearby box and filled the white waxed bakery bag with cookies. "No can do."

"Then perhaps you'd pass on a message and ask her to her to call her mother."

"Uh, sure. Is it an emergency?"

"I wouldn't say that, but Fiona, her mom, is anxious about a situation that needs to be quickly resolved, and it involves Nikki."

"I don't actually have her number. She emails me."

"Her mother hasn't been able to contact her by text or email."

"I guess Nikki had to change her contact info when she moved," Roger said.

Tricia nodded and pulled out her wallet to pay for the cookies. Roger made change and handed her the bag.

"When will the sale of the Patisserie go through?"

"With luck, before the end of the year. How's the tourist trade during the holidays?" Roger asked.

"Brisk. I don't think you'll have to worry about the winter doldrums. There're enough people in the village who supported Nikki through the slow months. If they like your wares, I'm sure they'll be just as loyal to you."

Roger raised his hand, crossing his fingers. "I hope to see you again, Ms. Miles."

"Tricia," she emphasized.

"Tricia."

She smiled and headed for the exit, wondering if he'd have an opportunity to pass her message along to Nikki anytime soon.

It was odd that Nikki seemed to have cut all ties to her hometown, her business, but especially her responsibility to her child. Nikki had considered selling the bakery the year before when she'd first become a mother—wanting to stay home with her boy. It had been Russ who insisted that she keep the bakery open because they needed the income. Now Nikki had abandoned both little Russell and her business, gambling that she'd make it big as a TV chef.

Did Nikki dream big, or was she just a fool?

SEVEN

Tricia arrived back at Haven't Got a Clue to find that Mr. Everett had come to work more than half an hour before his shift. "Grace is working at the Everett Foundation today, so I thought I'd ride with her to save gas." Mr. Everett had won the lottery several years before but had channeled the majority of that money into his philanthropic foundation that his wife, Grace, now ran. She, of course, was well-off, but they lived modestly in the home she had shared with her first husband.

"You're just in time for oatmeal cookies," Tricia said. She found a plate under the beverage station and placed the cookies on it before offering them to her employees. "They didn't have any thumbprint cookies, I'm afraid."

"These will do just as well," Mr. Everett said, and bit into his. But instead of a smile, he frowned, chewing slowly.

Pixie didn't seem to notice his reaction and selected one of her own. She bit into it, chewed, and her eyes narrowed.

"Anything wrong?" Tricia asked.

Pixie swallowed. "Well, I guess I was expecting something a little different."

"Different?" Tricia asked. She picked up a cookie and took a sniff. It smelled okay.

"Yeah, good. You know, like Nikki used to make."

Tricia took the tiniest of bites. There was oatmeal in the cookie, but it wasn't as sweet as she'd expected. In fact, it wasn't sweet at all.

"I think a crucial ingredient might be missing," Mr. Everett suggested.

"I'll say," Pixie agreed. "Do you think we should tell Roger?"

Tricia wasn't sure she wanted to be the bearer of bad news to someone she'd just met. "I don't think so."

"It might be a kindness," Mr. Everett said.

"Or taken as criticism," Pixie suggested.

"I'm sure it was just an oversight with this batch," Tricia said.

Pixie examined the cookie in her hand, then her gaze slid to the wastebasket nearby.

Tricia took the hint and discarded her cookie first, with the others following suit. Then she tossed the rest of the cookies in the trash as well. Unfortunately, there wasn't time to whip up a batch of cookies before Marshall came to pick her up for lunch. She'd try to make time that evening so they could offer their customers a sweet treat on Saturday.

It occurred to Tricia that she hadn't thought to tell Angelica about her lunch date, so she fired off a quick text, also asking if she needed anything for lunch.

Not a thing. See you for dinner at my place? came Angelica's reply less than a minute later.

Tricia sent her sister a thumbs-up emoji, then pocketed her phone. "Well, shall we finish our coffee before we begin the workday?"

Marshall's car pulled up outside Haven't Got a Clue at precisely eleven thirty. Tricia hopped into the passenger seat and buckled up. Marshall hadn't taken off and was looking at her expectantly, no doubt waiting for a hello kiss. She obliged, but it was quick, without a hint of passion. He turned his attention back to the road, checked his side mirror, and pulled away from the curb.

"How goes the Susan Morris investigation?" he asked.

"How would I know?"

"Tricia . . ." he chided.

"Apparently Chief Baker still seems to think Pixie might be responsible."

"Why's that?"

"Probably because she's handy to blame."

"Do you *really* think so?"

"I would hope he wouldn't stoop that low. He practically interrogated her on Wednesday night—and without a lawyer."

"Do you think she needs one?"

"I sure hope not, but the thought of going back to jail terrifies her."

"I should think so. What else?"

Tricia filled Marshall in on what little else she'd learned about the dead woman before changing the subject. "Where are we going this time?"

"On a picnic."

"Where?"

"Just up the road a bit."

Tricia laughed. "The last time I went on a picnic, it was in a cemetery."

"Oh, great. Now you've ruined my surprise."

"Really?"

"Of course not. A friend of mine has a piece of land just north of here with a pond and a gazebo. It's a very pretty spot."

"And what are we going to eat?"

"Something I had catered by the Brookview Inn."

"Oh, you're going all out," she said in jest.

"And why not? After that disaster of a vacation I dragged you along on, I owe it to you."

"The trip was not a disaster," Tricia said.

"It wasn't," he agreed. "Milford Travel sent emailed surveys to the guests and all but one has come back with high praise."

"Are you insinuating that I sent in the dissenting vote?"

"Not at all. That you didn't return it at all. I'm guessing it got caught in your spam filter."

Tricia thought about it: she didn't always check the spam for her personal account, but she did for the store. "I'll have a look when I get home."

"You've got a phone; can't you check it now?"

"What would you have me say?"

"Nothing," he said, sounding just a little defeated, his attention on the road.

Tricia studied his profile. "Part of me enjoyed the trip. The people were nice, the food was good, and the scenery spectacular."

"And the part you didn't enjoy?"

"That you had to work so hard. I knew that going in, but I didn't realize you'd be working as an indentured servant."

"Had you ever taken a guided tour before the trip?"

"No," Tricia admitted. "I thought you did great. You were knowledgeable and attentive to the guests."

"Just not attentive enough for you."

"You warned me before we left. And two weeks was way too long for me to be away from my home, my store, and my cat."

"Then a monthlong trek through China is out of the question."

"Sorry, but I'd have to answer yes."

Marshall was quiet for long minutes, and Tricia wished he'd switch on the radio to break the silence. Finally he spoke. "Do you still want to go on this picnic?"

"Of course I do. It's the first time in weeks we'll share a meal that doesn't include twenty other people."

"Now, that's not true."

"A scone and a cup of tea in a tea shop hardly counts."

Marshall braked and turned onto a dirt road that was lined with maple trees, their leaves giving a subtle hint that the full-blown colors of autumn would soon be upon them. As Marshall had said, the drive ended at a pond and a gazebo that looked newly built.

"Wow," Tricia said in awe. "It looks like the perfect place for a wedding."

"That's the whole idea. But the site won't be completely finished until next year. My friend has plans for a pavilion so that he can cater all kinds of parties. It'll even have a gas fireplace for winter gatherings."

"Sounds ambitious. How come I haven't heard about this before?"

Marshall raised an eyebrow. "It was reported in the *Stoneham Weekly News*."

Tricia frowned. "I no longer read that rag."

"Maybe you should."

Tricia nodded. "I do have a reason to speak with someone in that office—if I can gather up my courage."

"Why would you need courage?"

"I'll tell you about it over lunch. Speaking of which, shouldn't we get this picnic going?"

Marshall gave her a smile and reached for her hand. "Thanks for coming out with me today."

"Why wouldn't I?"

He shrugged. "Because."

"I'm here because I want to be with you. Even if we'd just gone to a burger joint, I'd still want to spend time with you."

His smile broadened, and he leaned forward and kissed her gently. Then again. And again.

EIGHT

Tricia returned late from lunch—quite late—
and perhaps just a little tipsy thanks to the wine
Marshall had brought to their picnic. But it was obvious that business was light at Haven't Got a Clue on that
Friday afternoon. A worried-looking Pixie kept looking
north up Main Street as though expecting a police cruiser
to barrel down the road and screech to a halt in front of the
store, a couple of cops spilling into the street and rushing
the door with cuffs in hand, ready to arrest her.

Mr. Everett had already left for the day, and Tricia glanced
at the clock and then back to Pixie. "Are you okay?"

"Oh, sure," Pixie said, and brushed at the shoulder of her
sweater as though to flick off nonexistent dust.

"I don't think you should worry about it."

It. They both knew what she meant. That Pixie could be
a suspect in Susan Morris's death.

"Why's that?"

"Because you've done nothing wrong."

"That never stopped the cops from nailing me before,"
Pixie admitted sourly.

Tricia decided to try another tack. "Have you got many
clients to see tomorrow at the day spa?"

Pixie worked for four hours Saturday afternoons as a nail tech at Booked for Beauty, Angelica's day spa. Considering she had no formal training, her nail artistry was exquisite, and already she'd had a number of repeat customers.

"Just five tomorrow, but I'll take walk-ins, too. You know I love working here, but I really enjoy all the girl talk at the spa. I missed all that once I—"

Once she got out of jail or once she no longer hung out with other ladies of the night?

Tricia didn't ask.

"I know what you mean. If I didn't have you to talk to, and Ginny and Angelica, I would be completely starved for female companionship."

"Did you ever have a lot of friends?" Pixie asked.

Tricia shook her head. "Angelica was the one who brought people home for parties and such. I was more the studious type."

"With your nose in a book?"

"You got it."

"What was the first mystery you ever read?" Pixie asked.

Tricia smiled. "*The Secret of Smugglers' Cove* by Margaret Leighton."

"How old were you?"

"Eight or nine. Years later I paid through the nose to hunt down a copy. How about you?"

"*The Mirror Crack'd from Side to Side* by Dame Agatha. I was thirty-seven."

Tricia smiled and looked at the clock. "It's only five minutes 'til closing. Why don't we call it a day?"

Pixie nodded and collected her purse from behind the cash desk. "It's such a pretty evening, I think I'll take the long way home."

Tricia knew that meant she'd avoid walking past the Stoneham police station. "Exercise is good for you," she agreed. "Have a good weekend. I'll see you on Monday."

Pixie forced a smile, and her voice broke when she said, "If I'm still around."

Tricia frowned, stepped forward, and gave her employee

and friend a hug, then pulled back, looking Pixie in the eye. "I'll see you on Monday."

Pixie nodded. "Okay."

Tricia watched as Pixie left the store with a good-bye wave and headed north. Sure enough, when she got to the intersection, Pixie crossed the road and started up Locust Street. She'd only have to walk up two blocks and double back to avoid the police station. Tricia sighed, shook her head, and then closed her store. After leaving a snack for Miss Marple, she locked up and hoofed it next door to the Cookery, where she let herself in and took the stairs to Angelica's apartment. Again Sarge gave her a hearty welcome and was rewarded with two dog biscuits.

"Oh, really, Sarge. Will you hush!" Angelica ordered. "Honestly, you'd think it had been years, not less than twenty-four hours, since he's seen you."

"I'm so lovable, he can't help himself," Tricia deadpanned. "Shouldn't you be sitting? What are you doing on your feet?"

Angelica frowned. "Walking, or perhaps shambling. I'm going stir-crazy," she admitted, and turned to retrieve the pitcher of martinis she'd already made, then took out the chilled glasses from the freezer. "So, how was your lunch with Marshall?"

"It was a picnic by the side of a pond. We sat on a blanket in the grass and drank chilled champagne and dined on baguettes stuffed with chicken salad. And for dessert—"

"You?" Angelica asked wryly.

"No! Profiteroles."

Angelica practically swooned. "Oh, I love them. We occasionally serve them at the Brookview for afternoon tea."

"I know. That's where they came from—like our dinner, I suppose?"

"You supposed right. Antonio had one of his employees drop it off. I'm going to gain ten pounds before my next surgery. I wonder if I should join the Y in Merrimack so I can do water aerobics."

"If you do, I'll go with you," Tricia offered, thinking about the weight she'd gained on her trip.

"Deal." Angelica poured their drinks and sighed. "It's been a long time since I was on a picnic."

"What's the weather supposed to be like on Sunday? Maybe we can have a cookout on your balcony instead of a big dinner inside. The weather won't hold for much longer."

"Isn't it supposed to rain?"

"There goes that idea. But it's lovely out now. Let's sit on the balcony again."

They picked up their drinks and Angelica led the way, with Sarge bringing up the rear, his dog biscuits long gone.

Once they'd settled themselves, Angelica spoke. "How was the rest of your day?"

"Busy, or at least making busywork for Pixie. She's paranoid she's going to be arrested for Susan Morris's murder."

"Well, if it happens, we'll get her the best lawyer money can buy," Angelica declared.

Tricia liked the fact Angelica included herself in that equation.

"Aside from that, there is something that's weighing on my mind," Tricia said.

"Oh?"

Tricia sipped her martini. "After I got home last night, I got a call from Fiona Sample."

"Oh? How's she doing?"

"Career-wise, fantastic. Not so happy on the personal front."

"Why's that?" Angelica asked.

"Nikki."

"Oh, your favorite subject," Angelica said, and rolled her eyes. "What's going on with her since she bolted for the West Coast looking for fame and fortune?"

"It seems that Russ wants Fiona to take charge of little Russell."

"But she's got her own family in Canada."

"Yes, and quite a few writing contracts she has to fulfill. She loves the boy, but—"

"She's not the kid's mother, and he's a handful," Angelica said.

"Exactly. I visited the Patisserie this morning and spoke with the new manager."

"Roger's a nice guy, but he doesn't make bread as good as Nikki does."

"Or cookies." She explained about the oatmeal cookie fiasco. "I assured him the business would make it through the long winter months, but after tasting his wares, I'm not so sure."

"That's too bad. Nikki may not have a winning personality, but she is a damn good baker."

"Anyway," Tricia continued, "Fiona wants me to speak to the women who work for Russ at his weekly rag."

"Is that a good idea? I mean, won't he look at it as interference?"

"I'm sure he will, but poor Fiona sounded so desperate, I feel like I should at least try."

"But you didn't get a chance today?"

Tricia shook her head.

Angelica sipped her drink. "I know Nikki went through a personality change when she started dating Russ—"

"From which she has never recovered," Tricia cut in.

"—but I don't get why she left little Russell behind. Two years ago she was desperate to stay home with that baby, and now she's just walked away. She's going to find it was the biggest mistake of her life. It was for me," Angelica muttered sullenly.

"When you left Antonio, you made sure he was well taken care of. You didn't abandon him financially, and you saw him as often as you could."

"But I still walked away. He's forgiven me, but I'll never forgive myself," she said bitterly.

Tricia reached over and touched her sister's hand, noticing the tears brimming in her eyes. "Hey, all's well that ends well," she said, invoking that old saw.

Angelica nodded. "I guess you're right." She took another sip of her drink. "What are the odds Patti or that other one—I can never remember her name—are likely to speak to you about little Russell? I never got the impression they were all that fond of Russ."

"A job's a job—and they surely want to keep theirs—but you're probably right."

Angelica nodded. "When will you try to talk to them?"

"The office is open tomorrow morning, and since the Chamber's hours have been slashed to half a day a week so as not to interfere with Russ's regular business, I'm not likely to run into him."

Angelica shook her head. "It's shocking. The Chamber's office hours should be scheduled for when businesspeople can interact with them. When I was its president, I had office hours five days a week—plus I fielded calls on weekends if necessary."

"You were a spectacular president, and it's painful to see how Russ has destroyed the organization you worked so hard to build."

"When his tenure is up, it's going to take years for the next president to rebuild trust," Angelica said, still shaking her head.

"I think I'll go over to the newspaper as soon as Mr. Everett comes in to work tomorrow," Tricia said. "Since we're between the summer tourist season and the leaf peepers, it should be pretty quiet in my shop."

"Which is why I was determined to diversify. Already, the day spa's local appeal is helping to float the rest of the Angelica Miles fleet."

"And how about Nigela Ricita Associates?"

"A completely different set of books, and that part of my empire is doing fantastically well." Of course, Antonio dealt with most of the day-to-day problems in that arena.

"Any word on Susan Morris?"

"She was a naval officer."

"Get out!"

"That's what she told Marshall when she interviewed for the assistant manager's job at the Armchair Tourist. And that earring I found in her car was of an anchor."

"I hate to think of how many of our veterans are down

on their luck and living hard," Angelica lamented. "And poor Susan among them."

"And now murdered. Pixie didn't know she was a vet, which seems rather odd, as they were close enough for Susan to accept a pair of Pixie's shoes."

"Not surprising. I'm sure Pixie doesn't go around introducing herself as an ex-prostitute, either."

"That was a long—" Tricia broke off. Actually, it *wasn't* such a long time ago.

"It could have been decades since Susan was in the service. She probably no longer identified as a sailor—if that's what she was—either."

Tricia nodded. "Well, let's drink a toast to poor Susan. Rest in peace."

Angelica raised her glass, and they both polished off the last of their drinks.

"It gets too damp to sit out here for too long," Angelica said, and gave a shiver. "Let's go in, and while you pour another drink, I'll haul out dinner. Tommy at the café made us a big julienne salad and sent over a pot of soup, too."

"I'm all for that," Tricia agreed.

She helped Angelica to her feet and then collected their glasses. As she turned, she glanced down at the dumpster that sat behind her building and a shiver ran up her back. It wasn't just the encroaching dampness that made her feel cold to her bones.

NINE

 Saturday morning arrived, and Mr. Everett was as punctual as ever. Since winning the amateur division of the Great Booktown Bake-Off three months before, he'd gained confidence in his baking ability and often arrived with a plastic container filled with his favorite thumbprint cookies. Tricia had completely forgotten she'd promised to bake something and was glad he'd come through with the treats.

"What kind of jam did you use this time?" Tricia asked.

"Gooseberry. It's tangy—with just the right amount of snap."

Tricia poured coffee for them both and sampled one of the cookies. "Oh, my—that's good."

Mr. Everett beamed.

They chatted for a few minutes as they got the store ready to open and finished their coffee. Tricia rinsed her cup in the store's washroom before announcing her intention of visiting the *Stoneham Weekly News*, although she didn't share why she was visiting.

"I won't be long," she promised.

"Take your time. I can handle anything that comes up, although I would like to spend some time downstairs in the office to update the inventory at some point today."

"An excellent idea," Tricia agreed, and grabbed her cell phone. "Give me a call if we get an influx of customers."

"Will do," Mr. Everett promised as Tricia hurried out the door.

The air was cool, but the forecast called for bright skies until late in the afternoon, with rain later on. Although Tricia felt unsure about her visit to the village's weekly paper, she was determined to enjoy the walk to get there.

Patti Perkins, Russ's receptionist, stringer, and all-around Jill-of-all-trades, sat behind her desk with a cup of coffee, staring at her computer screen, when Tricia entered the offices of the *News*. The desk across the way was empty, with no sign of an inhabitant. What was surprising was that Russ's office door was open but blocked with a baby gate. Penned inside was a whining little Russell, who appeared to be throwing plastic blocks against the walls.

"Hey, Patti," Tricia called.

"Tricia," Patti said, and smiled. "You're a sight for sore eyes. We don't see much of you these days."

"Well, we both know the reason for that," she said conspiratorially. "Where's your coworker?"

Patti's smile was short-lived. "She switched to part-time, and it wasn't her idea."

"Why's that?"

"Ad revenue is way down since we lost the Nigela Ricita account."

Angelica had made good on her threat after Russ had tried to smear Tricia's good name just three months before.

"I'm sorry to hear that," Tricia said, for Patti's coworker's sake—not Russ's.

"If you're looking for Russ—"

"I wasn't." Tricia nodded toward the office beyond. "Have you added part-time babysitting to your other office duties?"

Patti glowered. "It wasn't by choice." Little Russell's whining grew louder. "Russ says he can't get anything done if he takes the kid to the Chamber office."

Obviously, there was no love lost between Patti and little Russell.

"I raised my own kids and I resent having to take care of someone else's—especially for no extra pay," Patti groused.

"But?" Tricia asked.

"I need this job," Patti grumbled. A plastic block came sailing through the air, landing on Patti's desk. She tossed it back into the office to the sound of amused giggles from its inhabitant. "What can I do for you?" Patti asked Tricia.

"I came to speak to you on behalf of Russ's mother-in-law."

Patti's eyes narrowed in suspicion. "What for?"

"Russ is pressuring her to take little Russell off his hands."

Another block arced through the doorway, this time missing its target.

"And why did she want you to speak to me?"

"To see if you could reason with Russ."

Patti laughed. "I've been working for him for eight years, and in all that time I haven't had much luck with that. Why can't she take the kid? She's his grandmother."

"Fiona is a working mom herself, with two teens and a national book tour on the horizon. She's legally bound to finish and deliver the novels she'd contracted for, and she can't very well do that with a toddler underfoot—not to mention she lives outside of the US."

"Oh, yeah. I forgot about that."

"Would you be willing to speak to Russ on her behalf?"

"Hey!" little Russell called. "Hey! Hey!"

Patti let out a sigh, ignoring the boy. "And reap Russ's wrath?" She shook her head. "Uh-uh."

Tricia couldn't say she blamed the woman.

Patti leaned forward. "But I will tell you this—and you didn't hear it from me: if she doesn't take the kid, Russ is considering putting that little boy into foster care."

Tricia's mouth dropped open in disbelief. "You're kidding."

Patti shook her head. "Will his grandmother suddenly decide to take the boy on when she hears that?"

Tricia sighed, feeling sorry for the child no one seemed to want. "I have no idea."

"And good luck to the foster family that gets him. That boy is an absolute terror."

"Maybe he just needs love," Tricia suggested.

"Hey—I want a cookie!" Russell called.

"That and some stability," Patti agreed.

Tricia looked down and saw a mock-up of the next edition of the *Stoneham Weekly News* sitting on a stack of papers on Patti's desk. The headline read "Homeless Woman Strangled and Dumped." Russ's flair for attention-grabbing headlines was on full display. "Looks like Susan Morris's death is the top story in Monday's edition."

Patti shook her head. "Sad for the poor old lady. And after what she went through in the military."

That statement spiked Tricia's attention. "Oh?"

"Yep, we cover it all in our next issue."

Tricia reached toward the edited copy, but Patti was quick to move it out of her reach. "Russ would skin me alive if he thought I let you see the story. You can read all about it on Monday."

Two whole days? Where had the paper gotten the story on Susan—and what was it?

"Can you give me a hint about its content?" Tricia asked, idly noticing that it had gotten awfully quiet in Russ's office.

Patti shook her head. "I'm just surprised the *Nashua Telegraph* and the *Union Leader* haven't reported it. It's been a long time since Russ had a scoop."

And no doubt he'd be preening like a peacock over it. And how had Russ found out about whatever trouble had befallen Susan during her time in the military? By talking to Department of Defense personnel, or just plain searching the Internet?

If nothing else, she could try the latter.

"Anything else I can do for you?" Patti asked before a crash from the next room made her jump. She pursed her lips. "I told Russ his office isn't kidproof. If that boy has broken the computer or printer—"

Little Russell began to wail, and Patti got up from her desk.

"I'll see you later," Tricia called, and headed for the door, feeling sorry for the little boy and his reluctant babysitter.

* * *

Mr. Everett was waiting on a customer when Tricia arrived back at Haven't Got a Clue. She bagged the goods while he rang up the sale.

The little bell above the door jingled cheerfully as he bade his customer, "Come back soon!"

"That was a good sale," Tricia commented.

"They're all good," Mr. Everett said happily. He always looked at the sunny side of life.

"I need to do some computer research in the office. Do you mind if I do it now?"

"Not at all. I shall hold the fort. And if no one comes in, I'll sneak in a little reading."

"Sneak all you want," Tricia said, patted his back, and headed for the store's office.

After slipping into her office chair, Tricia started the computer and brought up her browser. But instead of Googling *Susan Morris*, she typed in her own name and that of her store: she hadn't thought to do it in quite a while. As expected, her recent TV interview was the first result of her search. She clicked on the link and it took her to the video. The clip was brief, only about ninety seconds long, and as others had remarked, she looked pretty good and her store came across even better.

She was still smiling when she typed in Susan Morris's name, but her good mood was short-lived when her screen was flooded. The name Susan Morris wasn't at all unique, as evidenced by the number of Facebook profiles that popped up. Tricia scrolled through the pictures of the women, but as she had no idea what Susan Morris the murder victim looked like, it was worse than futile. Since she knew that Susan had been an officer in the Navy, she tried adding various ranks before the name. Another washout.

Tricia stared at the blinking cursor on her screen. What if Susan had once been known under another name? Goodness knows, Angelica had changed her surname with each of her four marriages, returning to her maiden name only after her last—and what she had declared final—divorce. She was in no rush to return to the altar.

Tricia bit her lip and thought about what Baker had told her days before. Susan had a daughter named Kimberly something—a double name beginning with an *R*. Kimberly Rattler? Rudner? No, Radnor. Radnor-Herbert. Had Radnor been Susan's maiden or married name?

With nothing left to lose, Tricia typed in *Susan Radnor*. Another load of Facebook page profiles appeared. But when she tried typing in *Ensign Susan Radnor*—bingo! Up came a scandal that Tricia hadn't thought about since she'd been a kid in school: Tailhook. But even so, she only vaguely remembered what it was about, and the subject chilled her soul: sexual assault in the military.

Susan's name had been only briefly mentioned in the Wikipedia article that covered Tricia's screen. She clicked a link to a different entry and sat transfixed as she read about the Tailhook Symposium, what was meant to be a debriefing for Operation Desert Storm naval and marine aviation officers that took place at the Las Vegas Hilton back in 1991. How drunken naval and marine officers camped out in a narrow third-floor hallway, luring female naval officers—and even some civilians—into what was called "the gauntlet," where eighty-three women and seven men were sexually assaulted. Some of the women had been fondled, while others had had their clothes torn off and were manhandled as though in a mosh pit. The men weren't treated as badly. A pinch on the butt was what most of them experienced.

According to the article, Ensign Susan Radnor had testified against several higher-ranking officers and was said to have been retaliated against when said superiors were refused advancement in rank or were simply forced to resign their commissions—but none of the officers were named in the article. And it wasn't just the officers perpetrating the assaults who ended up with their careers in ruins. Fourteen admirals and the secretary of the navy were made to pay as well. The sad thing was, that scandal didn't put a dent in the ongoing problem of sexual assault in the military—something that goes on to this day.

After reporting the incident and not finding justice in the military, the loudest whistle-blower, Lieutenant Paula Coughlin, went public with her story and resigned her commission after suffering abuse and retaliation for telling the truth about what happened in that crowded hallway. It was the end of her career and her ability to find gainful employment in the private sector as well. She settled out of court with the Tailhook Association and sued the hotel for neglecting to provide better security.

The article didn't mention Susan's outcome. Had she sued or had she, too, been branded a pariah for daring to come forward and testify?

And was it likely that that long-ago scandal was the reason Susan Radnor Morris was murdered? If so, the officer or officers implicated had waited an awfully long time to retaliate against the woman. Did Russ Smith intend to imply that in his coverage of the murder? Or, despite her past, had Susan simply been at the wrong place at the wrong time?

Tricia wondered if Russ had dug up any real dirt on the murder. He wasn't a favorite among the villagers and had no friends—that she knew of—among the ranks of the Stoneham police force, either. But if one could believe his bragging, Russ had once been an ace reporter before buying his own weekly newspaper where he could be his own boss and call his own shots. Who could he have spoken with in Stoneham who would have known about Susan's life before she became a fixture in the village, albeit one who mostly coasted below the radar? Were there other homeless vets in the area? Could Susan have been a member of Alcohol or Narcotics Anonymous? Drug or alcohol addiction was a devastating side effect for members of the volunteer military who had been forced into seemingly endless rounds of deployment. But Susan's time in the military had been decades before. Had she suffered from post-traumatic stress disorder after what she'd experienced during the Tailhook incident and the months—and years—of economic and personal isolation afterward?

Tricia mulled over that question, wondering how she'd ever discover the truth.

TEN

 "I'm back," Tricia called as she reentered her store. Mr. Everett stood behind the cash desk with a book open before him but looked up as she approached. "Did we have any customers while I was downstairs?"

"Ah, Ms. Miles—just one," Mr. Everett said. "A six-dollar-and-forty-three-cent sale."

"That's better than nothing, I suppose."

"Quite," Mr. Everett agreed solemnly. "Things will pick up for the holidays."

Which were two months away. But the bookstore had done well during the summer tourist season, so there was no cause for worry.

Tricia poured herself another cup of coffee and offered one to Mr. Everett, who declined, but he did agree to join her in the reader's nook. Miss Marple took the opportunity to sit on the old gentleman's lap. He petted her, and the cat began to purr loudly, bringing a smile to his face.

"Mr. Everett, did you know Susan Morris?" Tricia asked.

"I'm afraid I never made her acquaintance," he admitted.

"Did you know she was homeless?"

He looked up from his pleasant task. "I do believe Pixie mentioned it to me."

Tricia shook her head. "She said Susan got used to living

in her car. What a sad situation. It's lucky there aren't more homeless people around here."

"Oh, but there are, Ms. Miles."

"Really? Do you know any?"

He shrugged. "For a while, I was taking food to some homeless men who've camped along the railroad line not far from Merrimack. Grace seemed to think it was too dangerous. Perhaps she's right. Unfortunately, not everyone in the camp retained all their mental faculties, and some could be cantankerous when it came to dividing up what was brought. It's a shame our society doesn't do more for the soldiers who fought on our behalf. Our foundation donates a considerable amount of funds toward the homeless in New Hampshire, and especially to one shelter in Nashua, but I'm afraid the need is greater than we're able to support and still maintain our other commitments."

"I'm sure you've done your best," Tricia said reassuringly.

"There is so much need in this world and not enough compassion, especially in these troubled times."

Tricia nodded, watching as the old man gently rubbed her cat's ears.

During their picnic the previous day, Marshall had proposed they try to find new ways to be together. Was it possible Tricia could talk him into visiting the homeless camp, or would he agree with Grace that it wasn't a safe space? Had any of those homeless vets been acquainted with Susan Morris?

Who else in the area would know about such hardships? And then it came to her: Libby Hirt. Libby ran the Stoneham Food Shelf, which shared space with the Stoneham Clothes Closet, both possible places the homeless might go for help. Of course, Tricia and Libby hadn't spoken in several years—not since the fiasco when Libby's daughter, Eugenia, got mixed up with a killer. She got five years of supervised probation for shooting a visiting philanthropist, which would end at the beginning of next year. During that time Eugenia had kept a low profile, and Tricia hadn't had an occasion to speak to her mother. She wondered what kind of reception she'd receive if she paid a visit to the Food Shelf. They did have Saturday hours. And what would Tricia's excuse be? She just happened to be in the neighborhood and wanted to chat about the homeless problem in the area?

Why not? Susan Morris was found behind Tricia's store. She'd been homeless. Wasn't it Tricia's civic duty to not only make sure that Pixie wasn't blamed for the woman's death but help the needy? She could do that by giving the food shelf a check. But would that look like she was trying to buy the information?

Tricia thought about it for a moment. One thing she had done after her home renovation was sort through her clothes. She had a big bag of things she'd meant to donate to the Clothes Closet but had never gotten around to doing it. What if she donated them and just happened to drop in on the Food Shelf? Of course, there was no guarantee that Libby would even be working on a weekend, but she was— or at least had been—the organization's leader.

"Do you know how late the Clothes Closet stays open on a Saturday?" Tricia asked Mr. Everett.

"If I remember correctly, they're the same as they are during the week: ten until two."

"I've been meaning to drop off a bag of clothes and wonder if I should do so today. Maybe it's a way I could help the homeless or those down on their luck."

"That's very generous of you, Ms. Miles."

Generous or self-serving?

Tricia wasn't sure she wanted to answer that question.

The church parking lot was filled with beat-up cars and even a few bicycles when Tricia arrived with her donation for the Stoneham Clothes Closet. The Closet and the Food Shelf rented space in the lower level, and business seemed to be booming.

Tricia retrieved the bag of clothes from her trunk and entered the building, where she was directed to place it in a big canvas laundry cart. It looked like the Clothes Closet had done well with donations that day, as the cart and another were piled high with plastic bags and cartons stuffed with clothing.

Afterward, Tricia took a moment to assess the charity's clientele. Most of the people looked like average citizens one might meet on the street. Were the mothers with small children and elderly couples perusing the racks just down on their luck, or were they members of the growing homeless population? Tricia had heard rumors that some dealers came through on a regular basis, looking for designer clothing that they could pick up for free and then resell. The idea appalled her, especially since the clothing had been given as a charitable contribution. But Tricia also knew the Closet had a no-questions-asked policy, and it was enforced. They made a point not to judge their clientele.

"Did you want a receipt for your donation?" asked a woman in a blue smock and a badge that identified her as one of the volunteers. "We're a registered charity, and your donation is tax deductible."

"No need," Tricia said, and smiled at the older woman. "You've got a good crowd today."

"Yes. The children are back in school and they'll be needing weather-appropriate gear. The nights are already quite chilly."

Tricia's gaze was drawn to a table piled with blankets and a couple of sleeping bags. "I didn't know the Clothes Closet dealt with anything other than clothing and shoes."

"We try to anticipate the needs of our clients."

Was she talking about the homeless?

"Ma'am," a woman's voice called out, "do you have any more kids' sneakers out back?"

"If you'll excuse me," the volunteer told Tricia, and moved to help the woman.

Tricia studied the four siblings who trailed after their mom. Used sneakers. Tricia had never worn another person's clothes or footwear. She'd never had to. She might not have had a happy childhood, but she'd had no worries when it came to a roof over her head and clothes to wear. Kids grew as fast as weeds. How did a mom on a budget keep four little ones in shoes that fit?

Feeling somber, Tricia left the Clothes Closet and walked along the sidewalk to the Stoneham Food Shelf next door. The door was unlocked. Tricia let herself in and found a number of people crowding the storeroom. Two elderly men stocked shelves with canned goods while two women worked at a shared desk, one on a computer and the other sorting through a stack of what could have been applications for the Food Shelf's services. Meanwhile, a woman with gray-streaked hair, dark slacks, and a pink sweatshirt held a clipboard and ticked off items on a list. Tricia was relieved to find that Libby was indeed working.

She stood across the way, watching as the others worked until Libby moved and caught sight of her.

"Tricia, is that you? What are you doing here?"

Tricia stepped forward. "Hi, Libby. I dropped off a bag for the Clothes Closet and I thought I'd stop in to see if you were here. It's been a while since we spoke."

"Almost five years," Libby said coolly. She hadn't forgotten Tricia's part in solving Pammy Fredericks's murder and Eugenia's involvement in the events that ensued.

"From what I've read in the news, the Food Shelf is needed even more now than it was when we first met."

"That's true," Libby said, as though relieved not to have to rehash the unpleasant past.

"No doubt you heard about the homeless woman who was found dead behind my store the other day."

"Everybody in the village has," Libby said.

"I understand she lived in her car. Was she a recipient of the Food Shelf's generosity?"

"We deal with emergency situations only. Susan may have been homeless, but she was able to take care of herself and wasn't food insecure—at least, most of the time."

"Then you knew her?"

"Yes. As a matter of fact, she sometimes helped out at the Clothes Closet. Twice a month, our volunteers are treated to a simple box lunch provided by the American Legion's ladies auxiliary. The church we rent space with also has free lunches on the third, fourth, and fifth Mondays of each month, and Susan was known to frequent them as well."

"How do you know that?"

"I volunteer to help make those lunches. I've gotten to know most of the regulars."

"That's very generous of you," Tricia said.

Libby merely shrugged.

"I understand there's a homeless encampment near Merrimack."

"A small group of people living in tents and cardboard boxes," Libby said.

"Does your group help them?"

"I wish I could say we did, but our organization's reach is Stoneham and a little beyond. We simply don't have the resources to help everyone in need."

Tricia nodded. "I must admit that while I've donated to charities that help the homeless, I don't know how to direct someone who finds him- or herself in that situation."

"First of all, give them some respect. You'd be surprised how downright nasty people can be toward those in need. After that, donate to shelters. There are more than thirty of them in New Hampshire."

"So many?" Tricia asked.

"There's a big demand—and not nearly enough beds."

"I had no idea. What else can I do?"

"Give them food."

"My friend and employee, Mr. Everett, has taken food to the people in the encampment. His wife was worried that at his age it might not be safe and asked him not to go back. Their foundation does make generous contributions to a shelter in Nashua."

"William Everett has always had a kind heart," Libby agreed. "I wasn't at all surprised to hear that after he'd won the lottery, he'd set up a foundation to help others in need."

"Libby," one of the men called.

Libby nodded to the man and turned back to Tricia. "I

only have help for the next half hour, and we have a lot to accomplish. I hope you don't mind if . . ."

"I'm sorry for taking up so much of your time, but thanks for speaking with me. I feel bad about Susan and I'd like to help others who're in the same situation."

"Money talks," Libby said with a pointed glare. Did she think Tricia was more talk than action? Maybe. Perhaps she knew of Angelica's Nigela Ricita empire: half the village knew or suspected. Tricia had never asked her sister about her charitable donations. What she did know was that Angelica had given a lot of people meaningful employment. People who work and earn a living wage contribute to the village's bottom line. Angelica had shared her success in so many ways. Was Tricia lacking in that respect?

"I hope we have an opportunity to speak again when you've got more time," Tricia added.

"That would be nice," Libby said, but it was apparent by her tone that if it was another five years before the women interacted, it would be too soon.

Tricia braved a smile and left the Food Shelf. After all, she had a business to run . . . and a lot to think about.

ELEVEN

 The day dragged on. Although the weather was still fine, it wasn't bringing vintage mystery enthusiasts to the village. The tour buses would return in a few weeks for the leaf-peeping season, and in November for the holidays, but then it would be a long five months when most of the shops along Main Street cut their hours and their owners lowered their expectations.

Since they hadn't had a customer in over an hour, Tricia decided to close the store half an hour early.

"I don't mind staying until my rightful quitting time," Mr. Everett assured her. "I could go back down to the office and sort some of those books that came in yesterday."

"It can wait until tomorrow."

"Sunday is my favorite day of the week," Mr. Everett confided. "I look forward to our family dinners all week. Grace does, too. We would be very lonely people if not for the kindnesses you and your sister have shown us."

"I look forward to those dinners, too," Tricia said. "Especially when I get to contribute. I think I'll ask Angelica if I can bring the dessert tomorrow. I could bake it in the morning after my walk."

"I wish she would let us contribute more," Mr. Everett lamented.

"Your presence is compensation enough. Now, hang up that apron and go home to your wife."

"Ah, but she's still working at her office. However, I shall go over there and see if she, too, is game to play hooky."

Mr. Everett traded his apron for his jacket and gave a cheery wave as he went out the door. Tricia turned the OPEN sign to CLOSED and pulled the blinds before she took out her phone and texted her sister.

We shut the Cookery down early, too. Come on over, Angelica texted back.

Tricia locked up, grabbed her jacket from a peg at the back of the store, and soon arrived at her sister's apartment over the Cookery.

"What a day," Tricia announced, hanging her jacket over the back of one of the chairs at the kitchen island.

"Busy?" Angelica asked, sounding surprised, her right knee resting on her scooter in front of the kitchen's island, where she poured the first martinis.

"Not at my store, but I ran a number of errands during the day."

"And was one of them your visit to the *Stoneham Weekly News*?"

"Yes."

"And how were you received?"

"With enthusiasm, until I told Patti Perkins why I was there."

"I could have told you so," Angelica practically sang.

"Yes, well, I learned something quite disturbing during our conversation."

"And what was that?" Angelica asked, handing Tricia a glass before she picked up her own.

"That if Fiona won't take little Russell, Russ is thinking about putting the boy in foster care."

Angelica's expression mirrored her horror. "I always knew the man was a jerk, but I never thought he'd stoop that low."

"On the other hand, living with a real family could be just what the boy needs. Kids are smart. Perhaps little Russell has already picked up on the fact his father doesn't love him—and probably never did. And what would Nikki think if she knew about Russ's plans?" Tricia asked.

Angelica frowned. "She's so full of herself since she's been hanging out with a Hollywood chef, I wonder if she even cares. And brother, is that sad."

Yes, it was.

"I don't know what to do. I mean, Fiona is between a rock and a hard place, if I may employ a cliché. She has a lot at stake, but I wouldn't put it past Russ to blackmail her into taking on his son because he's too lazy and heartless to live up to his responsibilities."

"Poor little Russell."

"And he's not the most well-behaved child, either. Patti thought any family that took him in would have their hands full."

Angelica sported a smug smile. "And our darling little Sofia is such an angel."

Compared to little Russell, she definitely was.

"Patti hinted the weekly rag has a big scoop on Susan that'll break on Monday."

"Oh?"

"Yeah, but if I could find it on the Internet, it can't be all that big a deal." And why hadn't the bigger newspapers in the area covered it? Did they brush off Susan's death as just another small-town death without digging deeper?

Tricia explained how she'd tracked Susan down online and that Susan's naval career took a nosedive after the Tailhook scandal.

"Susan was one of the victims?" Angelica asked, aghast. "Did she suffer from PTSD after the ordeal?"

"I don't know, but I wouldn't be surprised."

"To think that kind of thing was commonplace . . ." she muttered, taking another sip of her drink.

"And despite strides against sexual assault, it's *still* all too common," Tricia agreed.

"Poor Susan." Angelica sighed. "What else made your day so hectic?"

"Mr. Everett told me about a group of homeless vets who live near Merrimack. He used to give them food, but Grace was worried it wasn't safe."

"That's too bad," Angelica said, taking the frill pick that adorned her drink and slipping off an olive, then chewing and swallowing it.

"Which brings me to my next adventure, if you could call it that. I wondered who I could talk to about those homeless vets to see if they'd known Susan Morris. So I thought about Libby Hirt."

"Goodness, I haven't thought of her in years," Angelica said.

"Neither have I, I'm ashamed to say. Oh, I've sent the Food Shelf a donation every year, but maybe I could have done more. She certainly hinted at it."

"What do you mean?"

"I dropped a donation off at the Clothes Closet today."

"I wish I'd known. I've got a carton of things I've been meaning to give them, too."

"Sorry. But as I was there, it gave me an excuse to drop in on the Food Shelf, and luckily Libby was in."

"And how were you received?" Angelica asked, knowing full well the circumstances surrounding the situation.

"Coolly, but she was willing to talk about the homeless, including Susan. She volunteered at the Clothes Closet every so often—apparently to get a free meal."

"Who could blame her?"

"I thought I might head out to Merrimack sometime this week."

"Not alone you won't."

"Well, you're in no position to go with me."

"I was thinking more along the lines of Marshall."

"Me, too. It's too bad Russ and I are on the outs."

"With good reason," Angelica reminded her.

"Yes, but he's got the perfect cover, being a reporter and all."

"If you can call that rag he edits a newspaper. And why

can't you just pass yourself off as Lois Lane? Are the people there likely to check your credentials?"

"Probably not."

Angelica sighed. "I almost wish I could go with you. I've been cooped up for almost two weeks and I'm bored out of my mind. I wish I could go just about anywhere. Grocery shopping. Get my hair and nails done."

"Why don't you make an appointment at Booked for Beauty early in the week? I'll take you in the transport chair. Pixie or Mr. Everett will gladly cover for me."

"That would be nice. Thank you."

"What are we going to do about dinner tomorrow?"

"I thought I'd ask Tommy at the café to make a big pan of lasagna and a salad."

"That sounds good. And I'll bake something for dessert."

"Cake?" Angelica suggested.

"Cake it is. What kind?"

"Surprise me."

"You've got it. Now, what's on tap for our dinner tonight?"

It was after nine when Tricia returned to Haven't Got a Clue. She was about to head up the stairs to her apartment when a loud thud rattled the shop's back door, startling her. She took a step back, when another loud bang rattled the building. Someone was trying to break into her shop!

Backtracking to the front door, she made a hasty exit and stood out on the sidewalk. She hadn't yet set the security system for the night, so she did the next best thing and called 911.

"Stay outside the building. We're sending a patrol car," the dispatcher said, "but it might be a few minutes before anyone can get there."

"Okay," Tricia said as the banging continued. The perpetrator had to be kicking in the door. It was made of heavy steel, but eventually the jamb would give way and he'd be inside.

Tricia retreated to stand in front of the Cookery. Was this

break-in tied to the one exactly one week before? What if the person got into her apartment? Surely Miss Marple would hide, but a person who would break into a store might have no qualms about hurting a cat.

Tricia fought tears, worrying about her pet, but then heard the wail of a siren. The patrol car must have come from south of the village's main drag and gone up the alley behind Main Street. The siren cut off, leaving an eerie silence.

Her phone pinged with a text.

What's going on? Angelica asked.

Tricia answered. *Come inside my store—right now!*

But Tricia didn't obey her sister, and with good cause, as a second patrol car pulled up in front of Haven't Got a Clue and Chief Baker himself got out.

"Are you okay?" he demanded.

"Yes. Did your officer catch the guy?"

"Henderson pulled up and the guy took off. He ran down the alley, then climbed atop a dumpster and jumped the fence."

"So the guy didn't get in?"

"No, but only just. Come on, let's get you inside," Baker said, clasping Tricia's arm and pulling her back into her shop. He hit the switch inside the door, and the lights blazed. "Your security system didn't go off."

"I hadn't gotten around to setting it."

"Well, that was stupid."

"Hey!" Tricia protested.

Baker had the decency to look embarrassed. "I apologize. That was unprofessional of me." For the first time in a long time, he actually sounded sorry. "In the future, please set it as soon as you close for the day."

Tricia let out a shaky breath. "As you wish." But it was a pain in the butt to enter her store after dinner with Angelica and have to run to the back to reset the alarm every time she came in late. Still, Baker was right. This was the second attempt in a week, and someone seemed bent on breaching her security measures.

"I meant to tell you that you did well on that TV interview," Baker said nervously.

Tricia's mouth dropped open. "Someone nearly broke into my store and you want to talk about that silly interview?"

"I was only trying to make you feel better," he groused.

The police chief straightened, became all business, and stomped to the back of the store. The new locks had been broken, and the door's dimpled surface bore the scars of the attack. The lamp above the door must have been smashed as well, for the only illumination that came in through the entrance was from the flashing red-and-blue lights from the patrol car that had come as backup. It seemed like a gale was blowing in as well.

"Well?" Baker hollered to his officer.

"The creep got away," Henderson admitted.

"Dammit, Henderson!" Baker admonished him. He turned to face Tricia. "You should go back to Angelica's and wait. I'll get Nashua Emergency Enclosures to come and fix the door."

"Don't I need to make a statement?"

"You can do that later."

"What about my cat?"

"The door to your apartment is intact. If she was upstairs . . ."

"Then she's safe," Tricia finished, relieved.

Tricia pursed her lips to keep them from trembling. "You didn't seem at all interested in my attempted break-in last week. Will you take this one seriously?"

"You've got my full attention," Baker promised.

Then something occurred to Tricia. "Why are you still on the job on a Saturday night? Shouldn't you be with your fiancée?"

"Diana's busy tonight, which gave me a chance to catch up on some paperwork. I had the scanner on in the background. When I heard the address, I hurried over."

Tricia nodded.

"Go on. Go over and stay with your sister," he said gently.

Tricia shook her head. "No. I need to call the security company and have them send someone out to make sure the system is going to work. It may have been damaged as well. But I do need to call her to let her know what's going on."

"You can call the security company from Angelica's. I'll stick around until I know you and your store are safe."

Tricia frowned. Why was he being so nice to her after several years of indifference and sometimes downright nastiness?

Whatever brought on the change, she wasn't going to complain about it.

"I'd better make that call," Tricia said, and headed toward the front of her store and the exit. But as she looked back to the rear of her store, she found Baker watching her. Then, rather self-consciously, he turned to speak with his junior officer.

Feeling disconcerted, Tricia dug out her keys to reopen the door to the Cookery. And just what was she going to tell Angelica about Baker's apparent change of heart?

TWELVE

 The Nashua TV meteorologists had been correct in their predictions of rain. The sky was gunmetal gray, and the rain pounded the glass on the skylight over Tricia's bed. But, gloomy weather or not, Tricia hauled herself out of bed and began her day trying not to think about the events of the evening before. Angelica had begged Tricia to stay the night with her, but the thought of Angelica's guest room, which was decorated in pink and purple and designed to delight Sofia, didn't appeal to Tricia—nor did the idea of leaving her cat behind—and so she'd decided to stay in her own home, not about to be forced out by a thug.

That said, Tricia's sleep had been uneasy and disturbed by anxiety-filled dreams she could not remember upon waking.

After tossing on sweats, she stopped next door, picked up Sarge, and went on her usual brisk walk, grateful the little guy was well trained so she could handle her umbrella as well as his leash. Her thoughts kept returning to the second almost break-in at her store. She'd feel much better once the door was replaced later that day. She wondered what other fortifications she should consider installing. The front of the store, with its big display window and plate glass door, were even more vulnerable, but both attempts had been made at the rear of her store and home.

Walking gave her time to think about the timing of the break-ins. The first had happened just days after that silly TV interview. Could it have had something to do with the crime her security system had thwarted? But that didn't seem likely, either, as the attempts had been exactly a week apart. If someone wanted something she had, they had taken their time before trying to get it again.

After returning Sarge to his mistress and toweling him dry, Tricia went home and turned to her cookbooks. As per Angelica's request, Tricia decided to bake a cake for that evening's family dinner and flipped through the old cookbook that Angelica had given her over the summer for a dessert like her grandmother used to make. After checking the index, she read through several recipes, finally choosing an old favorite: applesauce cake.

Now that she had a few decorating tricks up her sleeve, she thought she might be able to pull off a pretty and tasty treat. While the layers were baking in the oven, she took a quick shower and dressed for the workday. Donning her Great Booktown Bake-Off apron, a souvenir from earlier that summer, Tricia waited for the layers to cool and whipped up a standard American buttercream icing, but instead of using vanilla extract she substituted pure New Hampshire maple syrup. A taste-testing proved it to be decadent, and she began making pink and purple roses. They looked revolting on the ivory frosting, but she was sure Sofia would be delighted.

Once the cake was finished and placed in the vintage Tupperware cake carrier that Pixie had found at a yard sale and gifted her with, Tricia headed down the stairs to her shop, with Miss Marple following in her wake.

The big piece of plywood that covered the opening where her security door had been was an eyesore, but she tried to ignore it as she went about the preparations for opening the store for the day.

Mr. Everett arrived soon after and was distressed to find that someone had again tried to gain illegal entry to the store.

"It occurs to me, Ms. Miles, that I should have reported

a rather disconcerting episode that occurred while you were in Ireland."

"What do you mean?"

"Several days before the first attempted break-in, a rather unsavory character came into the store. He didn't buy anything, and apart from studying the contents of our front display case, he used the washroom. I was preoccupied with customers, but it occurred to me that he'd taken a curiously long amount of time in there. When I went in back to investigate, I found him testing the door that leads to your apartment. When I asked what he was doing, he turned and ran for the door. I curse my faulty memory for not reporting the altercation until now."

"What did he look like?"

"I'm not sure I could describe him other than looking like a bum."

That covered a lot of territory.

"Thank you for bringing this to my attention, Mr. Everett. Chief Baker may want to speak to you about it. Would that be all right?"

"Of course. I'll do anything I can to help."

Tricia nodded.

"And now it's time for me to do my job and make coffee for our customers."

"Thank you." While he made the coffee, Tricia put some cash in the till.

"Looks like we're ready to begin the workday," Tricia said, determined to sound cheerful as she turned the CLOSED sign to OPEN. Just then the phone rang. She strode over to the cash desk and the heavy vintage telephone. "Haven't Got a Clue; this is Tricia. How can I help you?"

"Hey, lady."

"Marshall, what's up?"

"Nothing special. I just thought I'd check in to see what was new with you."

Tricia needed to tell him what had happened the evening before but paused, unsure if she should mention Baker's kindness. "Mr. Everett and I are all set up for another day of commerce. How about you?"

"The same. Let's hope this monsoon makes people think about travel—like getting away for the winter and the need to stock up on sunscreen. I've got a case I need to unload."

"It's barely fall," Tricia pointed out.

"One can dream. How about you?"

"Now that you mention it, I was wondering if you could spare me a couple of hours tomorrow?"

"What for?"

"Apparently there's a homeless encampment near Merrimack. I thought I might like to visit the people there to see if anyone knew Susan Morris."

"I don't suppose you'd listen to me if I told you to let the Stoneham police handle things."

"Probably not," Tricia admitted.

"And since Angelica's laid up, she can't very well accompany you."

"That's right."

Tricia heard him sigh. "I guess," he said reluctantly.

She continued despite his apparent lack of interest. "I don't think we should take either my Lexus or your Mercedes. It wouldn't look right."

"I see your point. Do you want me to dress in some old, raggedy clothes, too?"

"Well, I wouldn't go that far, but you don't have to wear a tux, either."

"Ha-ha," he deadpanned. "So, what do we do for transportation?"

"I'll bet Pixie would loan us her junker."

"We could have it washed and the tank filled as a thank-you."

"I like the way you think," Tricia said, wishing she could give Marshall a warm smile.

"When do you want to go?"

"I thought I'd order some subs to go from the grocery and maybe pick up a case of water. How about around ten thirty?"

"Yeah, I can do that."

"Great. And if you're not busy this evening, we're having our regular Sunday family dinner. I'd love it if you could join us."

A long silence followed her invitation. "I've already made plans for the evening," he said at last.

"Don't you like my little makeshift family?" Tricia asked, feeling hurt that once again he'd rebuffed her offer.

"I prefer to spend time alone with you. Is there anything wrong with that?"

Tricia sighed. "I suppose not. It's just . . ." He kept disappointing her in that regard. He didn't seem to want to make many concessions for her—and after she'd spent a boring two weeks following him around the Emerald Isle.

"Just what?" he asked.

"Nothing. I'll see you tomorrow," she said, trying to add a little cheer to her tone.

"Yeah. I'll meet you at your store."

"I'll see you then."

Tricia ended the call and set the receiver down. Marshall would no doubt be upset that she hadn't mentioned the second attempt to break into Haven't Got a Clue. But as she hadn't mentioned the first . . .

Tricia reached for her cell phone and scrolled through her contacts list to find Pixie's name. Pixie answered on the third ring. "Tricia, what's up? You haven't heard anything about an arrest for Susan's death, have you?" she asked excitedly.

"Unfortunately, no. I was wondering if you'd mind driving in to work tomorrow. I'd like to borrow your car, if you'll trust me with it?"

"What for?"

"To visit the homeless men at the encampment in Merrimack."

"Oh, Tricia, please don't go on my behalf. It might not be safe."

"That's why I asked Marshall to go with me."

"Oh, then that's all right."

It rather bothered Tricia that Pixie thought she needed to

be accompanied by a chaperone . . . but then, if she was honest, that's exactly what she expected of Marshall.

"So, can I borrow your car?"

"Sure. I'll park it in the municipal lot."

"Perfect."

"Do you guys need me to come in today?"

Tricia knew that if she mentioned the attempted break-in, Pixie would arrive in a hot minute. It could wait until the next day.

"Even if we were drowning in customers, which we're not, I wouldn't ask you to work on your only day off of the week."

"It might save me from that pile of laundry that's waiting."

"Everybody needs clean clothes," Tricia told her.

"Yeah, and those poor homeless people probably don't have any—and what they've got is going to be soaked, if it isn't already."

Tricia thought about the people in the encampment huddled under tarps and cardboard, trying to stay warm, and it made her appreciate her dry, heated store all the more.

"We'll see you tomorrow," she told Pixie.

"Bright and early. That is, if you think ten o'clock is the butt crack of dawn."

Tricia laughed. "I don't. 'Til tomorrow.

She ended the call and turned to find Mr. Everett standing before her, looking sad.

"Your gentleman turned down your dinner invitation again," he stated matter-of-factly.

Tricia nodded. "I wish he'd come, but . . . I think he feels uncomfortable in a crowd."

"Then it seems odd that he plans to be a tour guide. One would think being a people person would be requisite for the job."

"Yes," Tricia agreed, frowning. "One would."

Sometimes Tricia felt like it was a waste of time to bother opening her store between the busy tourist seasons, but the lack of rainy-day customers had one benefit: she and Mr. Everett had plenty of time to catch up on their reading and spent most of the day in companionable silence, flipping the pages of their books. They took a break late in the afternoon to visit Booked for Lunch to pick up their catered dinner, delivering it to Angelica's dumbwaiter, and Mr. Everett returned to Haven't Got a Clue while Tricia helped set up for the meal.

Mr. Everett closed the shop for the day, and the rest of the gang showed up at Angelica's apartment, arriving right on time—just after five. Tricia was greeted with hugs and kisses from her friends and family, which warmed her heart. Everyone made a fuss over Angelica's swollen foot, with Sofia crawling up on her lap to give her a big hug, but there was no mention of the attempted break-in at Tricia's store the night before.

Tricia brought out the stuffed leprechaun she'd brought back from Ireland for Sofia, who ran around the kitchen island squealing with delight and showing it off for everyone to see.

As usual, Ginny brought several bottles of wine and played sommelier, pouring it into glasses and describing its provenance before distributing it throughout the crowd. She found Tricia looking out the big window that overlooked Main Street and handed her a glass.

"Look at that rain. We may have to build an ark," Tricia mused before taking a sip.

"It's supposed to rain all week."

"I hope not," Tricia said, and laughed.

"Hey, Sofia loves her present. Thanks for thinking of her."

"She's a great kid."

Ginny proffered her glass. "Tell me what you think?"

They both took a sip. "Not bad," Tricia agreed. A thought occurred to her and she decided to test the proverbial waters. "I've been thinking a lot about what you said the other day at lunch."

Ginny looked puzzled. "What was that? Something profound, no doubt." She laughed.

"I spoke with Fiona Sample the other day."

Ginny's grin faltered. "I'm about three books behind in her cozy mystery series. I just haven't had time to read more than nutrition labels on cans since Sofia arrived." She took a tiny sip of wine. "What's Fiona got to do with my profound words?"

"I was referring to your *family* dilemma. Should you or shouldn't you have another child."

Every muscle in Ginny's body seemed to tense. "And?"

"What would you think about taking in little Russell Smith?"

Ginny's eyes widened to the point of caricature. "You're kidding, right?"

Tricia shook her head.

"Oh, Tricia, I've got my hands full with Sofia, my marriage, my home, and my job."

"It was just a thought."

"Two kids in diapers?" Ginny asked with what sounded like despair. "We're just starting to potty train Sofia. I heard it's a lot harder with boys—that they don't take to it as fast."

Tricia had never pondered the situation. "It seems that since Nikki just up and left, Russ doesn't feel he can care for his son and asked Fiona to take him."

"He's trying to foist off his son on her?"

Tricia nodded. "Unfortunately, she can't take him in because of her writing commitments. I was thinking maybe you could help her out."

"I'd be helping Russ out—and why would I want to do that?" Ginny demanded.

Tricia merely shrugged.

"Why don't *you* take the kid?" Ginny suggested.

"Me?" Tricia asked, aghast.

Ginny shrugged. "Why not? You're the only one who seems worried about him."

Tricia let out a breath. As a career woman, and especially after her divorce, she'd given up the idea of ever having children—at least biologically—and the thought of adoption had never entered her mind. At forty-six, she didn't want to even contemplate adding a child to what she considered an already unsettled life.

"I just thought taking little Russell might solve your dilemma about having another baby."

Ginny frowned. "And say we did take him in. Say we welcomed this boy into our home, took care of him, fell in love with him, and then Nikki comes roaring back on the scene and takes him from us?"

Tricia had to admit the scenario was entirely possible.

Ginny shook her head. "You of all people should know how downright mean and vindictive Nikki can be. She'd probably accuse me of trying to steal her son's affection."

That she would.

"I've been told Russ might be considering putting the boy in foster care."

"Oh, now you're really pulling the guilt card," Ginny said, sounding angry.

"I'm sorry. I just thought you should know the whole story."

"I have my own family to take care of," Ginny said resentfully. "And sometimes we struggle."

"Would you consider mentioning the possibility to Antonio?"

"Oh, yeah, I'll mention it all right," Ginny said, her cheeks flushing. "And I'd appreciate it if *you* didn't."

"Of course," Tricia agreed. What else could she say?

Ginny guzzled what was left of the wine in her glass, glared at the offending object, and stalked off in the direction of the kitchen, presumably for a tall refill.

Tricia joined the others, who were sampling the cheesy corn dip Tommy from Angelica's café had whipped up for the occasion. Tricia dunked a corn chip into the bowl of steaming dip and sampled it. Tommy was good at his job—maybe *too* good. How soon would it be before he decided to move on and find other employment, or would Angelica simply find him another position in one of her other enterprises, as she'd done with Tommy's predecessor? It was rare for someone to leave their job once hired by either Angelica or Nigela Ricita Associates.

Tricia was trying to decide if she should have another glass of wine, when Grace sidled up next to her. "I'm sorry we haven't had time to talk since your return from Ireland. We've been inundated with requests at the foundation."

"With so many appeals, you probably wouldn't remember if Susan Morris ever applied for a grant."

"The woman found in your dumpster?"

Tricia nodded.

"I knew you'd ask me that question, so I asked Linda to go through our files and look," Grace said—Linda was Grace's secretary. "We do keep track of who applies and whom we've had to turn down. There was no application from a Susan Morris."

"How about Susan Radnor?" Tricia asked.

"Linda only checked on that one name," Grace admitted. "Radnor, you say?" Tricia nodded and spelled it. "I'll have Linda look tomorrow and let you know if anything turns up."

"Thanks."

Angelica held up her empty glass. "Could anyone else use a refill?" she asked hopefully.

Seconds later Ginny swooped in and refilled everyone's glass—everyone but Tricia's. She didn't take offense and wandered into the kitchen to top off her own glass and wished that Marshall had accepted her dinner invitation. If Ginny was going to be prickly, it could be a long evening. But soon enough Tricia forgot about their conversation and lost herself in playing hostess for her sidelined sister. And, of course, the meal was a rousing success.

Ginny and Grace insisted on clearing the plates and tidying the kitchen, and Tricia's dessert was welcomed by one and all—especially Sofia, who insisted on having two roses. Antonio seemed fine with the idea, but Ginny maintained that Sofia would be bouncing off the walls from a sugar high and never go to sleep. Still, Sofia ended up with purple-stained lips and a bib smeared with pink frosting before she was wiped down and zippered into her rain jacket for the ride home.

Once Tricia had closed the Cookery's front door behind

the last of the visitors, she went back up to the apartment, poured two more glasses of wine, and joined Angelica on the other end of the couch.

"Another successful dinner," Tricia said, and extended her glass so they could clink glasses.

"Tommy's lasagna was almost as good as mine."

"Almost," Tricia agreed.

Angelica smiled. "The cake was excellent. Your culinary prowess has come a long way this past year. I'm so proud of you."

"Thank you."

Angelica sipped her wine. "Was it my imagination or did things seem a little strained between you and Ginny this evening?"

"They were," Tricia admitted. "I spoke to her about possibly taking little Russell."

Angelica winced. "Please say you didn't," she implored.

"I did."

"And her reaction?"

"Stupefaction, for one."

"A given," Angelica acknowledged. "And two?"

"She worried that she might become attached to the boy only to have Nikki show up one day and snatch him from them."

"That's a very strong possibility."

"And then she went on to suggest that I take the child in."

"You're the only one who seems to care about the boy."

"Another of her points." Tricia sighed.

"Can we talk about something less painful?" Angelica asked.

Tricia shrugged. "Tomorrow, Marshall and I are going to visit the homeless encampment near Merrimack."

"I guess I meant something cheerful," Angelica corrected herself, scowling.

"It could be cheerful for the people we meet. We're going to bring lunch."

"That's good of you. I suppose you'll be badgering them about Susan Morris, too."

"I didn't badger Grace this evening. She volunteered the information on Susan."

"That's because she anticipated your question. You have a reputation, you know."

"I'm well aware of my reputation." As the village jinx. But Tricia had never met Susan Morris before her violent death. Nonetheless, it did seem rather suspicious that her body had been disposed of in Tricia's dumpster—almost as though someone was daring the police to blame her for the crime. Except that she'd been out of the country at the time of Susan's death. And it could just as well have been Mr. Everett who'd found the body instead of Pixie.

"What if the people in this camp don't want to talk to you?" Angelica asked.

Tricia shrugged. "They'll at least get a sandwich and something to drink." She sipped her wine. "I wish you were coming along."

"To a dirty old homeless camp?"

"Not when you put it that way."

"Well, then why would you want me to join you? Because I can be more intimidating than Marshall?" Angelica asked.

"Well, he is shorter than me."

"So am I."

"Yes, but you're Nigela Ricita and you're invincible."

"Why, thank you," Angelica said, and smiled, but it was short-lived. "You *will* be careful, won't you?"

"Of course."

"And if you find out something, you'll go straight to Chief Baker with it and let the police follow up?"

"Don't I always?"

The scowl was back. "No," Angelica said emphatically.

THIRTEEN

Tricia didn't sleep well that night. She kept telling herself she wasn't nervous about her upcoming adventure, and to distract herself she read the first eight chapters of *False Scent* by Ngaio Marsh before she was able to fall into an exhausted sleep. When morning came, it wasn't her alarm that woke her but an impatient Miss Marple, eager for her breakfast.

When it came time to get ready for the day ahead, Tricia decided not to don her usual attire of dark slacks with a pastel sweater set and took a full ten minutes to decide what to wear that wouldn't look too showy or flaunt that she was better off than anyone in the camp. She chose jeans, a white turtleneck shirt, and a denim jacket, as well as brown boots that ended just below her knees. After all, she didn't know how dirty or muddy the camp was likely to be. As she dressed, Tricia wondered what kind of clothes Susan had worn to her job at Sweet As Can Be. If the customers had known she was homeless, would they have patronized the chocolate shop?

Tricia made it down to Haven't Got a Clue minutes before Pixie arrived and found the mail had arrived early, delivered through the slot in the door. She picked up the pile but immediately focused on the *Stoneham Weekly News*,

which had arrived as scheduled. Setting the bills and adver-
tisements aside, Tricia unfolded the paper and was disappointed to find a full-page ad for the big chain grocery store
in Milford, which was having a giant meat sale. Beef, pork,
poultry—you name it, it was on sale.

Tricia turned the page and found Susan Morris's murder
highlighted on page three. She quickly read through the
story but was disappointed that it didn't give her any more
information than what she'd been able to discover herself by
doing an Internet search.

Well, poop on that, she thought.

She thumbed through the rest of the paper and was rewarded with pages of white background interspersed with
ads for tag sales, the Bookshelf Diner, a book sale at the
Stoneham Public Library, and not much more. She was
about to toss the rag into the recycle bin when she caught
sight of a full-page ad on the back of the paper—an ad for
the sale of the *Stoneham Weekly News.*

What the heck?

Patti Perkins hadn't mentioned that when they'd spoken
two days before. She proofed the paper, so she had to have
known. Was she sworn to secrecy, or had she found it not to
be newsworthy enough to mention? After all, Russ had put
the paper up for sale several years earlier when he thought
he was about to get a job as a crime reporter at the *Philadel-
phia Inquirer.* Or had Tricia read her wrong by assuming
that Susan Morris's death would be the big story of the day?

Was it really surprising that Russ would want to bail on
the weekly newspaper he'd tried so hard to keep afloat? His
wife had left him for the possibility of a career as a TV chef,
and he was stuck with a child he'd never wanted and couldn't
seem to foist off on anyone else.

And just who did he think was going to see the ad and
buy a not-so-going concern?

The shop door swung open, and Pixie entered wearing a
trench coat that looked like something Ingrid Bergman had
worn in *Casablanca.* "Good morning," she called, already
untying the belt at her waist.

"And to you."

Pixie dropped her big leather purse before nodding toward Tricia's attire. "My, don't you look trendy."

"Really? I thought I looked rather casual."

"Not with those boots," Pixie said, eyeing the footwear.

"I don't have anything else."

"Then I guess you gotta go with what you've got." Pixie nodded toward the paper still in Tricia's hands. "Anything interesting in there?"

"Apparently Susan's murder isn't nearly as important as the big meat sale in Milford."

"That stinks," Pixie said. "I take it you haven't heard any more about the investigation."

Tricia shook her head.

"I have to admit, I've been thinking a lot about Susan and can't for the life of me figure out why someone would want to kill her."

"She didn't appear to have any enemies," Tricia agreed.

"That we know about," Pixie added. "I was thinking . . . maybe I should try to—"

"We've already had that discussion," Tricia warned. "If you step out of line, Chief Baker will crush you."

Pixie winced as though stung. "Wow—those are harsh words."

"He's looking for a killer. If he thinks he's got a strong enough case to present to the district attorney . . ." She let the words trail off.

"Maybe you could talk to him again," Pixie suggested hopefully.

Tricia sighed. "Okay. But I'll have to make it seem like a casual encounter."

"He usually has lunch at the Bookshelf Diner around one o'clock. He likes to sit in the back," Pixie said.

"It's not on my usual list of places to eat"—especially not since Angelica had opened her café, owned the local food truck, and had cornered the market for fine dining at the Brookview Inn under her Nigela Ricita umbrella—"but maybe I'll duck in later today."

"Well, my goal is to avoid the man at all costs. In fact, I brought my lunch," Pixie said, and picked up her purse, patting its side. "A good old baloney sandwich and a bag of chips."

Tricia cringed at such an unhealthy meal. But then Pixie's husband, Fred, worked for a meat distributor and got a good discount on cold cuts. But baloney? Tricia wondered if Pixie was taking a statin to lower her cholesterol. If not . . .

"I'll hang up my coat and then I'll get the coffee started," Pixie volunteered, then grabbed the empty carafe from the beverage station and headed toward the back of the shop. "Tricia!" she called, sounding distressed. "What happened to the back door?"

Tricia hurried to the rear of the store and explained. "Everything should be fixed by this afternoon. I'll be heading out in a little while. Do you think you can handle dealing with it if they come before I get back?"

"For the second time in a week? Yeah, I can handle it—and probably in my sleep."

The shop bell rang. The door flew open, aided by a strong breeze from the west, and Mr. Everett entered. Tricia turned and hurried to intercept him. "Looks like winter might come early," he declared as he paused to turn around and shake some of the drops off his umbrella before turning and closing the door. Since he had weathered more winters than either Tricia or Pixie, he might just know. "Good morning, Ms. Miles."

"And to you, too, Mr. Everett. What are you doing here on your day off?"

"Just visiting. And I thought I might take Sarge out for a walk or two."

"That's so nice of you."

Pixie returned, dressed in a navy shirtwaist dress with white cuffs and collar, looking quite prim and proper. "Hey, Mr. E."

"Pixie."

"What are you doing here on your day off?" And they went through the whole explanation once more.

"The coffee will be ready in less than five minutes. Anybody interested?" Pixie asked.

Tricia considered that she might be away from bathroom facilities for several hours and declined, but Mr. Everett gave an enthusiastic yes.

During the lull between summer visitors and the leaf peepers, things were slow for all the businesses along Stoneham's Main Street, so Tricia and her employees settled in the reader's nook for a chat and a friendly reconnecting. But Tricia kept her eye on the clock as the minute hand descended to the halfway mark. Sure enough, Marshall opened the door at precisely ten thirty.

"Hello," he called cheerily as he entered. Tricia stood and hurried to intercept him, grabbing his arm and turning him around. She didn't want to have to account for the plywood in the back of the store in front of Pixie and Mr. Everett. "My, don't you look pretty," he said, eyeing Tricia's attire. "Are those boots waterproof or just fashionable?"

"Both." Tricia turned toward Pixie. "I guess it's time we started on our mission. Is there anything we should know about your car?"

Pixie shrugged. "It's a stick, so I hope one of you knows how to drive it."

"That's me," Marshall volunteered.

"Um, I ought to mention that the steering is a little tough," Pixie said, seeming to shrink a little.

"'Tough'?" Marshall asked.

"Yeah, as in 'it ain't got power steering.' Left turns are kinda hard, so I always try to get where I'm going in the straightest line possible or with only right-hand turns."

"Isn't that inconvenient?" Tricia asked.

"Yeah, but I don't want to develop Popeye arms, either." Pixie smiled. "And now you know why I prefer to walk to work when I can." She dangled the keys on a Minnie Mouse ring, and Marshall grabbed them from her.

"I'm not sure when we'll be back," Tricia said, already opening the door.

"Don't worry about me. I've got my lunch, so I don't

have to go anywhere. Have fun!" Pixie called as Tricia hustled Marshall out of the store.

Fun? Visiting a homeless camp? Probably not. Tricia just hoped they weren't wasting their time.

Pixie's car, like her clothing, was considered vintage. The 1976 Plymouth Volaré was a bulky gray beast with a V-6 engine and, like she'd said, no power steering. Tricia watched as Marshall pulled onto Main Street and learned just how difficult those left-hand turns were going to be.

Instead of patronizing a chain sub shop, Marshall drove them to Milford and pulled into the parking lot of an independent shop and ordered twelve foot-long sandwiches, then they stopped at the grocery store and picked up a case of water bottles and were on their way to Merrimack.

"What are you expecting?" Marshall asked as they barreled down the highway.

"I don't know. But I have to admit, I'm a little apprehensive."

"And probably for good reason."

"I hope we'll find out something more about Susan Morris, but I'm not even sure if she connected with anyone in the camp. I mean, they have virtually nothing. She at least had a car to live in. She could lock it for security. According to what I've learned on YouTube, she did what was called stealth camping: making it look like her car was empty, blacking out the windows so that she could read by a battery light or a tablet. She had obviously studied how to live under the radar."

"That's sad," Marshall stated.

"But, according to Pixie, she wasn't all that unhappy with her lifestyle."

"I guess you can adapt to just about anything if you have to," Marshall said.

What he said was probably true. But living in such a tiny area . . . Tricia knew that for her, it would be an impossible task. Angelica would never last in the box that was the interior of a car—not with her claustrophobia. She could tolerate being in a car for about an hour; that was it. She often drove with the windows open—even in winter.

Marshall's attention was riveted on the road, and Tricia mulled over how she was going to tell him about the attempted break-ins. She finally decided to just come right out with it.

"A lot's been going on these past couple of days—so much so that I neglected to tell you that while we were in Ireland, someone tried to break into Haven't Got a Clue."

"What happened?" he asked, concerned.

"The security system was triggered, and it scared the burglar off. Pixie took care of everything."

"Thank goodness you weren't home when it happened."

"Well, it happened again on Saturday—and I *was* home."

Marshall shot a glance at her. "Why didn't you tell me?"

Tricia hesitated but then blurted, "I don't know. When you called yesterday, it just never came up."

"I would think you could've found a way to insert something that important—and dangerous—into the conversation." Yup, he was definitely annoyed. "Did you call the cops?"

"Of course. Officer Henderson came right away and chased the guy on foot. Unfortunately, he got away."

"Was there any damage?"

"The door was pretty beat-up and the locks just about destroyed. Nashua Emergency Enclosures came a couple of hours later. Right now there's a big piece of plywood over the back of the building. The door will be replaced later today. I was thinking they ought to put a steel slat in place so this can't happen again."

Marshall said nothing, but his hands tightened around the steering wheel.

"I'm sorry I didn't mention it sooner. I figured I could handle the situation by myself."

"I'll bet you told Angelica," he grated.

"Well, yes. She's my sister."

"And what am I? Chopped liver?"

"Marshall . . ." Tricia chided.

"Tricia, are you ever going to trust me?"

"Of course I trust you."

"But not enough to tell me about something that could have threatened your life."

Tricia let out a breath.

"Did Baker show up?" Marshall growled.

"Yes," she answered wearily. "And before you ask, I did not call him. He was working late and had his police scanner on when the call came through."

"Yeah. Sure."

Was there a point in protesting?

They spent the next fifteen minutes in silence, which felt awkward and yet not intolerable. It gave Tricia time to think. She looked out at the bleak landscape and wondered what she would say to the denizens of the homeless community. How would they react when a couple of strangers showed up at their camp offering food and drink? Would they be grateful or resentful about the intrusion of a couple of do-gooders?

Even if none of the people in the camp had known Susan, at least Tricia could comfort herself in knowing she was giving at least one meal—some sustenance—to people who had so much less than herself. Was it also a way to assuage her guilt?

The rain had just about stopped when Marshall turned off the highway, and they traveled along a dirt trail. He must have done his due diligence and Googled the encampment, because Tricia had no real sense of where to find those she considered in need. But then a smattering of mostly water-soaked tents appeared before them in a field. As they slowed, she took in a smoking fire pit with a group of raggedy-looking men gathered around it. Most were bearded, with long gray hair gathered in ponytails, and looking despondent. It wasn't far from what Tricia expected, but it pained her to see people living so rough.

Several of the men stood as Marshall stopped the car within ten feet of the fire pit. They didn't seem threatening, more apprehensive. They'd no doubt been hassled before.

"Ready or not," Tricia muttered, and opened the passenger-side door. Marshall opened his, and they got out together. After all the rain, the water table was high and Tricia's pretty boots were soon a muddy mess.

One of the men stepped forward. He looked to be in his late forties, with shaggy hair and a graying beard. "Can I help you?"

"Uh, yes. My name is Tricia Miles and I'm a business owner in Stoneham. I'm a regular contributor to the Stoneham Food Shelf and asked its director how else I could help you guys out. She suggested your encampment suffered food insecurity. We"—she indicated Marshall—"thought we'd stop by with some lunch."

"Do-gooders," another of the men muttered, and turned away.

Marshall called out and opened the rear passenger door. He pulled out the box filled with the wrapped sandwiches and set it on the trunk lid. "Anybody want a sub? They're assorted cold cuts with cheese. We also brought bags of chips and a case of water, too, if you can use it."

"We'll take it," the group's spokesman said, stepping forward. "Bobby, Jimmy, give the guy a hand, will ya?"

Two older men stepped forward as Tricia rounded the car and began handing out the bottles of water. The rest of the guys crowded around, taking their sandwiches and chips, some of them mumbled thanks, but most didn't—nor did they look Tricia in the eye despite her giving what she hoped was an encouraging smile.

When the last of the sandwiches was gone, Marshall grabbed the rest of the case of water and handed it off to another of the men. Most of the men went back to sitting around the fire pit, but their leader hung back. He hadn't immediately dug into his sandwich, and leaned against the Volaré's driver's-side fender. "Crappy car," he muttered.

"It's almost a classic," Marshall said.

"Like hell. What is it you guys really want?"

Marshall shot a look in Tricia's direction. "I don't know if you've heard, but Susan Morris, a homeless woman, was found dead in Stoneham last Wednesday. She was stuffed into a dumpster behind my store."

"What's that got to do with us?"

"I didn't know the woman, but I feel terrible that her life ended behind my property. I hoped you might be able to tell me something about her—and her circumstances."

The man shook his head. "Never heard of her." He turned to face the fire pit. "Anybody here ever heard of a Susan Morris?"

A muttered chorus of "No" erupted from the disinterested gathering.

The man turned back to Tricia. "Sorry."

"That's okay," Tricia said, disappointment coursing through her.

"Any other questions?"

Tricia shook her head.

One of the men got up from his seat at the fire pit and advanced on them. "Ya got anything else to eat?"

"I think there might be a few more bags of chips," Marshall said.

"I'll get them," Tricia said, and bent to retrieve the three bags of barbeque potato chips. As she straightened to face the newcomer, her breath stuck in her throat as she caught sight of the earring in his right ear. A silver anchor—just like the one she'd found in Susan Morris's car.

FOURTEEN

Tricia stood there, dumbfounded, just gaping at the man.

"The chips," he reminded her, and her hands were trembling so hard that she nearly dropped the bags as she handed them to him. She swallowed, suddenly feeling jittery.

"We ought to get going," Marshall said, eyeing her critically. But instead of asking what was wrong, he turned back to the group's leader. "My name's Marshall Cambridge. I've got a store in Stoneham, too. And you are?"

The man eyed him for long seconds before answering, "Hank Curtis. Will you be back with anything else to eat? Canned stuff is better, 'cuz then we can fix it ourselves when we need it, not just when someone shows up—ya know?"

"I hear you," Marshall said.

"What do you need?" Tricia asked, noticing that the man with the earring hadn't wandered off too far and seemed to be eavesdropping.

"Canned chili and spaghetti go over well. Tuna and chicken are good, too."

"We'll remember that," Marshall said.

"How many people should we buy for?" Tricia asked.

Curtis shrugged. "We usually number around twelve— give or take."

Tricia's heart sank. A dozen people living in such desperate poverty. How many more encampments were there like this in the area? "I hope I don't come off as judgmental, but how did you end up like this?" she asked.

"Circumstances," Curtis answered simply.

"What kind of work have you done?" Marshall asked.

"Food service. Twenty years of it in the military."

"What branch?" Tricia asked. Had Curtis been in the Navy and lied about knowing Susan?

"Army. I was a food service manager."

"You couldn't find the same kind of work after you retired?" Marshall asked.

Curtis seemed to squirm but then shrugged. "I had a hard time adjusting to civilian life. I'd been deployed to Afghanistan so many times, my wife and kids hardly knew me. Things got kind of bad and . . ."

"No drugs or drinking?" Marshall asked.

Again Curtis shrugged. "Maybe a little.

"And that's how you ended up homeless?" Tricia asked, truly interested.

Curtis wouldn't meet her gaze but nodded.

How terribly sad, Tricia thought.

Marshall cleared his throat and turned to Tricia. "Come on. We've got stores to run." He nodded at Hank and started back for the car.

But Tricia hesitated. "What does a food service manager do?" she asked.

"Look it up online. I'm sure you've got a computer. I haven't even got a damn flip phone." Curtis turned, his sandwich tucked under his arm like a football, and started walking away.

"It was very nice meeting you, Mr. Curtis," Tricia called after him.

Earring Guy laughed. "A good-looking woman like you can come back anytime," he said, and gave Tricia a toothy grin with gaps that made her cringe. It wasn't so much what he had said but how he had said it. Tricia gave him a rather forced smile and hurried around the back of the car for the front passenger seat while Marshall slammed the back door and piled into the driver's seat. Tricia buckled herself in as he started the car. He made a three-point turn and neither of them looked back, but Tricia glanced at the passenger-side mirror as they pulled away. Curtis stood there, just staring at them, until finally he disappeared from view.

"So, what gave you the heebie-jeebies?" Marshall asked at last.

"Did I tell you I found a silver anchor earring in Susan Morris's car?"

"No. And I guess I shouldn't be surprised after learning what you neglected to tell me about your store on the way out here."

"Marshall, please—"

"So, what about the earring?" he interrupted.

"The man who asked for the last of the chips was wearing what looked like its mate."

"Are you sure?"

"No doubt about it."

"Why didn't you ask him about it?"

"What was he going to tell me? He'd already answered no when Curtis asked if anyone knew Susan."

"I see your point. And what are you going to do with this information?"

"I guess I'll have to talk to Chief Baker."

Marshall glowered. "You didn't tell him about the earring when you found it?"

"At the time, I didn't know it would have any significance."

Marshall steered the car onto the highway once more. "I was going to invite you out to lunch on the way home."

"And now you won't?" she asked, feeling just a little hurt.

"I didn't say that," he grumbled. He didn't look at her.

"Would you like to go to lunch with me?" It wasn't exactly an enthusiastic invitation.

"Can we go to the Bookshelf Diner?"

"Why there?"

"Because Pixie told me Chief Baker often takes his lunch there."

Again, Marshall's fingers tightened on the steering wheel. "I guess," he grumbled. "The food's okay but not as good as at Booked for Lunch."

"I'll tell Angelica you said so. And as the chief isn't a fan of Angelica, I'll bet he doesn't want to patronize one of her businesses." Tricia thought about that statement. Did that mean the former detective didn't know Angelica owned the Brookview—where his wedding and reception were to be held—in her Nigela Ricita guise? Marshall had never asked Tricia about it, and she hadn't volunteered that information, either.

As they'd discussed earlier, they filled the Volaré's gas tank at the station on the outskirts of Stoneham, but as it was raining hard once again, they didn't bother to wash the car. It was almost twelve thirty when Tricia and Marshall arrived at the diner and found seats near the back of the restaurant, with Tricia taking the west side of the booth so that she could easily spot Baker should he come in. The diner didn't serve alcohol, so Tricia settled for a cup of coffee, while Marshall went for plain water. They ordered, and in no time their lunches arrived: a chef's salad for Tricia and a club sandwich for her escort.

They were midway through their meal when—just as Pixie had indicated—Baker came through the door and headed for the back of the restaurant, slowing when he caught sight of her. For a moment Tricia wondered if he'd do an about-face, but he continued and merely gave her a nod as he passed.

Marshall eyed Tricia critically. "Can you at least wait until we finish our meal before you run over to Chiefie?"

Tricia's brow wrinkled in confusion. "Why do I hear a note of sarcasm in your voice?"

Marshall frowned. "I seem to bump into your ex-lovers at an alarming rate," he muttered.

"What do you mean by that?" Tricia asked. It was her turn to be annoyed.

"Nothing," he mumbled, and took the last bite of his sandwich.

Tricia stabbed the lettuce and grape tomatoes in the bowl as if to punish them and polished off the last of her salad before she reached for her now tepid coffee. She signaled Hildy, the waitress, who topped up her mug.

"Can you bring the check when you get a chance?" Marshall asked.

"No dessert or coffee for you, sir?"

Marshall shook his head.

They didn't speak but watched as Hildy went back to the coffee urns, took out her receipt pad, and wrote up the bill, then came by the table once again. "I can take this when you're ready or you can pay at the register."

"Thanks."

Hildy went to check on some of her other customers, and Marshall folded his napkin before reaching for the slip of paper. "I've left Ava alone most of the morning and I have another appointment this afternoon, so I'd better run."

"Thanks for taking me to the camp this morning."

"You're welcome." He leaned in closer. "When am I going to see you again?"

"Call me," she said, giving him what she hoped was an encouraging smile.

Marshall's gaze seemed to stray to his right for a moment, then he picked up her hand and kissed the top of it. After his remark of minutes earlier, Tricia wondered if that gesture was meant as a token of affection to her or a message to the chief: that he'd missed out on something great by never committing himself to Tricia? She liked to flatter herself with the thought but then wondered what Marshall had meant about bumping into her lovers. Besides the chief, the only other person she'd dated in Stoneham was Russ Smith, and that had been a disaster of a relationship.

"Maybe I'll call later tonight," he said.

"Well, if you do, I'll be sure to answer the phone."

Marshall sidled out of the booth, stood, took a few bills out of his wallet, and set them on the table for a tip. "Until later."

Tricia watched as Marshall paid the bill, gave him a smile and a wave, and waited until he'd left the diner and was out of sight before she got up and hightailed it to the back of the diner. Baker was already chowing down on an open-face beef-and-gravy sandwich with fries.

"Do you mind if I sit down?" she asked.

Baker's mouth was full, so he grunted assent and nodded toward the other side of the booth. Tricia sat and waited for him to swallow before speaking.

"Thanks again for helping me out on Saturday night."

"You're welcome."

She didn't want to jump right into the painful part of the conversation and opened with an innocuous question. "How are the wedding plans going?"

Baker scowled, his brow furrowing. "Why do you care?"

Tricia's expression mirrored his own. "I was just making small talk."

Baker turned his attention back to his sandwich. "What are you really here for? As if I didn't know."

Tricia sighed. So he'd reverted back to his usual grumpy self.

"With everything that happened at my store, I didn't have an opportunity on Saturday night to ask how the investigation into Susan Morris's death is going."

Baker wiped his mouth with his napkin. "We're making progress," he said guardedly.

"Is my assistant, Pixie, still on your list of suspects?" Tricia demanded.

"I'm not at liberty to say."

"Oh, come on, Grant. You know she's no killer and she hasn't stepped out of line since she came to work for me three years ago. She's married, has a home and a stable life. She wouldn't do anything to jeopardize that."

"Says you."

"Yes, says me."

Baker cut another piece of his sandwich, chewed, and swallowed before speaking again. "No."

"No what?"

"No, she isn't a suspect."

"Well, you might have let her know that."

"I'm not in the habit of announcing my findings to those whom I might suspect of committing a crime."

"And there's a reason why people like Pixie distrust those in uniform."

"Did you stop by just to annoy me?" Baker asked.

"No, as a matter of fact. I might have some information you can use in your investigation."

Baker rolled his eyes.

"This morning Marshall and I went to Merrimack to talk to a group of homeless people."

"What were you doing there?" he snapped.

"Delivering food. I spoke with Libby Hirt at the Stoneham Food Shelf, and she suggested it would be a way of helping people in need."

"And to interrogate them, no doubt," Baker muttered.

"We did not interrogate anyone. In fact, I only asked one question: did anyone know Susan Morris?"

"Yeah, and how'd that go?" Baker asked with disdain.

"They all said no. But that wasn't true."

Baker raised an eyebrow. Now she had his attention. "And?"

She sighed. "The other day when I was poking around in Susan's car, I found an earring jammed into the edge of the glove compartment."

"And?" he said again.

"It was a scratched silver anchor. One of the men at the homeless encampment was wearing its mate."

Baker's gaze sharpened. "How do you know it was Susan's earring?"

"Oh, come on, Grant, how many people go around wearing anchor-shaped earrings?"

"Probably thousands."

"In one small village?"

"You just said you went to Merrimack—and Susan Morris hung around Stoneham. That makes the probability of it being Susan Morris's other earring plummet."

Tricia said nothing.

"What made you take it from her car—which, I might add, was tampering with evidence."

"Evidence you and your men missed," she countered.

His piercing gaze remained riveted on her face.

Tricia shrugged. "I don't know why I grabbed it. Maybe because it no longer had an owner or a mate. I guess I felt sorry for it."

Baker raised an eyebrow. "Sorry for an earring?"

Tricia didn't dignify his question with an answer.

"Why didn't you give it to me last Thursday?" he asked.

"I didn't think it could have any significance."

Baker frowned. "What else?"

"That's it."

Baker cut another bite of his sandwich. The gravy had begun to congeal, not looking at all appetizing. Again Baker chewed and swallowed before speaking. "You will turn over the earring so that I can investigate this. Not that it will go anywhere," he griped.

Oh, no?

"I'd be happy to give it to you. It could be the key to solving Susan's murder."

"Don't get your hopes up." He grabbed one of his fries, dunked it into the little paper cup filled with ketchup, and chomped on it. "What was the name of the guy wearing the earring?"

"I don't know."

"What did he look like?"

"Hairy and grubby."

"Come on, Tricia, you can do better than that."

Tricia sighed. "He had salt-and-pepper gray hair, a week or two of stubble, and wore muddy jeans and a gray hoodie."

"That describes half the guys in the camp."

So he had been to Merrimack to ask questions . . .

"He's the only one wearing a silver anchor earring," she reminded him.

Baker stared at her for long seconds, then turned back to his lunch. "I'll be over to your shop after I finish here."

"I'll be waiting for you," she said, and wriggled out of the booth. She said no more and walked out of the diner without a backward look.

Mr. Everett was nowhere in sight, and an older gentleman stood at the cash desk paying for a nice stack of books when Tricia reentered her store. Pixie waited on him, and the two were deep in conversation on the merits of the Travis Mc-Gee series by John MacDonald. Tricia was eager to speak to Pixie alone and forced herself to be patient as she hung up her jacket in the back of the shop. She was going to hang around but decided she'd better retrieve the earring so that Baker could take it and leave as soon as possible. Even with good news, Pixie was always nervous when in the presence of any police officer.

Tricia retreated to her apartment, plucked the lone earring from her jewelry box, and placed it in a plastic snack bag before returning to her store.

The gentleman customer had left the shop, and Pixie was looking out the big display window toward the north where the police station was located.

"I've got good news," Tricia said by way of a greeting. "I did as you suggested and had lunch at the Bookshelf Diner, where I just happened to bump into Chief Baker."

"And?" Pixie asked, sounding hopeful.

"You are not a suspect in Susan Morris's murder."

For a moment Tricia thought Pixie might collapse from

relief as she sagged against the big glass display case. "Oh, thank everything that's holy."

"I never had a doubt," Tricia told her.

"Yeah, well . . . I'm sure you, and probably Angelica, Grace, and Mr. E, were the only ones."

"Nonsense," Tricia chided her. "But I want to warn you that Chief Baker will be here in a matter of minutes, and I will completely understand it if you want to retreat to the office to avoid seeing him."

Pixie straightened in umbrage. "And let him think I'm afraid of him? Not a chance."

Tricia smiled. "You go, girl."

Pixie ducked her head in what seemed like embarrassment, but her lips curled into a smile.

The bell over the shop door jingled, and Chief Baker entered Haven't Got a Clue, adopting the usual cop swagger. Despite their tense conversation not ten minutes before, Tricia knew that wasn't the real Grant Baker. She'd known his much softer side in years past. And those green eyes of his . . .

Tricia gave herself a shake. It was better not to remember those times. It was far better to remember why they had broken up in the first place.

"You got here fast," she said in greeting, and didn't bother with any more chitchat, simply handing him the snack bag with the earring inside.

Baker shook his head. "You should have given this to me the night you found it."

Tricia sighed. "Well, you've got it now. Will you let me know what the guy wearing the other one says?"

"I'm conducting a murder investigation, not running a gossip mill."

"Fine," Tricia said flatly, and turned toward the cash desk. "See you later, Chief," she called over her shoulder, then faced Pixie. "So, how was business while I was out?"

Pixie's gaze jumped between her boss and the cop, who was still standing near the doorway.

"Not bad for a rainy day in September. We really should think about restocking the bargain shelves in the back."

Tricia heard the door open and the bell ring, then the door slam shut, but didn't acknowledge Baker's departure. "Maybe we can get on that this afternoon."

"Sounds like a plan," Pixie said, craning her neck to look out the big display window. "So, what's with the earring?"

Tricia shrugged. "I found it in Susan's car."

"What were you doing in Susan's car?"

"Um, folding her clothes."

"Uh-huh. Was the earring in a pocket or something?"

"Uh, no," Tricia answered quickly. Pixie seemed to be waiting for her to say something more, but Tricia changed the subject.

"Is there anything else about Susan you've remembered?"

"I've racked my brains, but . . . no. Remember, we weren't really friends. You, Angelica, and your Sunday dinner group are the only people I can truly call friends. I mean, there's no way I can hang out with the people from the old days . . . if you catch my drift."

Tricia knew that stipulation had been a part of Pixie's parole requirements. "Don't you and Fred have mutual friends?"

Pixie shook her head. "He plays cards with some guys on Saturday nights, but they aren't the chummy, invite-you-over-for-dinner kinda people. And they smoke. I'm a really bad ex-smoker. Since I gave it up, I can't stand the smell on my clothes and hair. And if someone tosses a butt on our driveway, I have a conniption."

"That's funny. I'd say that makes you a *good* ex-smoker."

"I certainly saved a lot of money since I quit."

Tricia nodded.

"Why does Susan's death bother you so much?" Pixie asked. "Just because she was found behind your store?"

Tricia shook her head. "It seemed like she had a terrible life."

"Oh, but she didn't. She was happy . . . at least, that's the impression she gave me. She felt she had a safe place to live and everything she needed, and I'm sure she was even more pleased when she got that job at the new candy store. Is it true they let you eat as much as you want until you're sick of it and never want to touch the stuff again?"

"That's the rumor."

"Then hiring a person like me would be a *big* mistake. I could live on chocolate alone." Pixie clasped her hands dramatically and practically swooned.

Tricia laughed, but before she could say anything, her cell phone rang. Withdrawing it from her pocket, she glanced at the number and the laughter died on her lips.

Fiona Sample was calling.

FIFTEEN

 Tricia looked up from her phone and turned to face Pixie. "Sorry, but I need to take this call downstairs."

"Not a problem," Pixie said, and Tricia hit the call icon. "Hi, Fiona," she said as she retreated toward the back of the shop and the stairs to the basement.

"I hope I'm not calling at a bad time."

"Not at all. It's been raining, and we're in between seasons here, so things are slow. What's up?" she asked, knowing what was coming.

"I was hoping you'd had a chance to talk to Russ's employees."

Tricia hit the bottom of the stairs, turning on the lights to the office as she entered. "As a matter of fact, I have. And I'm afraid I don't have good news."

"Oh, dear. I was afraid of that. What did they say?"

Tricia took the seat in front of the desk and computer. "I only spoke to one of them—Patti, his second-in-command—and she made it clear she didn't want to get into the middle of what looks like a sticky situation."

"But I thought Russ had two employees."

"One's been cut to part-time because ad revenue is down."

"I can't say I'm surprised by that. These days Russ seems to be alienating just about everybody he speaks to."

"He's certainly done a lot of damage at the Chamber of Commerce. But I'm afraid that's not the worst of it."

Tricia heard Fiona sigh. "You'd better get it over with and give it to me straight."

"It looks like Russ is ready to put his son in foster care."

"Oh, no! You can't be serious!" Fiona cried.

"That's what Patti told me."

"Nikki would never stand for that."

"Have you been able to contact her?" Tricia asked.

"No. And that manager she hired to look after the Patisserie was rude to me the last time I called to ask for her number. Have you met him?"

"Yes, and I can tell you that he hasn't got the culinary chops Nikki has. His cookies were dreadful, and the bread he's selling isn't much better."

"Do you think he's trying to run down the business so he can get it from Nikki for a bargain?"

"I suppose that's possible. There certainly aren't lines out the door like there were back in the summer when Nikki was still in charge, but then, until the leaves start turning in earnest, he can't depend on tourists, just local customers."

Fiona was quiet for a few moments. "Since we last talked, I decided to hire someone to track Nikki down."

"You mean a detective?"

"Thanks to winning the lawsuit, I've got the money. He might even have some information for me later today." She let out a weary sigh. "That girl needs to step up and take care of her child and her business and give up on the ridiculous idea of being a TV chef."

"Can't she do both?" Tricia asked. "It seems to me some of these celebrity chefs have multiple businesses. And those just coming up the pike already have cake shops or the like."

"That may be true, but Nikki has not been making good decisions for some time now. She likes to blame me for it because I was forced out of her life at an early age. Of course, I feel terrible about the past, but it can't be changed. When we were first reunited, everything seemed wonderful—possible. But then she started dating Russ."

Tricia listened patiently as Fiona conveyed a rather lengthy list of Russ's many faults, which Fiona assured her she'd never mentioned to Nikki. As a concerned mother, she worried that voicing such opinions could threaten their tenuous relationship, so she'd kept mum on the subject. But Tricia knew the truth in what Fiona said.

"I'm sorry I couldn't have been of more help," Tricia said with sincerity.

"And I'm sorry I put you in such an untenable position."

"To employ an old saw, you're the one between a rock and a hard place," Tricia offered.

Fiona sighed. "That I am."

"I don't know what else to do that would help," Tricia offered.

"You've been a good friend to me, and I'm sorry that Nikki can't see that you've been a good friend to her as well."

Tricia wasn't sure what else to say on that account, so she changed the subject. "There's something new that's come into the mix. Russ has put the *Stoneham Weekly News* up for sale. He put a half-page ad for it on the last page of the current issue."

"Really?" Fiona's surprise was evident by her tone.

"I take it this surprises you."

"Yes. Nikki told me that he had an unnatural attachment to that dusty little rag."

Tricia couldn't help but smile at the remark. "I feel sorry for both Nikki and Russ. They had everything going for them. I'm sad that they couldn't make it work."

"Is that regret something you feel when it comes to your life as well?" Fiona asked.

Tricia frowned and thought about her ex-husband, Christopher. She didn't think she would have gotten back together with him, but he'd been a charmer, and there was always that possibility . . . until he was killed protecting Angelica, of course. And when he was murdered, that option was yanked from her forever.

"Kind of," Tricia admitted. "But the past is the past and we can't fix it."

"Exactly," Fiona agreed, her tone filled with sorrow. She had to be thinking of the years she had spent isolated from her firstborn.

"I do hope you'll keep me informed on what happens to little Russell. I feel bad for that poor boy," Tricia said.

"Yes. If I don't call, I'll at least email you to keep you in the loop. Somehow this has to be resolved in the next week or so," Fiona said sadly.

"Thanks," Tricia said. She didn't know what else to say.

"Anything exciting happening in good old Stoneham?" Fiona asked.

Tricia considered telling her about Pixie finding Susan Morris's body behind her store but then changed her mind. Fiona might just grill her on the sordid details. Authors tended to do that.

"Everything's great."

"Good. Well, I'd best get to work researching a couple of topics for my next book. It's going to be a doozy."

"I can't wait to read it," Tricia said.

"Until later. Bye."

"Good-bye, Fiona," Tricia said, and the call ended, leaving her feeling just a little depressed. Still, Russell Junior wasn't her problem. Neither was what happened to Nikki or Russ. She switched on her computer, determined to put the Smith family and their troubles out of her thoughts. She wanted to look up what a military food manager's job entailed. A quick Google search later and she had her answer. She read the job description and was surprised to learn that not only did the position require a four-year college degree but it paid well. Such a manager had to be a jack-of-all-trades, with purchasing power, supervisory capabilities, and a host of other skills and responsibilities. Hank Curtis had had a very demanding job while in the military. There had to be more to his story than a rough transition to civilian life.

Tricia crossed her legs and realized she was still wearing

the knee-high boots, which were caked with dried mud and could use a good polish. She'd do that later, but first she needed to change back into her usual sweater-set work attire.

As she headed up the stairs to her apartment, Tricia thought again about Hank Curtis. Though no longer in the military, his authority in the homeless camp seemed absolute. Was it worth her time and effort to find out more about him?

When Tricia returned to Haven't Got a Clue, she found the workmen had arrived to replace the store's back door and jamb. Thankfully no customers were subjected to the constant banging and drone of power tools, and they left her with new locks, a repaired security system, and an itemized bill to submit to her insurance company.

Tricia spent the rest of the afternoon feeling distracted by all that had happened during that very busy day. Heavy rain made a return visit and the sky had prematurely darkened, making Haven't Got a Clue seem as gloomy as a dusty old museum. Mr. Everett would no doubt notice when he came back to work the next day and wield his lamb's-wool duster along the baseboard and shelves so that everything would once again feel squeaky clean.

When closing time rolled around, Tricia bid Pixie a good evening and was happy to shut the door behind her and head for Angelica's for their usual happy hour and dinner. But first she heeded Baker's advice and set the security system. As she unlocked the door to the Cookery, she pondered what treat Tommy over at Booked for Lunch had made for their dinner.

Tricia headed up the stairs to Angelica's apartment and was greeted—as usual—by an ecstatic Sarge. Angelica sat at one of the island stools and tossed the dog a biscuit she had at the ready, telling him, "Hush!" The barking ceased immediately.

"Does he need to go out?" Tricia asked, taking off her jacket, wondering why she bothered donning it when Angelica lived right next door. She hung it on a peg.

"No. June took him out for a comfort stop just before she left. How was your day? I want to hear every detail—a minute-by-minute description," Angelica said, sounding desperate.

Tricia eyed her sister. "You're that bored?"

"I'm about to go out of my mind."

"I don't understand. You do most of your work here at home anyway."

"Yes, but I visit my places of business on a regular basis. I'm at Booked for Lunch every day it's open. I visit the Sheer Comfort Inn at least every other day. And I pop in at Booked for Beauty a couple of days a week, too, if only to change my nail polish. Look at my fingers. It looks like they've been through a war."

Was that an opening for Tricia to discuss Hank Curtis?

"How about I make us a couple of drinks and then we can talk."

"You know where the gin is."

Although Angelica hadn't made a pitcher of martinis, she had installed the glasses in the freezer to chill them. In no time Tricia stirred the decanter with a glass spoon and poured. "Let's sit in the living room."

"I'm for that." Angelica settled herself on her knee scooter and zipped over to the sectional, where she moved to the chaise end so that her booted foot was raised. Tricia carried the tray with the pitcher and glasses into the room, setting it on the coffee table. Angelica poured and passed a stemmed glass to her sister before Tricia sat in the adjacent chair. "Now, tell all."

Tricia raised her glass. "Cheers." She took a sip. "First, I've got a question for you."

"Shoot."

"How much responsibility does Antonio carry?"

Angelica blinked. "A lot. Why?"

"I was thinking maybe if he had less to do, he might be more available for Ginny and Sofia."

"So they can have another baby?" Angelica asked eagerly.

"Not necessarily. I mean, they could have a live-in nanny if they wanted."

"That's true, and I've suggested it more than once. I also think Ginny's been a lot happier since I convinced her that there's no shame in having her house cleaned by someone other than her. I mean, it keeps someone else in a job."

"That's a good way of thinking about it."

"Thank you. But what did you have in mind when it comes to Antonio?"

"What do you think about hiring a food service manager? Someone who could coordinate the buying for the Brookview, Booked for Lunch, and the Sheer Comfort Inn. Someone who's good at logistics, overseeing personnel, and a host of other duties."

"It sounds like you're trying to put Antonio out of a job."

"Not at all. It would free him up to do other things for Nigela Ricita Associates. I've sensed he sometimes gets restless."

Angelica looked thoughtful and sighed. "We have discussed that in the past. And where would you find such a superman?"

"Well, I think I may have met him at the homeless camp."

Angelica looked skeptical. "Really?"

"He's a twenty-year Army veteran."

Angelica frowned. "Why's a man with that kind of experience homeless?"

This was where things got sketchy. "Uh, circumstances."

Angelica raised an eyebrow.

"Okay," Tricia admitted, "he kind of lost his sobriety."

"'Kind of'?" Angelica asked.

"It happens," Tricia explained.

"And is he still a druggie or tippler?"

"Hey, *we're* tipplers."

"We aren't homeless," Angelica pointed out.

"You're the one who rescues people and gives them not only jobs but hope. Heck, it was you who convinced me to take Pixie on. I've never regretted it."

"She *is* one of my success stories," Angelica agreed, taking a sip of her drink. "Do you think this man would even want a job?"

"I didn't bring up the subject. I thought I'd better run it past you first."

"Let *me* run the idea past Antonio and I'll get back to you."

Tricia nodded; she couldn't expect more at this point.

"Marshall and I spoke to the man who seemed to be in charge of the camp—the ex-Army guy. His name is Hank Curtis. I asked what we could bring on a future visit, and he suggested canned food. I thought I might go to Milford and buy some cases for them."

"When will you take it to the camp? And you're not going on your own!" Angelica declared.

"I don't know," Tricia said and avoided commenting on the second half of Angelica's statement. "Soon. I wish I could give them something a little more meaningful."

"I'd say food was pretty important."

"Yes, but . . . seeing those pitiful tents and big cartons really got to me."

Angelica nodded and toyed with the frill pick in her drink. "What else happened today?"

Tricia accepted the change of subject. "Fiona called again."

"Oh, dear."

"Yeah. I told her what I knew about Russ's situation. She wasn't pleased and has hired a private detective to track Nikki down."

"Well, it makes sense," Angelica said, and ate one of her olives. She gave a sigh. Sarge looked up at her from the floor, where he'd settled next to the couch, cocked his head, and looked at his dog mom with such devotion.

"I know you don't usually let Sarge on the furniture inside, but look at those little eyes. He wants to comfort you," Tricia said.

"Of course you do," Angelica cooed, and reached down to pet the dog's head. It took only a few seconds before she said, "Oh, all right. Come and sit on Mommy's lap."

The dog immediately leapt into the air with the grace of a gymnast and nearly knocked Angelica's drink from her hand. "Sit!" she implored as Sarge tried to give her doggie kisses.

Sarge sat but whimpered with gratitude.

"I know I'm going to regret this."

"Since we were speaking of the Smith family and their trials and tribulations, did you get a chance to read today's issue of the *Stoneham Weekly News*?" Tricia asked.

"Every last word. It took me all of five minutes."

"What do you think about Russ putting the business up for sale?"

"I'm not at all surprised," Angelica said. "As the new Chamber head, he's done nothing but alienate most of the businesses in town. I wasn't the only one to pull advertising. He can't stay in business if no one will patronize his little venture."

That was true.

"I'm not even sure the village needs a weekly paper," Angelica said. "Big newspapers across the country are failing. That rag is only good for lining bird cages and wrapping old dishes relegated to attics and thrift stores."

"That's sad," Tricia remarked. "In years past, Russ did do some actual reporting. If he hadn't been so obnoxious toward me, I might even feel sorry for him."

"Sorrier than for the men living in that homeless camp?"

Tricia thought about it. "No." She changed the subject once again. "What's for supper?"

"Stuffed peppers. It seemed like a nice meal for a cold, rainy evening."

"I'll say. I love that Tommy makes it with sausage instead of ground beef."

"Me, too. Would you mind putting them in the oven to reheat?"

"Not a bit. Then, when I get back, we can have another drink."

She drained her glass and headed for the kitchen.

Once the peppers were in the oven, Tricia set two places

on the kitchen island and returned to the living room to pour them new drinks, after which they clinked glasses.

"You didn't finish telling me about your little adventure this morning. Were you able to learn anything about Susan Morris during your visit to the homeless camp?" Angelica asked.

"No. But remember that earring I found the evening we looked in her car?" she said, and resumed her seat.

"Uh-huh."

"A man at the camp was wearing its mate."

"Get out."

"No lie. I ran into Grant at lunchtime"—she deliberately didn't mention that it was at the Bookshelf Diner, Angelica's competition—"and told him about it. Afterward, I gave him the earring. He's going to check it out."

"How can you be sure it's from the same set?"

"I can't, but it's got to be a clue, don't you think?"

Angelica looked skeptical. "What was the camp like?"

"Sad. Tents, tarps, and cardboard. Nobody should have to live like that."

"What will they do when the weather turns for the worse?"

"I don't know. Maybe they go south if they can."

And if they didn't? What then?

Tricia didn't want to continue discussing that subject and instead told her sister of the repairs to her shop's back entrance. The tale didn't seem to entertain Angelica.

"So, what have *you* been doing all day?" Tricia asked.

"Wrote emails. Studied spreadsheets. Nothing very interesting. But, thanks to your suggestion the other day, I made an appointment for both of us at Booked for Beauty to get a haircut and our nails done. Do you think you could carve out an hour or so to do it?"

Tricia was due for a trim and to have her hair highlighted. "Sure. When?"

"Tomorrow. I've got a morning appointment so we can go out and have lunch afterward."

No way was Tricia going to beg off when it meant so much to Angelica to get out, but all these restaurant meals and take-out dinners from Booked for Lunch had to be playing havoc with her weight. Not many things frightened her, but getting on the scale was definitely high on the list of things that did.

"I'll look forward to it," she said.

"Good. I'll text you in the morning. And going to the day spa will give you an opportunity to talk to Randy about Susan."

"Does he have anything interesting to report?"

"He interviewed her twice. That must mean something," Angelica offered.

Yes, it might.

Suddenly, Tricia was looking forward to getting her nails done.

SIXTEEN

 Upon arriving back home, Tricia reset the security system and trudged up the steps to the apartment above her store. After such an event-filled day, she expected to feel exhausted, but her mind was filled with so many thoughts and she felt so restless, she knew trying to sit and read would be futile. So instead she pulled out one of her cookbooks and chose to make a batch of lemon crinkle cookies. She assembled the ingredients and made the dough and had just put the first batch into the oven, when her phone rang. Only two people would be calling her at that time of night: Angelica or Marshall.

It was Marshall.

"To what do I owe the pleasure?"

"I was just thinking about you. Were you thinking of me?" he asked.

"Sorry, but no. I was thinking about my day and then decided to make cookies for tomorrow's customers. But I'm glad that you called. I wanted to thank you again for going with me to the homeless camp today."

"It was my pleasure."

Oh, he lied so effortlessly.

"And thanks for indulging me about going to lunch at the Bookshelf Diner, too. I know we both prefer other venues."

"The food was okay; the company was definitely better."

A smile tugged at Tricia's lips. "Aw, thank you."

"Is the chief going to look for your pal with the earring?" Marshall asked, and Tricia detected more than a hint of ire in his tone.

"Yes, although he didn't say when. But let's not talk about that. What's on your mind tonight?"

Marshall sighed. "I've had a few days to think about the Ireland trip," he began.

Oh, dear. This sounded ominous.

"And?"

"I didn't enjoy it," he admitted.

Tricia blinked. "What aspect?"

"Making sure everyone's luggage was accounted for, resolving problems with the hotels, but mostly running and fetching for everyone and not having a chance to enjoy the trip myself. I love Ireland. This was my third trip and I don't feel like I got to enjoy one minute. Except," he quickly amended, "for the fleeting time I had with you."

"I thought you realized that going in."

"I did to some extent. But the only thing that made the trip bearable *was* you."

Tricia let out a sigh. Was he just trying to flatter her? "Come on, you must have enjoyed *something*."

"By the time I got to eat, my meals were usually ice-cold. I was the last one on the bus and the first one off, worried that any of my charges might fall and get hurt—and then it would be my responsibility to find whatever medical help they'd need and then I'd have to figure out how to get them back home."

"But nobody fell."

"This time," he asserted.

"What else?" Tricia prompted.

"I never had a chance to relax. And I worried that because of the stress, I might snap at any minute."

"Let me assure you, it wasn't apparent to anyone on the tour."

"Thank goodness."

Tricia wished she could see his face, stroke his cheek, and gaze into his dark eyes. "So it sounds like you may have made a decision."

He let out another long breath. "I've already talked to the folks at Milford Travel and turned in my notice . . . not that I was actually getting paid. That trip was an internship of sorts, and I'm not sorry I did it. It gave me an opportunity to test the waters without making an actual commitment to them or anyone else."

"Does this mean you no longer want to travel?" Tricia asked.

"Hell no. But I don't want to travel with a group and be responsible for making sure everyone is happy. Give me a backpack and a plane ticket and I'm off."

"How soon?" Tricia asked, not sure she wanted to hear the answer.

Marshall laughed. "Don't worry. Travel is not in my immediate future."

"Then you're sticking with the Armchair Tourist?"

"Well, sort of. Now that I've got a great manager in Ava, I'm free to expand my horizons."

"In what way?" Tricia asked with trepidation.

Ding! The stove's timer went off.

"Hang on, I've got to get my cookies out of the oven."

Tricia set the phone down, rescued the tray of crinkles, and set them on the counter to cool. She set her phone on speaker. "I'm back. Now, where were we?" she asked, and started dropping dough onto another prepared baking tray.

"I was about to say how tremendously impressed I am with what your sister has done. She's built up quite an empire here in Stoneham—as Nigela Ricita and under her own name."

Tricia felt her gut tighten. "I didn't know you were aware of her NR connection."

"Tricia, half the village knows."

"So I've been told, but no one's mentioned it to me."

"Why blow a good thing? Everything she's done has been of benefit to the village. She's given people jobs and brought prosperity back to what was a dying backwater."

"Bob Kelly started the whole Booktown resurgence," Tricia said, hating to mention the man's name. She'd never forgive him for the things he'd done—the lives he'd ruined—and all in the name of greed.

"Yes, but Angelica expanded on that, and as far as I know, she's never asked for special favors from the Chamber, the board of selectmen, or anyone else."

"She's pretty special," Tricia agreed.

"Does it ever make you feel . . ."

"Like less of a success?" Tricia thought about it while she put the second tray of cookies into the oven. "I could do what she's done: she's encouraged me hundreds of times to open another business, to get involved in other things . . ." Like her recent disastrous attempt to volunteer for the Pets-A-Plenty Animal Rescue.

"So why don't you do it?" Marshall asked.

"It's not that I lack ambition, but I love what I'm already doing. And for the first time in my life, I've surrounded my-self with people who love me. People who aren't going to abandon me."

Marshall didn't comment. Was he feeling just a little bit guilty for not trying harder to be a part of her makeshift family?

"I've got my family, my cat, and my business," Tricia continued. "From my perspective, it's already a pretty full life."

"When you put it that way, it makes me envious; I'm still searching for what I can do that'll fulfill me."

"Any clues as to what that might be?"

"Maybe," he admitted. "I've been poking around, asking questions."

"Do you think you'll be leaving the area?" Suddenly the idea of losing him gave her pause. She wasn't sure she wanted more than what they already shared, but she wasn't ready to give up on it, either.

"I've been looking at various options in southern New Hampshire. Believe me, I have no plans to leave the area anytime soon."

Could a share in the proposed wedding venue they'd visited on their picnic be one of those options?

"I'm glad to hear that. I've gotten used to having you around. I wouldn't like that to change anytime soon."

"Thank you."

"Thank you. Now, why don't we talk about something a little less serious?"

"Like what?"

"Like wouldn't you like to come over to my place and have a few of these wonderful lemon cookies and a nice big glass of—milk? Mmm . . . they smell so good," she teased.

"I could. But only if you'll have a couple with me."

"I could do that."

"And . . . maybe later we could . . ."

"Marshall, I thought you'd never ask."

The next morning, after making a light breakfast for herself and Marshall, Tricia decided to forgo her walk and head for the big grocery store in Milford. She locked the door to Haven't Got a Clue and walked to the municipal parking lot to retrieve her car. In minutes she arrived at her destination, where she spoke to the store manager and rustled up cases of canned food topped with pull tabs, as well as another case of water, and then drove back to Stoneham. Just as she pulled into a parking space, her phone pinged. It was Angelica, texting to say they had an eleven thirty appointment at the day spa. She texted an acknowledgment and was about to put the phone back in her purse, when it rang. Tricia looked at the number and hit the call answer icon.

"What's up, Grant?"

"I did what you said. I went to the homeless camp in Merrimack yesterday afternoon to look for your so-called guy with the anchor earring and nobody there knew a thing about it. Nobody knew what I was talking about, either. Now, did you do anything to let the guy know that he might be scrutinized?" he asked, his voice hard once more.

"Well, I never said a word, if that's what you mean, but

he may have noticed me noticing that earring. But their leader, a man named Hank Curtis, did ask the group if anyone knew Susan. After the guy heard that, all he had to do was take the earring off. I suppose others covered for him when you started asking questions."

"My thoughts exactly. Would you be willing to return to the camp and look for the guy?"

"I guess so, but I'd prefer to do it in a humanitarian way."

"Such as?" Baker asked.

"Curtis mentioned they could use canned goods more than sandwiches. I went to the grocery store in Milford this morning and bought a few cases of food to give them. If you want to act as a liaison, not to harass but to show them that they have nothing to fear from the police, then I'd be pleased to help you do so."

"I'm running a murder investigation," he reminded her curtly.

"Is it likely anyone at that camp would betray one of their own, even if they knew the person to be a murderer?"

"It would be in their best interest to do so. Committing one murder is hard. Committing a second is a whole lot easier," Baker said.

Tricia didn't like to think about that possibility, especially since she might be looked at as someone asking far too many questions.

"Have you got time today to pay a return visit to the homeless encampment?" Baker asked.

"I will make myself available anytime you want to go."

"Good. I'll pick you up in front of your store in ten minutes."

"I can't leave until Pixie comes in to work. Can you give me twenty minutes?"

"Oh, all right," Baker growled, and ended the call.

Tricia started her car, drove to the alley behind her store, and unpacked the cases. After disarming the security system, she moved the boxes inside. Then she put them on a dolly, pushing it to the front of the store. She had just enough time to drive her car back to the municipal lot and return to

Haven't Got a Clue to change into her boots once more. She grabbed the container of cookies and brought them with her. By the time she made it down the stairs, Pixie was coming through the door.

"Going somewhere?" she inquired as she put away her key to the shop.

"Back to the homeless encampment. Would you be a dear and make the coffee and set out these cookies for our customers?"

"It would be my pleasure."

Baker's vehicle arrived outside the shop, and he honked the horn. Tricia pushed the dolly out the door.

The SUV's passenger-side window rolled down. "What are you doing with all that stuff?" Baker demanded.

"I told you if I made a return visit, I would be bringing them supplies. Now, are you going to help me put them in the back of your vehicle or not?"

The window went back up, and Baker got out of the car and stamped toward the sidewalk, grumbling under his breath. He helped her move the boxes into the SUV and left her at the curb.

"I'll put the dolly away and be right back."

Baker slammed the driver's door.

Pixie intercepted Tricia. "I'll put that away for you. Do you know how long you'll be gone?"

"Probably a couple of hours."

"Well, have a good time," Pixie said cheerfully.

"With Chief Baker?" Tricia asked.

"Oh, yeah. I forgot you were going with him. Try not to kill him."

Tricia couldn't help but smile. "I'll see you later."

Pixie gave her a wink. "You bet."

Tricia returned to the vehicle and climbed into the passenger seat.

"Nice boots," Baker said, and slammed the gearshift into drive before pulling away from the curb.

Before Tricia could voice a reply, Baker turned up the volume on the police scanner, effectively ending any chance there was for conversation. Tricia always planned for such occasions and pulled her current read from her purse. She could entertain herself, thank you.

Twenty minutes later Baker turned off the main road onto the dirt track that led to the homeless encampment. Tricia marked her page, closed the book, and returned it to her purse, setting it under the seat.

Baker pulled the SUV over to a grassy spot off the dirt road and killed the engine. When they got out, the ground beneath Tricia's boots still squelched. She'd never had the desire to camp and couldn't fathom how these people lived in such primitive conditions. Knowing they had no choice, her sympathy for them grew. She followed Baker as Hank Curtis and another man walked toward them.

"You back to hassle us?" Curtis asked Baker in a none-too-friendly tone.

"No," Baker said neutrally.

"The chief volunteered to help me deliver these cases of food. And I brought another case of water—just in case you need it."

"Thanks," Curtis said, mumbled "I'll give you a hand" to Baker, and walked around to the back of the vehicle.

While they worked, the rest of the men gathered closer—but not too close—to watch. Tricia counted and saw there were ten, including Curtis, and searched their faces, but, as before, a few refused to look her in the eye. She couldn't say she blamed them.

Finally, Tricia recognized the gray hoodie belonging to the man who'd worn the anchor earring. Because he kept his head ducked, she couldn't see if he'd removed it.

Curtis tore open the box tops. "Everybody gets two each."

"Who gets the extras?" one of the men demanded.

"Me. I'll keep 'em for Eddie and Bill."

"They ain't here. They shouldn't get any!" shouted another.

"Hey!" Baker barked, and the two malcontents backed off, probably intimidated by the uniform and his take-no-prisoners voice of authority.

One by one the men approached the SUV, some grabbing the food and hustling away, most of them glaring at Baker. The guy in the hoodie stepped forward and, just as Baker had suspected, he'd removed the earring. Tricia handed him two cans but said nothing, only giving him a smile at his muttered "Thanks." With only a few more people in line, Tricia made sure to watch where the man went.

"Well?" Baker asked Tricia once all the food had been distributed.

"It's that man over there with the gray sweatshirt."

"Follow me," Baker said. It sounded like an order.

"What's going on?" Curtis demanded.

"Nothing. I just want to talk to that guy in the hoodie. What's his name?"

"Joe King. What do you want with him?"

"As I told you the other day, I'm investigating the homicide of Susan Morris. Ms. Miles here believes she saw Mr. King wearing an anchor earring."

"Yeah, so what of it?"

"It could be considered evidence, depending on where and when he got it."

"Joe was in the Navy. Spent four years on an aircraft carrier," Curtis said.

"Did he know Susan Morris?" Tricia asked.

"I don't know. Do you mind if I tag along? I look after my people," Curtis explained, which was the mark of a good leader.

"All right," Baker agreed, and led the way across the muddy grass.

King was crouched before a one-man tent with a substantial rip in its side, squirreling away his canned rations, as the group approached. "Joe, Chief Baker wants to talk to you."

King rose, looking uncomfortable. "What about?"

"I understand you have a silver anchor earring," Baker said.

"So, what if I do?"

Baker reached into his pocket and pulled out an inkjet

copy of the earring Tricia had found, blown up to take up half the page. "It looks like this."

"I know what it looks like," King muttered.

"So, have you still got it?"

"I lost it the other day."

"Well, isn't that convenient? Where did you get it?"

"A chick gave it to me years ago."

"How many years?"

"I don't remember."

"Was it Susan Morris?" Baker asked.

"Who?"

"The woman who was found dead in Stoneham last Wednesday."

"Nah," King said, looking away.

"Perhaps you'd like to come to the Stoneham police station to talk about it," Baker said, resting his right hand on the butt of his sidearm.

"No, I wouldn't."

"Then I'll ask the question again: Did you know Susan Morris?"

King glanced at Curtis as though looking for guidance, but Curtis's expression remained impassive.

He let out a breath. "Yeah, I knew her."

"How well?" Baker asked.

King shrugged. "Not very."

"How did you meet?"

"I was panhandling in town—"

"Which town?"

"Merrimack, and the cops were about to run me off, when she drove past and asked if I needed a lift. I was wearing a cap that said, 'CVN-68.'"

"What does that mean?" Tricia asked.

"The *Nimitz*," Curtis explained.

Tricia had heard of that particular ship.

"She said she was a former naval officer. She took me to a diner, and we traded war stories . . . so to speak. She was nice to me. It's been a long time since someone was nice to me," King practically growled.

"What else?" Baker demanded.

"She dropped me off at the end of the road." King jerked a thumb over his shoulder.

"So, how'd you get the earring?"

"I saw it on the floor of her car. She said she'd lost the other one. I'd had a gold stud before and lost it. I figured, why not wear it? Hurt like a sonofabitch to put it in: the hole had almost closed up."

"When was this?"

"Back in the summer."

"Why'd you take it off?"

"I told you: I lost it."

"How convenient that you lost it right after I came to speak to the group about Ms. Morris's death."

"Hey," Curtis protested, "he's got no reason to lie."

"He sure as hell does if he killed the woman," Baker countered.

"I didn't kill nobody," King declared, his voice rising.

"What's your alibi?"

"For when?"

"Last Tuesday. Where were you? Who can vouch for you?"

"I don't even know what day this is. How would I remember what happened a week ago?" King objected.

"Think about it, Chief. Joe's got no car: How was he supposed to get to fancy-schmancy Stoneham? How would he have tracked down the lady? What reason could he possibly have to kill someone who was nice to him?" Curtis asked.

That was a good question.

Baker glared at the two men.

"Are you going to haul him in for further questioning?" Curtis challenged.

"Not right now." He turned to King. "I'll take down your personal information and do a check on you, and I might be back to ask you more questions. But if you pull a disappearing act, I'll put an APB out from here to Hawaii and haul your ass back here. You got it?"

"I got nothin' to hide and nowhere to go," King asserted.

Baker pulled a small notebook from his jacket pocket,

and Tricia stepped back to give King some privacy. Curtis did likewise. "Do you believe him?" she asked.

Curtis hesitated before answering. "Mostly."

"What does that mean?"

"That I really don't want to talk about it," he said bluntly.

"A woman is dead," Tricia reminded him.

"Yeah, well, railroading an innocent man isn't going to bring her back, either."

"The chief isn't trying to railroad Mr. King, but he has information on property that belonged to the dead woman. He has to follow through. That's his job. He has to answer to his superiors. As a former army officer, I'm sure you understand the chain of command."

Curtis threw a glance in Baker's direction. "Oh, yeah."

Tricia watched as Baker put away his pen and notebook, pivoted, and stalked off in the direction of the SUV. She left Curtis and struggled to catch up with Stoneham's top cop.

"Is everything okay?" Tricia asked, concerned.

"Oh, yeah. Everything's just peachy keen. Get in the car," he ordered.

"Grant," she admonished.

Baker got in the driver's side and slammed the door. Tricia hurried to get in the passenger side, suddenly afraid he might take off without her. As soon as she shut her door, he started the engine.

"Grant, what's wrong? It can't just be talking to Joe King. Is there anything I can do to help?"

"I'm sorry," he said, shoving the gearshift to drive. "Things are a little stressed at work."

"Are you getting pushback because of Susan Morris's murder?"

Baker gripped the steering wheel. "Yeah, that's it."

Why didn't Tricia believe him?

"I understand that kind of stress. You must be looking forward to taking some time off for your honeymoon."

"We've got the weekend; that's it," he said tersely as they bumped along the rutted dirt track.

"Why so short a time?"

"Because Diana has a trial that starts the Tuesday after our ceremony."

"I'm sorry to hear that. Have you got plans to go somewhere after the trial?"

"We've talked about it," he said evasively.

"Where would you like to go?"

"I was thinking about the Caribbean in January or February. New Hampshire sucks in winter."

"It's not my favorite time of year, either, but the spring, summer, and fall more than make up for it."

"I guess," he muttered. "So, how was your trip to Ireland?"

Tricia winced at the sneer in his voice. Should she confide in him and tell the truth, or ignore the question entirely? She decided to fudge. "It was a working vacation for Marshall, but it's a beautiful place with wonderful people and stunning scenery."

"Was it the best time of your life?" he pressed.

Oh, dear. Now Tricia wished she hadn't brought up the subject. "Not necessarily," she answered honestly, "but I wouldn't hesitate to go there again. Where would Diana like to go for a belated honeymoon?"

"She doesn't. I mean, she isn't interested in travel. She says she wants to be a homebody. But her idea of a home is more like a mansion," he said with disapproval and then shook his head. "I'm sorry. I don't mean to disparage her in any way. It's just that I don't think we need a castle. What we need is . . ." But then he didn't elaborate.

Was there trouble in paradise? It seemed a change of subject was warranted.

"What will you do to check on Joe King?"

"Ask questions. Call the Veterans Administration."

"Do you think he'll take off?"

"There's a good possibility."

"It did sound logical that he'd have a hard time getting to Stoneham."

"He could have hitchhiked. Hell, he could've called an Uber, for all I know."

But the fact that he hadn't hauled the guy in meant that he believed at least some of King's story.

Once again Baker turned the police scanner on, indicating he was done talking. Tricia pulled out her book once more, knowing she'd get in at least another chapter or two before they returned to Stoneham.

But as they traveled westward toward Booktown, Tricia found her thoughts wandering. She couldn't help Susan, but there were others who could benefit from a word in the right ear. And she knew just which ear to speak to.

SEVENTEEN

Tricia had Chief Baker drop her off at the alley behind Haven't Got a Clue so that she could remove her muddy boots and leave them at the back of the store until she could clean them. She entered Haven't Got a Clue and saw that Pixie was busy helping a woman customer.

"Tricia?"

"I'll be right back. I've got to get a clean pair of shoes," Tricia called, and unlocked the door marked PRIVATE, then crept up the stairs to her apartment, where she changed clothes and put on a pair of flats. Returning to the store, she saw that Pixie was still conversing with the woman.

"Tricia, this is Kimberly Radnor-Herbert. She's Susan's daughter."

"Oh," Tricia said, taken aback. "Oh, I'm so sorry for your loss."

"Yeah, me, too," Kimberly said wearily. The woman was younger than Tricia would have thought, stylishly dressed in a maroon tunic over black leggings and wearing a black hat, silver earrings, and a heart-shaped pendant. She tossed her long dark hair over her shoulder, and her big blue eyes glistened with unshed tears.

"Kimberly wanted to see where her mom was found."

"Just for closure," Kimberly said sadly. "Pixie was nice

enough to show me, then invited me back inside your store for a cup of coffee."

"Why don't we sit," Tricia said, indicating the reader's nook, and the three of them took seats. "I never met your mother," Tricia began, "but I understand she had some real troubles."

"She made her life a lot harder than it needed to be," Kimberly admitted, wiping at a tear that threatened to spill from her left eye. "I can't tell you how many times I asked her to come back to Utica to live with me and my family—but she always had an independent streak. That's why she joined the Navy straight out of high school. She wanted to see the world. The one thing she liked about being in the service was the travel. These past few years she got the wanderlust once again and said being stuck in one place would kill her. I worried that something bad would happen to her by living in her car, and I'm sick to know I was right."

"Did she make friends easily?" Tricia asked, thinking about the story Joe King had told her and the chief not an hour earlier.

Kimberly shrugged. "Sometimes."

"She was always friendly when we interacted," Pixie said.

"After what happened in Vegas, Mom wasn't all that comfortable around men," Kimberly admitted.

That didn't match the story Joe King had spun just an hour before.

"Because of her name change, I assumed she married at some point after that," Tricia said.

Kimberly shook her head. "She started calling herself Morris, and why she chose that name, she never said. But I'm not sure she ever made it legal, either."

Tricia decided against inquiring if Susan had been married to Kimberly's father, instead asking, "Was she proud of her time in the service?"

"Up until Vegas. Then everything soured. Mom tried to sue but didn't get far. She didn't have the stamina to fight the government like some of the other women." She said the words with some regret.

"What happened to her?"

"She resigned her commission and was unfortunate enough to meet my biological father."

"I take it he wasn't a big part of your life."

"He was *never* a part of my life. She could have—*should* have—gone after him for child support. It would have made our lives so much easier. She was so beaten down, she didn't have the stamina to fight."

"Sounds like a tough life," Pixie sympathized, and reached to pat Kimberly's hand. Tricia knew that Pixie's home life had been far worse but was heartened that her second-in-command could muster empathy for this stranger.

"Do you remember her wearing silver earrings with an anchor on them?"

"Sure: I bought them, and one of my kids gave them to her for her birthday a few years back."

"Did she like them?"

"She used to wear them exclusively," Kimberly said.

"So it's not likely she would have given one of them away."

"Not a chance. When she downsized her possessions, she kept those earrings. Why do you ask?"

"I found one of them in her car. I saw a homeless man wearing the other one."

Kimberly shook her head. "That can't be. Mom never would have given one away."

"Would she have picked up a male panhandler and taken him to lunch because he wore a cap with an aircraft carrier's hull number?"

"I don't think so."

"Would you be willing to talk to the police about that?"

"I spoke to a Chief Baker last week, but, sure, if you think it will help."

"It would prove that the man was lying about how he got the earring. And if he'd lie about that . . ."

"Do you think it's possible he killed my mother?" Kimberly asked, and Tricia wasn't sure if it was excitement or dread that tinged her voice.

Gut feeling? Maybe. But Tricia wasn't comfortable making an accusation with such flimsy evidence. And why would Joe King lie about the earring, especially knowing that he could be looked at as a possible suspect in Susan Morris's death?

"Do you know how I can get in contact with Chief Baker?" Kimberly asked.

"Does she ever," Pixie said with an eye roll.

"Now, Pixie . . ." Tricia warned.

Pixie had the decency to look guilty.

"I'd be glad to take you to the police station. It's just a couple of blocks down the road."

"Thank you," Kimberly said, her voice breaking. "I want to make sure whoever killed my mother pays. She didn't deserve to die. She deserved so much more than life ever gave her."

Tricia found herself leaning forward to capture the woman in a hug, feeling bad that she'd previously wondered if Susan's daughter had cared about her. Now she knew and patted Kimberly's back as she sobbed for her loss.

Tricia wasn't sure if, when her own mother passed away, she would experience an emotion other than relief.

She felt guilty considering the possibility.

Chief Baker hardly had time to research Joe King's claims before Tricia showed up with Susan's daughter in tow. He was not pleased to learn that Susan Morris's anchor earrings had meant so much to the dead woman—that she would never have relinquished one of them to a virtual stranger. But at least he was kind to the grief-stricken woman—as kind as he'd been to Tricia three days before. Then again, if nothing else, Grant Baker was always professional. Well, except when he dealt with Angelica.

Afterward, Tricia walked Kimberly back to her vehicle, which was parked on the street.

"Your mother's car is still in the municipal parking lot. What's going to happen to it?"

"There's no way I can deal with it on this trip, but earlier

Chief Baker assured me it would be okay to let it sit in the lot for a couple of weeks. I'll probably come back with my husband in a week or so to collect it." She shook her head. "Mom would have hated to think that she'd inconvenienced us so much. She was that kind of person."

Tricia nodded. "I'm sorry we had to meet under such terrible circumstances. After speaking with people who knew your mother, I'm sure I would have liked her, too."

"She was a great mom, a patriot, a kind soul, and just an all-around nice lady who loved life and her family—even if her wanderlust kept her away from us much too often. That someone would kill her . . . I still can't wrap my head around it."

"Chief Baker and his officers are good at their jobs. I'm sure you'll have some kind of resolution soon."

Kimberly offered Tricia a wan smile. "Thanks. I needed to hear that."

"Will you be staying in the area for a few days?"

Kimberly shook her head. "Mom's funeral will be on Friday. I only came up here because . . ."

But she didn't have to say any more.

Tricia gave the woman another hug. "Travel safe."

Kimberly nodded. "Thanks."

Tricia waited on the sidewalk until Kimberly's car pulled away. Then a ping from her cell phone made her pull it from her jacket pocket. It was a text from Angelica.

Did you forget our spa appointment?

Yes, she *had* forgotten it.

Be right there.

Less than a minute later Tricia entered the Cookery to find her sister sitting in one of the few upholstered chairs the store possessed. She'd taken Tricia's advice and was wearing slacks, a pink sneaker on her unscathed foot, and the ugly black boot on her sore foot. She'd set the crutches against the wall but grabbed them as soon as she saw Tricia approach.

"Do you think you can walk that far?" Tricia asked, concerned.

"We won't know unless I try."

It was a slow journey up the block, crossing Main Street, and another two blocks to the day spa, but it gave Tricia time to tell her sister about her morning's adventures.

"You've had a busy day," Angelica grated, her voice strained. Tricia was pretty sure her sister wouldn't be able to walk back home, but Tricia could remedy that by retrieving her car and driving her sister there.

Booked for Beauty's manager, Randy Ellison, greeted them at the door. "Darling Angelica, come in, sit down. Can I get you a coffee? We've got some yummy chocolates from Sweet As Can Be as a sincere welcome home."

"Oh, Randy, you are such a dear. Just plunk me in one of the chairs so I can get some pressure off this darn foot."

Randy led her to the closest chair—one Tricia had never seen used before.

"Who's going to do my hair?" Angelica asked.

"Why, me, darling girl," Randy said as he whipped a plastic cape across Angelica's sweater and fastened it at the back of her neck.

A blush rose to Angelica's cheeks. "I am so honored." She nodded toward her sister. "Is someone available to give Tricia a trim, too?"

"Mindy!" he called, and one of the women who'd been sitting in the lounge area in the back rose to her feet. She wore Booked for Beauty's standard uniform of dark slacks, a white blouse, and a black full-front apron with the shop's name embroidered in white. Beneath it was her name. Mindy hadn't cut Tricia's hair before, but she had no misgivings about letting her have a go at it. Everyone Randy employed at the salon had also been vetted by Angelica herself.

"Can we sit here together?" Angelica asked, indicating the chair next to where she sat.

"Of course."

Mindy didn't look as happy about the arrangement, as all her tools of the trade were apparently housed at another station, and she had to retrieve them. Meanwhile, Randy got the sisters settled and fetched them both a cup of coffee.

Once he returned, Angelica wasted no time getting to the point.

"Wasn't it just terrible about Susan Morris dying right in the alley behind Main Street?"

"That poor woman," Randy agreed. "Did you want a wash first, Angelica?"

"Ordinarily I'd say yes," she said, eyeing the line of sinks that flanked the far wall behind the lounge, "but I'm content to sit here and rest my foot."

"That's fine," Randy said, and reached for a plastic spray bottle that was filled with water for just such occasions.

Mindy arrived with her rolling rack of tools and asked Tricia what she wanted done to her hair, which caused Tricia to miss whatever answer Randy was saying. Thankfully, she stopped talking, so Tricia could listen in on Randy and Angelica's conversation.

"And it was too bad, too, because she seemed a lovely woman," Randy said. "Just not right for our demographic."

Was he trying not to say Susan had been too old to be their receptionist? While Randy wasn't much older than Angelica, he was at least two decades older than most of the women he employed as beauticians and nail techs. Furthermore, what Randy had said wasn't true. Susan *had* mirrored the shop's clientele. Despite the hip posters on the wall and the trendy music that issued from speakers concealed in the shop's ceiling, Booked for Beauty wasn't some cut-rate franchised salon. The clientele was older and could well afford the prices it charged.

"Why didn't you hire her? After all, you interviewed her twice," Tricia pressed as Mindy covered her with yet another plastic cape. She was tempted to ask Randy if Susan's age had been the reason. Their only concession to an older worker had been to hire Pixie for a short stint on Saturday afternoons. Angelica had done it out of kindness, only to find that Pixie was sought after by customers for her talent and charm.

Randy frowned, and Angelica shot Tricia a warning glance.

"Because . . . because"—Randy faltered—"because she was too fearful."

"Fearful?" Tricia asked.

Randy nodded. "She put on a brave front. But I noticed that while we talked, anytime the door opened, her gaze would dart around the room as though she was looking for an escape route . . . as though she thought she might be attacked. Of course, after reading the story about her tragic experiences in the *Stoneham Weekly News* on Monday, I can understand where she was coming from. But even without knowing that, I could tell she wasn't a good candidate to work in this environment. While we talked, a gentleman came in for a buzz cut. She kept looking at him, and her expression was more than wary; it was fearful."

Tricia nodded as Mindy snipped the locks at the base of her neck.

"I'm a hairdresser by trade, not a shrink. I have a business to run," Randy said, shooting a glance in Angelica's direction. "Susan just wasn't a good fit."

"Did she tell you much about herself?" Angelica asked.

"Just that she'd been in the military and had a daughter. Other than that, no." But then Tricia noticed Randy turn thoughtful. "Well, she did say that she wanted to change her living situation. At the time I had no idea she was homeless. Had I known, I might have made a different decision And I know—because she waited on me—that she did just fine working at the village's new candy shop. And she seemed happy there. I was glad for her. It's not often one finds joy in one's work."

"I hope you don't mean you're unhappy working here at Booked for Beauty," Angelica declared.

Randy smiled and patted Angelica's shoulder. "Not in the least, dear lady."

Angelica laughed, and Tricia gave the spa's manager a smile. It wasn't at all surprising that Susan was fearful of men after her experience in Las Vegas, but it was sad that, decades later, she hadn't gotten over the ordeal. Then again, when she thought about it, Tricia had never really recovered from her mother's rejection.

Susan had likely suffered from post-traumatic stress disorder at a time when it wasn't well understood—and women *and* men were expected to "just get over it."

Did Tricia suffer from the same complaint? She didn't think so. She could go days without even thinking about her mother or the times when, as a child, she'd been ignored for days on end.

But Tricia felt empathy for the dead woman. Unfortunately, that meant nothing now—at least as far as Susan was concerned. She'd been killed and Tricia still had no idea why.

EIGHTEEN

 Angelica protested when Tricia said she would get her car to drive her sister back to her apartment, but not enough to deter Tricia. Angelica was in no hurry to go home, and they ended up at their usual lunchtime eatery, Booked for Lunch, where Angelica was given a round of applause and many well wishes from the staff and regulars.

They took their usual seats at the back of the little café, and Molly filled their water glasses. "What'll you have, ladies?"

"I'm starved," Angelica said. "Do you think Tommy could rustle me up one of his open-faced Reubens?"

Molly nodded. "And for you, Tricia?"

"Splurge!" Angelica encouraged.

Tricia again thought of those pounds she'd gained and frowned. "Oh, what the heck," she said, and turned her attention back to Molly. "I'll have a club wrap with everything on it."

"Red onion?"

"The works," Tricia said. "And don't forget the chips."

"You got it."

Molly turned and headed for the kitchen.

"My, a club wrap. That's adventurous of you," Angelica commented.

"There's no way I can eat the whole thing, so I'll either keep it for tomorrow or offer it to Pixie." At the mention of her subordinate's name, Tricia realized she hadn't told Pixie she was taking Angelica to the hairdresser or that they were out having lunch. She whipped out her phone and sent a terse apology.

Not a problem, Pixie texted back. *Mr. E and I have already figured out our lunchtimes and we'll be here waiting when you get back. P.S. Mr. E took Sarge for a walk, so you don't have to hurry back.*

"I can't believe I forgot all about my own business," Tricia told her sister.

"You've got good people working for you. I'm sure Pixie had already figured it out."

"Yes, and Mr. Everett has taken your dog for a comfort call, so you won't have to go home to a puddle—or worse."

"That darling man. We are the luckiest people in the world, aren't we?" Angelica said.

"Yes. And you've given me the perfect opening to ask if you've spoken to Antonio about hiring Hank Curtis."

"Yes, I called him this morning about hiring a food service manager for all our various eateries."

"And?" Tricia asked.

"He thinks it's a good idea. Food service was never his specialty, but he's done a good job. Antonio agrees if we hired someone for that job, it would allow him to do what he loves best."

"And what's that?"

"Taking on new and exciting projects."

"What else can you guys possibly do in Stoneham?" Tricia asked.

Angelica looked startled. "Oh, my dear, there's so much more we could do for the village. For one, I'd like to see that warehouse where Russ has located the Chamber torn down. It's an eyesore, and the lot is ideal for retail. We could bring in some kind of business that can thrive on the tourist trade during the summer and local and Internet sales during the off-season. I'd also like to build a professional building and lure in a dentist and doctor or two. There's that tract of land next to the dialysis center, across from the Brookview Inn, that would be perfect for professional space. We could use a pharmacy, a pizzeria . . . I could go on and on about the possibilities."

"It sounds like Curtis would be a great fit."

"I don't know about that," Angelica said, "but I'm not opposed to interviewing him."

"*You'd* interview him?"

"Antonio and me."

"But wouldn't that jeopardize your"—Tricia lowered her voice to a whisper—"secret identity?"

Angelica giggled. "You make me feel like Wonder Woman. And the answer is no, not at all. I'll bring my laptop to the Brookview's conference room and employ my voice-altering app."

"You've got a voice-altering app?" Tricia asked.

"Doesn't everybody?" Angelica asked incredulously.

Tricia certainly didn't.

"Anyway," Angelica continued, "how are you going to get the guy to come into the village for an appointment? I don't suppose he has a car."

"Not that I saw." She let out a breath. "I suppose I could pick him up and take him back to the camp."

"That sounds a little risky."

"If you're seriously considering giving him the responsibility to take over your food management service, you'll have to show some trust in him as well."

"I suppose you're right," Angelica conceded, and shrugged. "If you bring him to the Brookview, you can sit with me in the conference room and listen in on the conversation."

"I'd like that."

"Great. Now all you have to do is convince this Curtis fellow to agree to an interview."

"I'll do that. Maybe this afternoon."

"Good."

"How soon do you want to speak with him?"

"The sooner, the better."

"Tomorrow?"

"If you can arrange it. I've got nothing else to do."

Molly arrived with their lunches, first placing Tricia's in front of her. It looked good enough to photograph, but Tricia knew in a heartbeat that she'd never be able to finish her meal. Yet, after just the first bite, she wasn't sorry she'd ordered it, either.

Angelica attacked her Reuben, which was smothered in melted Swiss cheese. She took a bite and nearly swooned. "Goodness, this is tasty."

The sisters ate in silence for a couple of minutes before Angelica spoke again. "By the way, I forgot to mention there's been a development in the Baker nuptials."

"Oh?" Tricia asked, wondering if the bride might have changed her colors from the golds of autumn to a more muted shade.

"The ceremony—and the reception—have been canceled," Angelica said with an almost sly lilt to her voice.

Tricia's mouth dropped open and for a moment she thought she'd heard wrong. "You're kidding, right?"

Angelica shook her head and let out a breath. "I'm beginning to think that weekend is cursed. Two weddings planned and both canceled. At least we hadn't ordered the linens and everything else that such a wedding entails. Antonio and the rest of the staff will be spreading the word that the date is open for other functions. The contract the bride signed calls for her to pay a fat cancellation fee. I seriously doubt we can rent the space on such short notice, but at least we'll be compensated for our trouble."

"Did she give you a reason?"

"Antonio spoke to the jilted bride, who was quite upset."

"Grant called it off?" Tricia asked, dumbfounded.

"I guess so. But then, you shouldn't be surprised. He wasn't willing to make a commitment to you, either. Maybe cold feet are just part of his genetic background. I don't suppose he gave you any hint he might pull such a stunt when you last spoke."

Tricia pursed her lips and thought about it. "No, but he spoke about the lack of a honeymoon just this morning."

"Why didn't he just tell you he'd called it off?"

"I don't know. Maybe because he thought I'd say something about our own breakup. Of late, he's sure been crabbier than usual . . ." Except when she'd reported that her store had nearly been broken into for a second time. Then he'd been almost solicitous. Had he already been thinking about calling off the wedding? Was that the reason he'd been working late that Saturday night? Had he already delivered the bad news to his Diana? ". . . but I just thought he was probably antsy about tying the knot again." Tricia shook her head. "Poor Grant. I don't think he has a clue about what he wants in life."

"Well, I certainly don't have that problem," Angelica quipped. She signaled for Molly to return to the table. "When you get a chance, could you bring me a cup of coffee?"

"Sure thing. How about you, Tricia?"

Tricia shook her head. She barely had room for half of her wrap—and a good portion of the chips. Boy, did she like potato chips. She wondered how she could have survived without them for nearly three decades of her life. But she found herself chewing slower as she thought about Grant Baker and his ditched fiancée. All those wedding plans down the proverbial toilet. When Tricia got married, it wasn't just a question of buying a dress and a ring. Not with the circus that had surrounded her nuptials. And, of course, her marriage had ended in divorce—and she wasn't the one who'd called it quits, either.

As she thought about it, her indignation grew. Here she was feeling sorry for Grant when he'd just betrayed the woman he'd (apparently) claimed to love. Just as Christopher had done to her.

Tricia took a savage bite of her wrap and chewed.

Men. Were they all rats?

NINETEEN

After making sure Angelica was settled in her apartment and had everything she needed within reach, Tricia returned to Haven't Got a Clue with her leftover lunch wrapped in waxed paper. Angelica's businesses were jumping on the green bandwagon—and about time, too. But before she had an opportunity to head upstairs to deposit the brown bag into her refrigerator, she was reminded of why she did not think all men were finks. Mr. Everett quietly hummed to himself as he wielded his lamb's-wool duster. And she thought about Antonio, who was the partner in his family who was eager to welcome a second child.

Tricia paused to speak to her employee. "Thank you, Mr. Everett, for taking such good care of the store—and my sister. We really appreciate how you've stepped in to help her out these past two weeks."

"It was my pleasure. And if I can be of any other help, I do hope you and she will let me know."

"We certainly will," she said, and leaned over to kiss his cheek. Of course he blushed a furious red, but he did look pleased.

After putting her leftovers in the fridge and making sure Mr. Everett could handle the store until Pixie returned from lunch, Tricia collected her car and started off for the homeless encampment. On the way, she stopped at a big-box store and bought a cheap flip phone. If Hank Curtis couldn't communicate with the outside world, there was no way he'd be able to keep a job. She bought a hundred minutes of service and had the associate at the counter set up the phone, then continued on her way to the camp.

Catcalls and whistles erupted when she parked her car beside the muddy field, and as happened during her last two visits Curtis was the one who walked out to greet her.

"Sorry about the guys. They're just messing with you. Just can't stay away, eh?"

"I'm sorry, but I didn't bring more provisions. I came to see you."

"What for?"

"To see if you'd like to interview for a job."

Curtis's eyes widened. "Doing what?"

"You were a food manager, right? To manage food."

"For who?"

"I'm friendly with the staff at Nigela Ricita Associates."

"I've heard of them," Curtis said cautiously.

"I inquired if they might be willing to interview you as a food service manager for their collective businesses, and they said yes."

"When?"

"As soon as possible. How about tomorrow?"

"Tomorrow?" he echoed, sounding shocked as the color drained from his face.

"Why wait?"

Curtis looked down at his attire, then swung his gaze up to look at Tricia once again. "Why would you do that for a stranger?"

"People in Stoneham do things like that for others all the time."

"Yeah, I heard."

"Heard what?"

"That there's a bunch of do-gooders in the village."

"And what's wrong with that?"

Curtis shrugged and gave a mirthless laugh. "Nothing, I guess."

"What have you heard?" Tricia asked.

"That the big fancy restaurant has an ex-con as its head chef."

"And?"

"That you hired a former prostitute as your assistant manager."

"And?"

"That Nigela Ricita has hired over a hundred locals since she came to town and opened a shitload of businesses."

"That she has."

"And now she wants to interview me?"

"She doesn't live in the area, but you'll meet with the Brookview Inn's manager, Antonio Barbero, and Ms. Ricita will speak to both of you via Skype."

Curtis looked uncomfortable.

"What's the matter?" Tricia asked.

"It's been a long time since I interviewed for a job."

She eyed him critically. "You'll need to clean up a bit. Maybe shave?" Tricia suggested.

"You got something against beards?"

"Not at all. But yours could use a trim. So could your hair."

Curtis grabbed at the ponytail at the back of his neck. "Yeah," he sheepishly admitted. "I guess they could."

"*Is* tomorrow morning too soon?" Tricia asked, trying to pin him down.

"It doesn't give me much time to prepare."

"I could pick you up early in the morning and take you to the barbershop and to buy you a shirt and tie."

"Why? What's in this for you?"

She gave him a watery smile. "It brings out the do-gooder in me."

"What if something comes up and you have to cancel or something? I'd lose out on this opportunity."

"That won't happen—but just in case . . ." Tricia reached into her jacket pocket and brought out the flip phone, handing it and the paperwork to him. "I bought this on the way over. You've got a hundred minutes to get started."

Curtis stared at the small phone in his hand, and for a moment Tricia thought he might cry. But he had been a soldier. He nodded and pocketed the device. "Thank you."

"You're welcome. I'm sorry I can't guarantee you a job, but this could still be a new beginning for you."

"Maybe," Curtis agreed. "How can I ever thank you?"

"You haven't got the job yet."

"I know, but you're right." He glanced over his shoulder at the muddy field. "I'm ready to go back to a sticks-and-bricks place to live. A place with running hot water, and a fridge with food in it. Believe me, lady, I'm more than ready."

"I don't think I've ever introduced myself to you," Tricia said. She smiled and held out her hand. "Tricia Miles."

They shook. "Nice to know you, Tricia. Is there anything I can do for you?"

"Yes. Please tell me what you know about Joe King."

Curtis seemed to mull over the request but then shrugged. "Not a lot. Some of the guys don't share much about themselves. He was here for a while before he told us he was in the Navy, but we'd already figured that out."

"Because of that earring?"

Curtis shook his head. "No, a tattoo."

"What else?"

"He's only dropped a few hints about his past, but he did say something happened and he was given a dishonorable discharge."

Tricia frowned. "He wasn't, by any chance, involved in the Tailhook scandal, was he?"

Curtis looked at her, taken aback, and then shook his head. "He was just a punk-ass sailor. Although whatever happened was back in the nineties."

Had Susan recognized King from another point in her naval career, or was there a chance he *had* been at the Tailhook Symposium? The officers involved had been pilots. King had served on an aircraft carrier. Could he have gone there in some minor capacity and been swooped up in the scandal? Could King have been one of the men who'd assaulted Susan all those years before? If so, was it possible she'd confronted him? A lot of officers had lost their commissions—but no one was ever criminally prosecuted. Still, the outcome had been life changing for everyone who'd been at that Las Vegas hotel back in the early nineties, and none for the better.

Tricia looked at her watch. "So, how about I give you a call in the morning to let you know what time I'll pick you up and what you can expect?"

"Okay."

"Great. I'll see you tomorrow."

She turned for her car.

"Hey, lady—Tricia," Curtis amended. "Thanks."

"Thank me if you get the job," she said, and got in her car.

Curtis stood in the muddy grass while Tricia turned the car around on the dirt track and started off. She didn't wave, figuring the other men in the camp would just heckle Curtis. However, she did look in her rearview mirror to see him just standing there—grinning.

After returning to Haven't Got a Clue, Tricia retreated to her basement office and called Antonio. They set up an appointment for the following morning for Curtis to interview with him at eleven o'clock. Tricia figured she could pick Curtis up around eight thirty, get him some new clothes and a shave and haircut, and make it to the Brookview in plenty of time. Afterward, Angelica could either take an Uber or catch a ride back to her apartment with a staffer, or else Tricia could ask Pixie or Mr. Everett to give Angelica a lift while Tricia took Curtis back to the homeless camp. She knew neither would mind in the least.

With that settled, she went back upstairs to her store.

An influx of shoppers visited Haven't Got a Clue on that sunny September afternoon, and Tricia found herself helping customers, ringing up sales, and hauling boxes for restocking from the basement. She began eyeing the clock as the hands moved toward five o'clock. Just another hour before the store closed.

In years past she'd hosted a Tuesday night book club, but interest had waned and it had fallen by the wayside. She missed it. As she hadn't had a book signing in months, Tricia wondered if she should start putting out the word that she was booking authors for the holiday season. She thought about heading back to the basement to make a list of authors who'd previously visited her store, when her cell phone rang. Angelica was calling.

"Hi, Ange, what's up?"

"I've been invited out to dinner!" she said with delight.

"By whom?"

"Ginny. They want my advice on redecorating their little house in the woods."

"How do they have time to cook with their killer work schedules?"

"Brookview Catering saves the day once again!"

"What kind of redecorating are they thinking about?"

"Possibly adding an addition to the house. You know what that might mean?" Angelica hinted gleefully.

Oh, dear. Were they facing an addition to their family at a time when Ginny wasn't certain she wanted another child?

"I assume Antonio is going to pick you up."

"Yes. In fact, he'll be here within the next ten minutes, unless he gets caught at work."

"I'm sure you could pull some strings to set him free," Tricia said.

"Maybe. What will you do about dinner?" Angelica asked.

"Don't worry about me. I have the other half of my club wrap from lunch. I've got food, a bottle of wine, and a stack of books in my to-be-read pile. I'll be fine."

"You *are* a big girl now," Angelica agreed. "I don't know what time I'll be home: Sofia goes to bed early, and that's when the three of us can have an in-depth chat. If I see your light on when I return, I'll call you tonight. If not, first thing in the morning."

"Okay. Have a good time."

Angelica sighed. "That remains to be seen. And don't worry about Sarge. Antonio has promised to take him out before he leaves."

"Okay. Good night."

They ended the call.

"Anything wrong, Ms. Miles?" Mr. Everett asked with Pixie right behind him, both looking concerned.

"Not at all. But it looks like I won't be around the shop much tomorrow."

"What's up?" Pixie asked.

"One of the homeless men near Merrimack is a retired vet—"

"There are lots of those around," Pixie muttered before Tricia could finish.

"His expertise is in food service management. I've finagled an interview for him with Antonio for tomorrow morning, but he needs a little spit and polish before he's presentable."

"It's commendable of you to take an interest in the welfare of one of our former servicemen," Mr. Everett said.

"Why did you decide to help him of all people?" Pixie asked.

"I don't know. Maybe because he reminds me of you?"

"Me?" Pixie asked, startled.

"Yes. Thanks to his years in the Army, he seems to have authority over the homeless men, but I think he's capable of a lot more than sitting around a fire pit in the rain. Look what having a purpose did for you, Pixie. You've got a stable job, a husband, and a home."

"Ya got me there. I never thought I'd have a real job, let alone a husband and a house. And, of course, you guys." She gave Mr. Everett a gentle punch to his shoulder, which made him blush. "Well, I wish that guy all the luck in the world," she added.

"As do I. You must tell us how the interview goes," Mr. Everett chimed in.

"I will."

The shop door opened, the tinkling bell drawing Tricia's

attention, although it wasn't a customer who crossed the threshold but Nikki Brimfield, her son straddled over her left hip.

"Nikki! I thought you were in California," Tricia blurted.

"I flew in last night," she said, setting the little boy down but keeping a firm hold of his hand, for which Tricia was grateful. The kid was rambunctious, to say the least, and Tricia could picture him pulling the covers off the paperbacks or chewing on the hardcovers.

Nikki turned to Pixie and Mr. Everett. "Could you give us a few minutes?"

"Oh, sure," Pixie said. "We've got things to do down in the office, don't we, Mr. E?"

"Uh, yes. It was very nice seeing you again, Nikki."

"And you."

Nikki watched as Tricia's employees escaped to the back of the shop and around the corner to the stairs before she spoke again. "I hear I have you to thank for my return." Her tone was neutral, and Tricia wasn't quite sure what to make of the statement.

"I—"

"My mother tracked me down. She said you told her Russ was going to put our son in foster care."

Wow—that detective Fiona had hired sure worked fast.

"That's what I heard," Tricia said, deciding not to name her source. "Is that true?"

"Unfortunately, yes." Nikki looked down at the fidgeting boy, and her lips trembled. "If I hadn't turned up, Russ was going to surrender him by the weekend. He's sure in a hurry to get on with his life."

Tricia could have accused Nikki of the same thing, thanks to her flight to California, but chose not to mention it.

"I understand you're still tripping over bodies," Nikki said rather snidely.

"My assistant, Pixie, found Susan Morris, not me."

"Yeah, but somehow you're always involved in these things."

Again Tricia decided not to comment.

"I thought after I turned her in to the cops, they would've run her out of town, but I guess she just got a warning."

"You turned her in to the police?" Tricia asked.

"For parking in the municipal lot and sleeping in her car, among other things," she said sourly. "The board of selectmen ought to make a law to take care of people like her. Let one person do it, and the village will be overrun with scum."

Wow. Talk about a lack of compassion.

"How did you find out Susan was living in her car?" Tricia asked.

"I happened to drive into the lot one evening back in June and saw slits of light from where she hadn't done a good job of blocking her windows. The cops made her leave that night, but I guess they had no problem with her parking there during the day, more's the pity."

"She had a job, you know."

"Yeah, I heard—at the new candy store." Nikki shrugged, sounding uninterested. Same old Nikki. "Anyway," Nikki continued. "I came by to say thank you for looking out for my baby boy."

Then again . . .

"I suppose you'll be taking him back to California."

"Yes. I've got an apartment, and I'm a finalist in the Divine Desserts Competition. I'm going to win, and when I do, they'll offer me a shot at my own prime-time show, along with a book deal and a national tour."

"Congratulations," Tricia said, her voice flat. If Nikki couldn't muster a modicum of warmth, Tricia was content to do likewise. "How long will you be staying in the area?"

"We're leaving on the red-eye from Boston tonight. I packed up everything I thought he would need and am having it shipped. It was only a few boxes. He can have all new toys when he gets to his new room. Isn't that right, Rusty?"

"Rusty?" Tricia asked. She'd only heard the boy called little Russell.

"As of today, his name is Rusty. I think it suits him, don't you?"

Tricia eyed the boy, whose gaze was fixed on Miss Marple, who had retreated to the top of one of the bookshelves. She'd had her tail pulled enough by Sofia and wasn't amused by the game. "Yes. He looks like a Rusty." Tricia changed the subject. "I suppose you'll be heading straight to Boston from here."

"Not quite. I still have one more task to do."

"And what's that?"

"Fire Roger Sykes. I've heard nothing but complaints about his baking. Mother thinks he's trying to ruin the business to get it for a cheaper price."

"But I understood you had already made a deal to sell him the Patisserie."

"He's been telling people that, but our deal was for him to run it on a month-by-month basis. My lawyer added a clause that I could terminate the arrangement at any time, and I'm grateful he insisted on it."

"Do you have anyone in mind to run it?"

"Steve Fenton. He worked for me for a couple of years before he went out on disability. He's better now and jumped at the chance to keep the shop going until I can figure out what I want to do next. He'll do right by me—and my hard-won customers."

"Did you know Russ is selling the *News*?"

"I had a conversation with Patti in his office. Apparently she doesn't feel any special loyalty to Russ now that her livelihood is in jeopardy."

"Well, I'm glad everything seems to be working out for you."

Nikki's smarmy smile was back. "Yes, I'm entitled to a part of the paper's selling price. I'm very pleased."

"Will Russ have a shot at the Patisserie?"

Nikki's eyes narrowed. "Not a chance. I saw to that when we first got married. It's mine free and clear."

Nikki seemed to have all angles covered.

Tricia straightened. It was time to bring this conversation to a close. "Well, I hope you have a smooth flight."

"Thanks. But before I go, I want to . . ." Nikki pursed her

lips, hesitating. "I want to apologize to you. I see now that you never had any interest in Russ, and I can't for the life of me think why I was ever jealous of you."

Tricia couldn't think of anything to say on that account, either, and merely gave Nikki the barest hint of a shrug.

Rusty pulled at his mother's hand. "Wanna go for a ride in the car."

"Yes, honey. We're going now."

"Good luck with the show—and your career," Tricia said.

"Luck has nothing to do with it," Nikki said. "I'm no loser—in business or in life," she said with deadly assurance. "Good-bye, Tricia."

"Good-bye."

"Come on, Rusty," Nikki said, picking up the boy and settling him on her hip once more.

"Who's Rusty?" the boy asked.

Nikki started for the door, and Tricia waved to the little guy, who giggled and waved back. And then they were gone.

Well, that was an unexpected turn of events, Tricia thought, shook her head, and headed for the back of the store. She turned the corner and found her employees sitting on the top step of the stairs to the basement. "Did you hear what Nikki had to say?" she asked.

"Um, a little," Pixie admitted.

Mr. Everett eyed Pixie with surprise but then turned to Tricia. "I assure you, Ms. Miles, I wasn't eavesdropping." He pointed to his left ear. "My hearing isn't as good as it used to be."

"Well, Nikki's visit, and what she told me, won't be a secret by tomorrow." Tricia filled them in on the pertinent information.

"I'm glad she's giving that Sykes guy the boot. His baked goods are terrible," Pixie said.

"And Steve Fenton will do a fine job. He worked in the bakery department of my grocery store the last few years it was open," Mr. Everett added.

"That's good to hear," Tricia said. She looked at the clock. It was already fifteen minutes until closing, and as

they hadn't had a customer in over an hour, she decided to
pack it in for the day. She bade her employees a good night,
locked the store, set the security system, and turned off all
the lights.

Heading up the stairs to her apartment with Miss Marple
scampering up ahead of her, Tricia reflected that it had been
a very long day with far too much activity. She was glad for
the opportunity to finally sit down and relax. The only thing
pending was news from Angelica and her dinner with Antonio and Ginny.

Then again, maybe she'd turn out the lights so that Angelica wouldn't call that evening.

Tricia wasn't sure she could take any more traumatic
news that day.

TWENTY

•

Despite the events of the day, Tricia found herself feeling restless as she rattled around her way-too-quiet apartment, missing her usual happy hour conversation with her sister. She couldn't help thinking about what was going on at the Wilson-Barbero house and changed her mind, deciding she might as well leave her lights on and accept Angelica's call filling her in on all the evening's details.

She sat at her kitchen's breakfast bar, poured herself a glass of wine, and dined on her leftover wrap before she settled into her personal reader's nook in her master suite with the intention of finishing *False Scent*, and she had another book at the ready to pick up as soon as she did.

But then her cell phone rang, rousing a sleeping Miss Marple, who'd taken up residence at the end of the chaise. Tricia immediately recognized the number and punched the call acceptance icon. "Marshall—what's up?"

"I'm standing in front of your door with a bottle of chilled Dom Pérignon, and there's nobody I'd rather share it with."

"What's the occasion?"

"Why don't you let me in and I'll let *you* in on my big announcement."

Trivia's heart sank. The last time Marshall had been this

excited, he'd embarked on the whole fantasy of being a tour guide. Still, she tried to instill a note of cheer in her voice. "I'll be right down." She stabbed the end call icon on her phone and headed downstairs, making sure to turn out the bedroom light before she did.

Sure enough, Marshall stood behind the door with a sappy smile plastered across his features. "Come in." Tricia beckoned.

But before she could turn away, he grabbed her arm, pulling her against him for a kiss—and a very nice kiss it was. "Not here," she laughed, taking his arm and tugging him inside the darkened shop. "Follow me."

Hand in hand, they made their way through the store and to the stairs that lead to Tricia's apartment, where Miss Marple sat waiting with what could only be described as an annoyed expression. After all, her beauty nap had been interrupted.

Marshall closed the door to the stairs behind him and followed Tricia into the kitchen to grab a couple of wineglasses.

"Are you going to keep me in suspense?" she asked.

"Only until I pour the wine."

Tricia bent down, resting her elbows on the island's marble top, her chin cupped in her hands, watching him wrestle with the bottle's stopper. "Just a hint?" she wheedled. "The suspense is killing me."

"Well, I don't want you to die," he said as the cork went flying and the champagne fizzed out the top of the bottle. He grabbed a glass, pouring it in, then grabbed the other, doing the same. Once the bubbles died down, he topped off both glasses, handing one to Tricia. "A toast," he said and raised his glass. "To the new owner of the *Stoneham Weekly News*."

Tricia's mouth dropped open in shock. "Honestly?"

Marshall grinned. "Yeah, why not?" He clinked his glass against Tricia's and took a sip.

Feeling just a little overwhelmed, Tricia gulped her champagne. "Do you even have any journalistic experience?"

"Not since high school, but isn't it mostly a matter of getting ad revenue and inserting local color stories here and there?"

"I suppose so," Tricia said, and they drank some more, the bubbles tickling her nose. "I think I need to sit down," she said, grabbing Marshall's arm. He snatched up the bottle and let her lead him to the sectional in the living room, where the lights were already turned down low. Marshall set his glass and the bottle down on the coffee table and then removed his suit coat, tossing it on a chair. Miss Marple immediately jumped up and began to sniff it.

"Miss Marple—down!" Tricia commanded, but the cat took no notice of her. "Down!" she warned again.

"Oh, leave her alone," Marshall said as he sat down beside Tricia. "I've got a lint roller that'll take care of any cat hair she leaves."

"Yes, but you're setting a bad precedent."

"Let the cat celebrate along with us—just for tonight."

Tricia frowned. "Oh, all right.

After moving the bottle within reach, the two of them sat down next to each other, with Tricia resting her head on Marshall's shoulder. It was she who spoke first.

"Now tell me all about how you came to buy that horrible little rag."

"It won't be horrible once I get my hands on it."

"You've got your work cut out for you," she said.

"Yeah. The business has a lot of problems, but I'm up for the challenge."

"I don't doubt it. When did all this come about?" Tricia asked. It certainly wasn't news to Nikki.

"This morning. We wrote up a basic framework. Now it's up to the lawyers to hammer out the final deal. I figured you'd be having dinner with Angelica, so I waited until you usually come home to tell you. Besides, do you know how hard it is in this burg to track down a chilled bottle of Dom Pérignon?"

Tricia laughed. "I'll bet. But you could have called me.

As it happens, Angelica was invited out this evening, so I've been on my own."

"Damn. You should have let me know. I'll bet you ate dry toast for dinner."

"I had lunch leftovers, so I'm good. But I'm more interested in hearing about your new venture. How soon will you take possession of the paper?"

"That's up to my lawyer to figure out, but I'm hoping it'll be before the holidays, although Russ seems in a hurry to seal the deal, so maybe it'll happen even sooner than that. My first job will be to get the business back in the black."

"And what's your plan?"

"First of all, I'm going to talk to all the advertisers, especially those who've backed away from supporting the *News*."

"And that includes Angelica?"

He nodded.

"And then?"

"Consult with a graphic designer. At the very least, I want to get a new masthead. I don't suppose the paper has had a refresh in decades."

"Russ is so cheap, he makes Ginger do the paper's graphics, and she's admitted to me that she doesn't feel comfortable in that role. Will you hire more staff?"

"I don't know. I'll have to do a feasibility study."

"Have you spoken to Patti and Ginger about it?"

He shook his head. "I met them when I went to Russ's office, but there was no opportunity to talk to them. If he hasn't already told them, they probably suspect."

Interesting. Nikki had spoken to Patti that afternoon. Maybe Patti was afraid to jump the gun and say anything until she knew for sure if her job was secure.

"Did Russ give you a reason for selling the paper?"

"Apparently he plans to leave Stoneham—and, according to him, the sooner the better. It seems he wants to get away from the memories of his ex-wife."

"I spoke to her this afternoon."

"On the phone?"

"In person. She picked up their son and is flying back to California with him tonight. Did you know Russ was about to put that little boy in foster care?"

Marshall exhaled a long breath. "No, he didn't say a thing about the kid."

That was so typical of Russ.

"While in town, Nikki also took care of other business."

"Such as?"

"She fired the manager of the Patisserie and hired someone else to take over. From the sound of it, she doesn't plan to return."

Marshall shrugged. "It looks like Russ is getting everything he wants."

"Did he mention what he plans to do about the Chamber presidency?"

"He's going to resign."

"That rat. He hasn't even served a year in the position, and he seems to have taken great delight in destroying the organization."

"I guess he's going to call a meeting sometime soon and turn in his resignation. This is your chance to run for the job. And this time you'll win."

Tricia frowned. "I don't know if I'm up to the amount of work it'll take to rebuild it."

"It's something to think about. You know it would make Angelica happy."

"Yes, it would. It's broken her heart to see what he's done—how he's hurt the village and all the Chamber members. Did Russ mention his personal plans for the future?"

"He just said he wanted to start a new life."

"Well, I certainly won't miss him, and neither will a lot of other people."

"Let's not talk about Russ anymore," Marshall said. "I want to celebrate—and maybe you will, too," he suggested.

"You mean because we'd be getting a decent person who cares about the truth editing our local paper?"

"No, because it means I won't be leaving you to gallivant across the globe."

Tricia laughed. "Oh, that. I guess I'm very glad to hear that, too."

"You *guess*?"

"Okay, I am absolutely thrilled to hear you say that."

Marshall smiled and gave her a light kiss. "I can think of another way to celebrate."

"Really?"

"You've got that great big soaker tub in the upstairs bathroom. Wouldn't it feel good to light a few candles and let hot water and lots of bubbles ease away the tensions of the day?"

Oh, yes—and Tricia still harbored a lot of tension. She hadn't even begun to tell him about the events of her day.

"That sounds like a marvelous idea," she said, getting up from the couch. "You take the bottle and head upstairs while I turn off all the lights."

He kissed her again and grabbed the bottle. Tricia followed and paused at the light switch on the wall.

She didn't want Angelica's call to spoil what could very well be the best part of her day.

There was no call that evening. Had Angelica anticipated that Marshall might stay at Tricia's apartment for the second night in a row when she'd suggested a signal, or had it just been wishful thinking on her part? Tricia didn't know or care.

As she and Marshall were both early risers, Tricia made a light breakfast for them both, then kissed Marshall goodbye. They both had busy days ahead of them.

Tricia had showered and dressed for the day and was catching up with emails when the phone finally rang.

"Hello, dear sister," Angelica practically sang.

"Hello to you. Is everything okay? Do you need me to come over to take Sarge out?"

"Thanks, but no. Antonio took him out last night, and I've already taken him out this morning. June will help out during the day."

"She's a good egg," Tricia agreed. "Will you be spilling all about your evening?"

"Not until you confess that you got lucky again last night."

"I'll never tell," Tricia said, but then giggled.

"I thought as much when every light in your apartment was off last night when I arrived home."

"How did your evening go?"

Angelica sighed. "Pretty much as expected. Antonio is over the moon that they're pregnant for a second time, and Ginny—who has to actually carry the new baby—is not."

"Oh, dear. No wonder she overreacted when I suggested she and Antonio take in Little Ru—er, Rusty."

"Who's Rusty?"

"That's what little Russell wanted to know."

"What?" Angelica asked, confused.

"I'll get to that in a minute. First, tell me more about Ginny's reaction."

"Oh. Well, if you ask me, if she had her druthers, she wouldn't carry this baby to term."

"Are you saying what I think you're saying?" Tricia asked.

"I'm pretty sure there's a tubal ligation in her future," Angelica said succinctly. "Of course, she knows she's going to love this baby once it arrives, but she's feeling totally overwhelmed right now. She would have preferred this to happen in a year or two—not now."

"When did they find out?"

"Ginny bought a pregnancy test at the drugstore on Monday morning. She made an appointment with her ob-gyn in two weeks; it's the first she could get."

Had Ginny suspected she might be pregnant the previous week when she brought up the subject during their meal at Booked for Lunch? Had she been in denial on Sunday, during their family dinner, when she had a glass or two of wine? Now that she knew for sure, Tricia was positive wine and spirits were out of the picture for Ginny for the foreseeable future.

"I'm happy for Antonio and sad for Ginny at the same time. This wasn't what she wanted."

"I know, but she'll make the best of the situation," Angelica said.

Yes, Tricia had no doubt she would.

"And I'm hoping we like this Curtis fellow we're interviewing today. It would take a load of bricks off Antonio's shoulders. Ginny is going to need more support with two little ones underfoot."

"Did you mention they could hire a nanny?"

"It may have come up in conversation," Angelica admitted. "In fact, I'm going to encourage them to start interviewing. And I'll talk to Ginny about working from home a couple of days a week once the new baby arrives."

"Those sound like good ideas. Did the three of you talk about renovations to Ginny's little house?"

"Oh, yes, and that at least pleased Ginny. They've been living in cramped quarters ever since Sofia arrived." Angelica launched into all the different scenarios in which the tiny house could be enlarged on that wonderful, big lot, and taking great delight that her advice seemed welcome and valued.

Once Angelica ran out of steam, Tricia dropped her own bombshells.

"Nikki came back to Stoneham to claim little Russell?" Angelica asked, aghast.

"She's renamed him Rusty," Tricia pointed out. "Perhaps she wants to banish Russ from their collective memories. And who could blame her? Russ was never in line for the title of Father of the Year."

"And Marshall is buying the *Stoneham Weekly News*?"

"That's right."

"Wow. That's a lot to take in at one time."

"Tell me about it," Tricia agreed.

"I will definitely start advertising with the paper again once Marshall is in charge," Angelica declared. "For my own brand and for Nigela Ricita Associates."

"Do you want me to tell him so?"

"No. I want to hear his pitch first. I'll let him work for it. That way he'll gain more pleasure from it."

Yes, Tricia had to agree, he probably would.

"Has anybody ever told you that you have great wisdom, oh, sister of mine?"

"Not so far," Angelica said.

"Good. Then I won't have to ruin that record."

"You are the worst," Angelica accused.

"No, I'm the best."

Tricia heard her sister let out a breath. "Okay, maybe. But just for today. I might claim that title tomorrow."

"And I will gladly relinquish it. For a day," Tricia asserted.

"Then you'll just have to earn it back on Thursday," Angelica said.

"Can do." Tricia looked at the clock on the wall. "I've got to get my butt in gear if this interview with Hank Curtis is going to happen this morning."

"Very well. I've got a lot to accomplish by then, too. I haven't worked out how I'm going to get to the Brookview."

"I'll ask Mr. Everett. He's more than willing to do anything for either of us."

"He's such a dear man," Angelica agreed.

"I'll set it up and let you know."

"Thank you. Then I guess I'll see you at the Brookview around eleven."

"Count on it," Tricia said, and the sisters ended the call.

Now Tricia just had to make everything work.

TWENTY-ONE

Tricia arrived at the encampment at precisely eight thirty, but when she got out of her car and looked around, she didn't see Hank Curtis, whom she'd expected to meet her. Some of the other men were sitting in front of the fire pit, drinking coffee and eating—some from the cans of food she'd brought two days before.

"Where's Hank?" she asked.

"Gone."

"What do you mean 'gone'?" she asked, shocked. "Forever?"

"Nah, for a walk," one of the grubbier men said.

"But he was supposed to meet me here to go on a job interview this morning."

"He don't want no job."

"That wasn't what he told me yesterday."

The old guy shrugged. "That's what he told us last night."

Tricia frowned. If Curtis hadn't worked in several years, maybe he was just overwhelmed.

"When did he leave?"

"Ten, twenty minutes ago."

"Which way did he go?" she asked.

He pointed farther down the road.

"Thank you," Tricia said, and stalked off in the direction

of her car. She got in and took out her phone, calling the number of the flip phone she'd bought the day before. It rang and rang but wasn't answered.

She set the phone aside, started the engine, and took off down the road, driving slowly. The dirt track was some kind of service road, probably for the railroad, and there were plenty of places to hide among the brush and trees if Curtis decided to do so. That said, she wouldn't have thought he was the kind of man to run away from a challenge. Had she made a mistake in suggesting that Angelica interview him for a job that carried a lot of responsibility?

Tricia kept watch as she slowly rolled down the lane, and it took a good five minutes before she saw a figure shambling along up ahead. What was she going to say to the man? She wasn't sure, but she did know one thing: she wasn't going to beg him to go on the interview.

As she approached Curtis, Tricia hit the button on the driver's-side armrest and rolled down the passenger-side window. "Need a lift?"

Curtis turned, and Tricia braked.

"Where are you going?"

"I needed some fresh air," he said.

"It's all around you."

"Okay, then maybe I needed to think."

"About what?"

He let out a breath. "That I'm not ready for this."

"Why not?"

"I've got problems."

"So does everybody else in the world," she said.

"Just thinking about getting a job makes me want to have a drink," Curtis admitted.

"Did you?"

"Not yet."

"Good. Now hop in."

"I told you, I'm not ready for a job," he asserted.

"How do you even know they're going to offer it to you?"

Curtis blinked, as though the thought hadn't occurred to him.

"Come on, if we don't buy you some new duds and get you to the barber, you *won't* get the job."

To say Curtis looked perturbed was putting it mildly. But after a few long seconds he jerked open the passenger-side door and got in the car. Tricia did a three-point turn and headed back toward the encampment.

"Buckle up," she ordered, rolling up the window, and he meekly complied.

"Look, I appreciate you setting this up, but you can drop me off at the camp," Curtis said.

"No can do," Tricia answered, keeping her gaze straight ahead. "I went out on a limb for you, and you're going to see this through."

"You can't make me," Curtis said, sounding like a petulant child.

Tricia laughed. "No, I can't. But I figure a guy who went through multiple deployments to Afghanistan can muster the courage to speak with a young man and an older woman and make out okay."

"This Nigela Ricita woman is a powerful person," Curtis said.

"She can't bite you from a computer screen."

"What if I have a panic attack?"

"I've got a paper sack you can breathe into."

"What if I say something stupid?"

"And what if you don't?"

"What if I get the job? Where would I live? How would I get to work?"

"Ms. Ricita and her associate, Mr. Barbero, are aware of your circumstances. I'm sure something could be worked out."

Tricia braked as they drove past the camp, but when Curtis didn't leap from the car, she sped up and headed for the main road.

"Where are we going first?"

"First, to one of the big-box stores on Route 101. We'll get you a clean change of clothes and then I'll take you to Booked for Beauty."

"A beauty parlor?" he protested.

"It's a day spa. My sister owns it. It's unisex. Everybody in the village goes there."

"You own a store, too, right?"

"Yes. Haven't Got a Clue. I sell vintage and current mysteries."

"And your sister's a hairdresser?"

Tricia laughed. "No. She's an entrepreneur. She has a bookstore, a café, the day spa, and an interest in a bed-and-breakfast." Among other things. "She's partnered with Nigela Ricita Associates on the B and B, and should you get the job, you would probably be speaking with her when it comes to sourcing for it and the café."

"Plus that swanky inn?"

"Uh-huh. I'm sure, after working in the military, you're more than up for the job."

"How do you know I wasn't a screwup?"

"Were you honorably discharged?"

"Yeah."

"With full rank and retirement?"

"The retirement money is a tangled mess, thanks to the divorce; otherwise I wouldn't be sleeping in a tent."

Tricia nodded. She'd heard similar stories. "I think you'll find Nigela Ricita Associates to be competitive when it comes to pay." Tricia glanced to her right to see Curtis merely shrug.

Once on the highway, Curtis peppered her with questions about the Brookview Inn, Booked for Lunch, and the Sheer Comfort Inn. She was happy to answer them all, glad he was finally showing more interest in the whole experience.

They parked in front of the store with the big bull's-eye, and half an hour later Curtis was decked out in business casual attire, including new socks and shoes.

"I'm going to pay you back for this," Curtis muttered, which Tricia took as a hopeful sign that he actually might sell himself on the interview. Once they were back in the car, Curtis had a more serious question for Tricia. "Why are you doing this for me?"

Pixie had asked the same question. "When I heard your

credentials, I thought you might be a perfect fit with NR Associates."

"Yeah?"

"And Mr. Barbero and his wife are dear friends of mine. They have a young daughter, and he works a lot of hours. Maybe with you taking on a big part of his job, he'll have more time for his family."

"Maybe. But there'll be a learning curve."

"I don't doubt it."

"You sound awfully confident," Curtis groused.

"To be truthful, I don't have a stake in this at all. But I figured if I could help you out—or anybody else, for that matter—I would."

"Do-gooder," Curtis muttered.

"I like the sound of that," Tricia said as a smile tugged at her lips.

They were quiet for a couple of minutes, then Curtis spoke again. "I met her."

"Who?"

"Susan Morris."

Tricia's fingers tightened on the steering wheel. "Where?"

"In Stoneham. At that free-clothes place."

"The Clothes Closet."

"Yeah. She was working there. She helped me pick out some stuff"—he gave a wry laugh—"so I could go on a job interview."

"Did you?"

"Yeah," he said, sounding dispirited. "Sometimes clothes don't make the man."

"What was the job?"

"Dishwasher at some diner in Milford."

"And?"

"I didn't get it." He shook his head ruefully. "Me, a dish-washer. What would the enlisted men under my command have said about that?"

Tricia could imagine, and it wasn't a pretty picture.

Curtis shrugged. "It's probably just as well they didn't hire me. I was going to have to hitch a ride to get to work every day. It would've been hard to get back to the camp at night. But losing that job kind of shattered whatever confidence I had left."

"From what I saw, you take care of those guys at camp. You don't seem all that shattered to me."

"I put on a good front," he said sourly.

"And what did you think about Susan?" Tricia asked.

"She was okay."

"Did you know she was homeless?"

"There are degrees of homelessness. She had a car—in my book, that's pretty good shelter—and she had options most of us don't."

"Did she talk about her daughter?"

"Yeah. She told me she had an open invitation to stay with her and her family, but she still had places to go, places she wanted to see."

Maybe Susan would have traveled south once winter hit. Instead, she ended up going south, all right. Probably cremated in a plastic container.

And there seemed to be no rhyme or reason to her death.

In no time they arrived in the village. And because they were between seasons, Tricia was able to park on a street not too far from the day spa.

Randy Ellison met them at the door. "Welcome, Tricia, and this must be your friend, Mr. Curtis. Would either of you like some coffee? We've got some more of those marvelous chocolates from the Sweet As Can Be candy shop, too. Just the thing for a sweet tooth."

"Uh, no, thanks," Curtis said.

"I need to call Pixie and check up on my store, but I'll take a rain check," Tricia said.

"Fine. Step this way, Mr. Curtis. Marlene will be taking care of you this morning."

"Thanks."

Tricia stepped outside and took out her cell phone, calling her store.

"Haven't Got a Clue; this is Pixie. How may I help you?"

"Hey, Pixie. Is everything all right?"

"Peachy keen," Pixie told her. "And Mr. Everett has already picked up Angelica and taken her to the Brookview."

"Oh, good. I'm not sure when I'll get back to the store. I'll probably be taking Mr. Curtis back to the encampment, and I might stop for lunch along the way."

"Not to worry. We'll be fine, won't we, Miss Marple?"

If her cat replied, Tricia didn't hear it. "Great, I'll talk to you later," she promised, and ended the call. She put her phone away and walked back into the spa, taking a seat in the waiting area, where she pulled out her current book and settled in to read. Twenty minutes later a virtual stranger appeared before her. Not only had Marlene trimmed Curtis's hair, but she'd trimmed his beard, making him look more like a college professor than a homeless vet.

Tricia stood. "Wow, you look terrific—and years younger."

"That's a plus for anybody over fifty looking for work," Curtis admitted.

"Nigela Ricita Associates doesn't age discriminate."

"So I've heard." Curtis glanced at the big clock on the wall. They had just ten minutes to get to the Brookview.

"Let me settle the bill and I'll be right with you," Tricia said. She stepped up to the reception desk with her credit card in hand, and two minutes later they headed back to her car.

"Are you ready?" she asked.

Curtis's hands were clenched into fists. "Ready as I'll ever be."

Tricia patted his shoulder. "You'll do fine."

Curtis didn't look convinced. They got into Tricia's car and off they went.

The Brookview Inn wasn't all decked out for fall, but a few hints of color, in the form of pumpkins, were visible on the big open porch as Tricia drove up the driveway. She parked in the lot behind the historic edifice, and Curtis followed her in through the building's back entrance.

They arrived at the lobby, where the door to Antonio's office was open. Tricia knocked on the jamb. "We're here."

Antonio got up from behind his desk. "Come in."

Tricia rushed forward and gave him a hug. "I'm so happy to hear about the good news."

Antonio blushed. "I am very pleased. Ginny . . ." He gave a shrug.

"She'll come around. She's a great mom and she's going to love this baby just as much as she loves you and Sofia," Tricia whispered. Antonio gripped her hand in a gesture of thanks. Then he became all business and offered his hand to Curtis. "It's very good to meet you, Mr. Curtis."

"Thanks for inviting me."

"I'll just close the door and let you two get down to business," Tricia said. "We'll talk later," she told Curtis.

"Feel free to wait for Mr. Curtis in the conference room," Antonio said, nodding his head in that direction.

"Thanks." Tricia gave Curtis a thumbs-up. "Good luck." She closed the door and wasted no time hightailing it down the hall to the conference room, where Angelica was seated at the head of the table, with her foot propped on another chair and her laptop already open and connected.

"So, you got here okay?" Tricia asked without preamble.

"Mr. Everett was such a dear to bring me here. And he made sure I was settled in before he would leave. I may attempt to make him a batch of thumbprint cookies this weekend and give them to him at our family dinner as a thank-you."

"I'm sure he'd love it," Tricia said as she removed her jacket and took a seat at Angelica's right. "When will Antonio contact you?"

"Any minute now. Antonio's decided that if he likes Mr. Curtis, he'll invite him to the dining room for lunch. That would give us the opportunity to have lunch, too. I've been cooped up for so long, I'm going stir-crazy. And that way I'd get an opportunity to meet the guy as well."

"He's pretty nervous." Tricia told her sister how the dish-washing job hadn't panned out.

"Oh, the poor man. Let's hope he makes a better impression today."

"Great. Then I can fill you in on what we talked about this morning."

"Fine."

Tricia nodded toward the laptop. "Are you sure that voice-altering thing is going to work?"

"It's worked before whenever I've had to talk to staff as Nigela."

"Will I hear a difference?"

Angelica shook her head. "It's all on their end."

"What do you use for a picture?"

Angelica laughed. "A stock photo I bought off the Internet for five bucks. I had it photoshopped so if it shows up on an ad or something, it won't look suspicious."

"Good idea."

The call came through, and Tricia and Angelica straightened in anticipation. But within a minute or so, Tricia found her mind wandering as Antonio and Angelica got into the meat of the interview. Hearing about ordering food in bulk and supervising a staff wasn't nearly as interesting as she would have thought, but Curtis was doing a good job of selling himself and his skills, which pleased her. She pulled her book out of her purse to take a reading break. Still, her mind wandered back to what Curtis had told her concerning Susan Morris—the fact that the situation was so ordinary. Susan had had her volunteer job with the Clothes Closet, she had worked at the chocolate shop, and she had been well liked and kind to people. Why would anybody want to kill her?

Angelica tapped Tricia's arm to get her attention and then put the computer's microphone on mute. "I like this guy. He seems to know exactly what we need and how to accomplish it. What do you think about me offering him the job on a contingency basis? Perhaps as a consultant? We could give him a month to prove himself and then see where it goes."

"It sounds fair. What about his accommodations? He's got no car and nowhere to live."

"He can stay in one of the inn's bungalows. We can move him to a room or even to the Sheer Comfort Inn if we have to."

"Yes, but won't you be fully booked by the end of the month?"

"We'll figure something out." Angelica turned up the sound once again. When an opening appeared, she spoke up.

"I'm quite happy with what I've heard, Mr. Curtis. I wonder, would you consider working with us on a trial basis as a consultant? That way we could decide if you're a good fit for our organization, and you can decide if you'd be happy working with us."

"That sounds good," Curtis said, his voice higher than Tricia had heard before.

"Shall we say five thousand and room and board for a thirty-day trial?"

"Uh . . . yes. That sounds fair."

"Good. When can you start? Tomorrow?"

"I . . . I . . . yes, of course."

"Good. Mr. Barbero, perhaps you'd like to take Mr. Curtis to lunch and go over the job requirements in more detail."

"As you wish, Ms. Ricita."

"Good. I've got another meeting in a few moments, so I'll say good-bye for now, Mr. Curtis. And I hope we get to speak again soon."

"Uh, thank you. Thank you for this opportunity."

"You're welcome. We'll talk again soon," she promised, and cut the connection, letting out a breath. "Whew! I'm glad that's over. I'm starved. Let's go to the dining room and eat."

TWENTY-TWO

Antonio and Curtis had already retreated to the dining room by the time Tricia and Angelica caught up with them. Tricia stopped by their table, and both men immediately stood. She waved them to sit.

"So? How'd it go?" she asked Curtis.

"Great. I've been offered the job on an interim basis."

"That's wonderful," Tricia said, feigning surprise, happy to see that Curtis seemed to be a man transformed—much more confident than he'd been earlier that morning.

"I'd like you to meet my sister, Angelica."

"Ms. Miles," Curtis said, standing once again and holding out a hand.

"Very happy to meet you. Tricia's told me a lot about you." She handed Tricia one of her crutches, and they shook on it.

"You and Mr. Curtis will be able to get to know one another in the coming days," Tricia informed her. "You will be working with him on the Sheer Comfort Inn account."

"I'll look forward to it," Angelica said, and batted her eyelashes at him.

Tricia cleared her throat. "We'll be having lunch here, too," she told Curtis and Antonio. "When you're done—"

"If you wouldn't mind taking me back to the encampment so I can get my things and say good-bye to my . . . my friends, I'd really appreciate it," Curtis said.

"I'd be happy to. Have a good lunch," Tricia said, and gave Angelica a nudge, handing back the crutch.

The sisters sat several tables away by the window overlooking the brook. A waiter approached with menus. "I'll bring you some water and be back in a moment."

Angelica kept leaning to look around Tricia and peer at Antonio and Curtis's table. "He's much better-looking in person than on a tiny computer screen."

"Curtis?"

"Who else are we talking about?"

"Did you have to make eyes at him just now?"

"I did not make eyes. I was just admiring . . . *his* nice eyes."

"Sure."

By the time they ordered, they were on to other subjects, and enjoyed a delightful lunch accompanied by glasses of wine. Since Angelica needed a lift home, she decided to hitch a ride with Tricia. And so, Angelica rode shotgun and Curtis took the back seat.

"I can drop you off at your shop," Tricia told her sister.

"I've got nothing on my agenda today," Angelica said, looking over her left shoulder to the man in back. "Why don't I just tag along for the ride?"

"Fine with me," Tricia said.

"I should have mentioned it earlier, but I won't be staying at the camp," Curtis said.

"Oh?" Tricia asked, again feigning surprise.

"Mr. Barbero—Antonio—has offered me accommodations at the Brookview Inn, at least temporarily."

"He's a nice man," Angelica quipped.

"It's part of the deal. They offered me a monthlong trial period."

"And how do you feel about that?" Angelica asked.

"With my background, it's more than fair. It'll sure feel good to sleep in a real bed tonight. But I do need to pick up my gear at the camp—such as it is—and I appreciate the ride back there to get it," he told Tricia with sincerity.

While Tricia played chauffeur during the twenty-minute ride, Angelica peppered Curtis with questions about his past work experience, told him how she ran things at Booked for Lunch and the Sheer Comfort Inn, and indicated that she hoped to save money sharing a food manager with the Brookview Inn.

They were so involved in the discussion that they didn't see what Tricia saw as she approached the location where the encampment had been. She slowed and took in what looked like piles of trash scattered across the landscape.

"What happened?" she cried as she and the others turned to take in the devastation.

"It looks like a tornado hit," Angelica said.

"Everything's gone," Curtis said in a hushed voice.

"But where are the people?" Tricia asked.

She stopped the car, and the three of them got out. Curtis tramped across the grass to where the fire pit had been. The ground beneath was scorched, but it and the tents and large cardboard cartons that had acted as homes for the destitute were gone. Large tracks were dug into the soft earth. No natural phenomenon had caused that kind of damage.

A movement to her left caused Tricia to whirl. She recognized one of the homeless men she'd spoken to that morning.

"Bobby, what happened?" Curtis asked.

The older man's eyes were bloodshot, and it looked like he'd been crying. "First a couple of cops from Stoneham came to talk to Joe. It got kind of heated, and Joe took a swing at one of them. They arrested him and hauled him away. Not ten minutes later some guys in a white pickup showed up towing a Bobcat excavator, saying this was private property and that we had to leave. Well, we told them we weren't gonna, but they didn't listen. They just unloaded the Bobcat and started smashing down our tents and tarps. They didn't even give us a chance to salvage nothin'. Now all I got is the clothes on my back and nowhere to go," he said, his voice breaking.

"That's terrible!" Tricia cried.

"Where are the others?" Curtis asked.

"They took off on foot, but I stayed to tell you. I knew you'd be back." The old man sized up Curtis's new clothes. "You sure spiffed up. Did you get the job?"

"Yeah," Curtis said, his voice husky. "I got it. I start tomorrow."

"Wow. Good going."

"What can we do to help you, sir?" Angelica asked.

The old man wiped the back of a hand under his nose and sniffed. "Nothin'."

"No," Tricia said emphatically, looking at Angelica. "Let me call Grace. The Everett Foundation has made sizable contributions to the big homeless shelter in Nashua. I'm sure she could pull some strings to get you in today."

"I don't like shelters," the old man declared. "They gots lots a rules."

"Bobby, go," Curtis said. "Just until you get settled and can figure out your next move."

The old man surveyed the empty field. "I guess you're right. I really got no choice."

It took the rest of the afternoon to deliver Bobby to the homeless shelter and make sure he had a cot for at least the night. Tricia checked in with Pixie, letting her know the situation, and Grace kept in touch, promising she'd follow up the next day to see if the Everett Foundation could be of any further assistance to Bobby. He shook hands with all three of them and then they piled into Tricia's car and headed back to Stoneham.

"Is it even legal for people to just show up and bulldoze a homeless site?" Angelica asked, apparently as upset as Tricia over the entire ordeal.

"Technically, we were trespassing," Curtis said. "We

were lucky they didn't come along and break up our camp months before now."

"It does seem suspicious that it happened right after Chief Baker showed up," Tricia observed. Much as she wanted to know why King had lied about the earring, trashing the only place the homeless men had as a sanctuary seemed incredibly cruel. Had Baker set things in motion, or was it just a coincidence that the men in the pickup had arrived immediately after he'd left the encampment? Tricia intended to find out.

It was almost happy hour by the time Tricia dropped Curtis off in front of bungalow number two behind the Brookview Inn. Unlike Bobby, Curtis had two changes of clothing in addition to his new attire, although Tricia wasn't sure when the former had last been washed. The Brookview's housekeeping team could take care of that, and she was comforted to know he could get three square meals a day at the inn's restaurant as well.

Tricia rolled down her window as Curtis exited the car with his shopping bag of stuff in hand. "I don't know how to thank you, Tricia. I don't know what I would have done with nowhere to go—again."

"Make the most of this opportunity. Succeed. That would be the only reward I need."

"I'll make you proud. I promise."

"I'll talk to you soon," Tricia said.

"It was nice to have met you, Mr. Curtis. I look forward to working together," Angelica called.

"Call me Hank, ma'am."

"Only if you call me Angelica."

"Will do," he said, and straightened, giving both women a salute. They waved good-bye and Tricia closed her window before she drove out the inn's back entrance.

"What a day," Angelica muttered, sinking back in her seat, and then winced.

"Is your foot bothering you?"

"Yes, I should have had it raised during lunch. The swelling will probably be worse for a couple of days."

"I'm sorry. But I couldn't just abandon poor Bobby."

"Oh, I'm with you a hundred percent. I'm just glad Grace could help the man out. And I wonder what happened to the other guys who were living in that field."

Tricia shrugged. "We'll probably never know, although I have a feeling Hank will try to track them down. A good commander always looks after his men."

Angelica nodded and changed the subject. "I never had a chance to coordinate with Tommy about making our dinner, and I'm afraid my cupboards are pretty bare."

"Come to my place and I'll fix us something, even if it's only eggs and toast."

"That sounds fine to me, but Sarge will need to go out. If June hasn't already done it—"

"Don't worry, I wouldn't let the little guy suffer."

"I feel bad that I've neglected him all day."

"Mr. Everett was aware of our change of plans; I'm sure he saw to it Sarge was well looked after."

"I'm sorry my silly foot has taken him away from his work at your store so often these past couple of weeks."

"Nonsense. He's loved every minute of feeling useful. And, anyway, things have been pretty slow at the shop. He would probably have only worn out his lamb's-wool duster."

Angelica laughed. "You're probably right."

It was five fifty-five when Tricia pulled up in front of Haven't Got a Clue. Pixie emerged and greeted them both, grabbing Angelica's crutches from the back of the car and helping her inside while Tricia parked the car in the municipal lot. Pixie was putting on her coat to leave when she returned.

"I'm sorry I was gone all day," Tricia said, "but we had to help that poor homeless man."

"Of course you did. Mr. Everett left about twenty minutes ago to take Sarge for a walk, so he'll be fine. You and Angelica can have your usual happy hour gabfest." She sighed. "Fred and me usually have a cocktail before we flip a coin to see who's going to burn dinner."

"Oh, come on, you're not that bad a cook."

"You haven't tasted my baked chicken." Pixie grabbed her purse and headed out the door. "See you tomorrow!"

Tricia locked up and set the security system and thought about the timing of the two attempted break-ins, which had occurred on successive Saturday evenings. Why would someone intent on getting into her store wait a week before trying it a second time?

She was still thinking of that when she stepped into her apartment and found Angelica ensconced on the chaise end of her sectional, feet up, her boot off, and looking like she'd been there for hours.

Tricia hung up her jacket and plopped into the chair by the coffee table, sinking in and kicking off her shoes. "This has been a very long day. I don't want to move from this spot."

"Oh," Angelica said in what could only be described as disappointment.

"Don't tell me you've still got the energy to go somewhere else tonight."

"Well, sort of," she admitted. "Despite my swollen foot, I can't tell you how much I enjoyed today. Not that I liked witnessing that poor homeless man's troubles, but, thanks to Grace, we *did* get to help him out. And I've had such a terrible case of cabin fever, I feel like I'm going *crazy*," Angelica cried.

"But you were out nearly the whole day," Tricia protested.

"As I just pointed out, not all of it was fun."

Tricia frowned. "What do you want to do? Go to a movie?"

"Definitely not! I've watched too many movies during the past few weeks."

"How about I take you to a bookstore?" Tricia suggested with a smile.

"I'd only have to walk down the stairs for that," Angelica griped.

"Do you want to go out to dinner?"

"No. I'm actually getting sick of restaurant food. Eggs and toast will be fine. But I want to be where people are hanging out—where there's noise and music."

"The Dog-Eared Page?" Tricia asked.

"Exactly."

"Then that's what we'll do. Do you want me to go next door to get the transport chair?"

"Not really." She looked down at her puffy foot. "I can put weight on my heel, and with the crutches it's not too bad. Besides, I've got nothing planned for tomorrow and can sit with my foot up the whole day. But for now—or rather in an hour or so—I feel the need to get up and be among healthy people."

"All right. Then, shall we have wine instead of martinis?"

"Perfect. We can have the good stuff at the pub."

"Sounds good to me," Tricia said, and rose from her chair. "I haven't got much more than cheese and crackers as a snack."

"Fine with me. About now I'd eat my sore foot."

"I'll be back in a jiffy."

Tricia retreated to the kitchen, poured the wine, and assembled stuff to nibble on, including some olives and the last of her stash of grapes. She lifted the tray and took it into the living room, where she found Miss Marple had taken up residence on Angelica's lap and was purring happily. Of course, that didn't last long, because the cat knew that happy hour always meant a treat for her, too.

Once everyone had been taken care of, Tricia flopped down in her easy chair and kicked off her shoes once again.

"What shall we drink to?" Angelica asked.

"A normal day. I haven't had one in I don't know how long."

Angelica raised her glass. "To a normal day."

They drank and then Tricia stifled a yawn. She wasn't sure she was up for what passed as an evening on the town, but a promise was a promise. And yet she had a feeling that, apart from her weekly lunch with Ginny the next day, she wasn't going to have an ordinary Thursday. She needed to make time to speak with Grant Baker.

She had a lot of hard questions for him to answer.

TWENTY-THREE

As the sisters slowly walked south on the east side of Main Street, Tricia wondered if the chill in the air would bring them their first frost of the season by morning. Then again, it was still rather early for that. But a cold wind from Canada could change everything in a heartbeat.

Traffic was almost nonexistent, and they crossed the street in front of the Dog-Eared Page, where they could already hear cheerful Celtic music playing from within. Tricia held the door open for Angelica to enter, but her sister stopped abruptly, and Tricia had to stand in the ensuing draft while Angelica took in the space.

"Noise! People! I love it!" she declared.

"Yeah, well, they'll be cursing you if you don't move and let me close this door."

Angelica threw a sour look over her shoulder and then hobbled over to the first empty bistro table. She sat down, handed Tricia the crutches, and eased her sore foot onto the closest chair.

"Ah, that's better."

Tricia set the crutches against the wall, then removed her coat and hung it on the back of the adjacent chair. "Take off your jacket and get settled while I get us a couple of drinks at the bar."

"Bring a bowl of chips back with you, too, please."

"I've only got two hands."

Angelica pouted.

"Oh, all right!"

As Tricia approached the bar, she noticed a number of acquaintances from the Chamber of Commerce who'd also chosen to patronize the pub that evening—including its president. But Russ sat alone at a table in the rear of the pub, nursing a beer with his back to the crowd. It was him all right—and his Chamber constituents were doing a fine job of ignoring him.

When she got to the bar, Tricia was surprised to find the manager making drinks instead of the regular bartender. "Hi, Shawn. Where's Yoshi tonight?"

"Hey, Tricia. She's taking a break. We haven't seen you since you got back from your visit to the land of the little people." Shawn's Irish brogue always made her smile.

"I loved it. I've been busy, but I'm here now," she quipped.

"I hear you didn't get much of a welcome back, either."

Tricia frowned. "What do you mean?"

He shook his head, his expression somber. "I mean finding that homeless woman in your dumpster."

Tricia nodded. Everybody in the village seemed to know about that. "Did you ever meet Susan?"

He nodded. "Oh, yeah. One night the week before last, I caught her throwing her trash in one of our bins out back." He grimaced. "Well, if you can call it trash. I call it crap—literally."

For a moment Tricia didn't understand, and then she remembered the slop bucket in Susan's car. When she and Angelica had scoped out the vehicle, it was empty, the bag inside unsoiled. Had Susan emptied it just before she was killed?

"Did you catch her just the one time?"

"Yes, but I'm sure she'd been there before. I told her in no uncertain terms not to come back, but I assume she'd been dumping her crap all over the village—probably in a different locale every night so that no one would catch on."

Pixie had also mentioned that Susan disposed of her . . . waste. Tricia assumed the woman put it in the cans that resided on the fringes of the municipal parking lot. Had there been complaints about Susan? Had she been warned not to sully the cans? As it was, they didn't smell all that good on a hot day. And many people who walked their dogs along Main Street often deposited their droppings in the cans as well. It made sense that none of the business owners would want that kind of litter in their garbage totes or dumpsters—especially the establishments that served food, like the pub.

Then she remembered that Nikki had practically crowed about turning Susan in to the police. Had she caught her dumping her waste in the Patisserie's dumpster? The idea made Tricia shudder. Freegans often dug through trash looking for viable food. From personal experience, Tricia knew there were freegans living in the Stoneham area and the Patisserie threw out a lot of stale baked food.

And what about the sanitary considerations? Diseases like hepatitis, E. coli, salmonella, cholera, and even polio are spread through feces. The thought made Tricia shudder. No wonder Shawn had run Susan off.

"What can I get you and Angelica tonight?" he asked, nodding at Tricia's sister across the way. Angelica smiled and waved. "The usual?"

"Of course. And Angelica would like a bowl of chips, too, please."

"We're out of crisps. Will pretzels do?"

"The saltier, the better."

Shawn rummaged under the bar, came up with a bag of pretzel sticks, and poured them into a bowl before handing it to Tricia. "I'll have one of the girls bring your drinks to the table."

"Thanks."

"How's Angelica's foot?" Shawn asked.

"Getting better."

"Great. If I get a chance, I'll try to stop by to say hello."

"She'd like that."

Tricia returned to the table and plunked the bowl down in front of her sister.

"No chips?"

"Not tonight."

"That's okay. I'll enjoy these anyway. Too bad we don't have some peanut butter to dunk them in," Angelica said, and helped herself to several while Tricia seated herself. Peanut butter with a martini? No. Just no.

Tricia looked toward the bar, where Shawn was already in deep conversation with another patron. "I just had a short but very interesting conversation with Shawn."

"About what?"

"First, let me ask you a question. Is it illegal to dump your garbage in a business's dumpster?" Tricia asked.

Angelica shrugged. "I believe it is in some states, but more than that, it's just not nice. Why do you ask?"

"Because apparently Susan was dumping her trash—and her bodily waste—in commercial dumpsters across the village."

Angelica wrinkled her nose. "Eeuuww! Is that what Shawn said?"

Tricia took a couple of pretzels and nodded. "He said he caught her red-handed. I'm just wondering if that was enough to get her killed."

"By Shawn?" Angelica asked, appalled.

"Of course not. But what if someone else caught her doing it—and maybe not for the first time?"

Angelica shook her head. "That would seem like one heck of an overreaction. And who in Stoneham would do such a thing? Wouldn't it have just been better to call the cops or simply scare her away?"

"What if they'd tried both things and she came back anyway?"

"But why would someone drag her body all the way to your dumpster?" Angelica asked.

Tricia shrugged. "Maybe they didn't have far to go. Or if the killer didn't know who she was, he—or she—might have just done the deed and then stuffed her body behind Haven't Got a Clue to deflect detection."

Angelica shook her head. "I don't see that happening. It's too simple."

"And what if it *was* just that simple?"

"I guess there's only one way to find out."

"And how's that?"

"Talk to some of the other business owners along Main Street."

"Most of the stores are unoccupied after six o'clock. It makes sense that Susan would dump her trash at times she wasn't likely to get caught," Tricia said.

Angelica shrugged. "I guess that sounds logical. But many of the buildings have apartments. Maybe one of the tenants saw Susan or her car driving down the alley."

"I'm sure she would have done so in stealth mode—with her car lights off."

"But there're streetlamps, and they're bright enough that someone looking out a window would have seen her or her car."

Tricia was sure Marshall would have mentioned it if he'd seen Susan skulking around—that is, if he'd recognized her out of context.

"Here you go, ladies," said Bev, the waitress, who had formerly worked for Angelica at Booked for Lunch. She picked up a couple of cocktail napkins from the tray she held and placed them on the table before setting their drinks upon them. "How's the foot, Angelica?"

As Angelica launched into a detailed account of her surgery and subsequent recovery, Tricia did a little mental arithmetic. Main Street boasted at least twenty businesses, and several of the storefronts were currently vacant. Still, that didn't mean the apartments above them were also empty. Most of the buildings were three stories, with storefronts and one or two apartments. That could be an awful lot of people to canvass.

"Bev!" Shawn called, indicating several drinks before him on the bar.

"Gotta go. I'll talk to you later."

Angelica waved to get her sister's attention. "You're thinking of something?"

"Just wondering how long it would take to do a little nosing around."

Angelica frowned. "Why not just call Chief Baker and tell him about your stinky discovery?"

"And have him tell me I'm full of crap—if you'll pardon the pun?"

"It's his job."

"I want to test my theory first. If it seems to pay off, of course I'll mention it to Grant. I also want to know if he's responsible for the destruction at the homeless camp."

"I'll be interested to hear the answer to that," Angelica said. "When will you start your interviews with potential witnesses?"

"First thing in the morning."

Tricia wasn't kidding when she told Angelica that she intended to canvass the neighborhood to ask about Susan. The next morning she was up by six thirty, showered and dressed, and was out the door by seven fifteen, hoping to run into some of her neighbors who commuted to Nashua and beyond for work.

She walked up and down Main Street instead of her usual exercise route and ran into a middle-aged woman who came out of the door that led to the apartment above the Happy Domestic. "Excuse me, do you have a minute?" Tricia asked.

"Not really. I'm heading to the municipal lot to pick up my car."

"Do you mind if I walk along with you?"

"Why not?" The woman started off at a brisk pace. "You own the mystery bookstore, don't you?"

"Yes. I'm Tricia Miles."

"Marie Painter."

"Cool name."

"It would be if that was my occupation. I'm an admin at St. Joseph Hospital in Nashua. What did you want to ask me?"

"I'm sure you heard about the woman who was found murdered in the alley behind Main Street last week."

Marie frowned. "Everybody did."

"Did you see her hanging around the village before that?"

"I don't think so."

"She was known to dump trash in the dumpsters behind the businesses here on Main Street. She liked to do it under the cover of darkness."

Marie paused, looking thoughtful. "Maybe. Not a lot of cars use the alley after business hours. I'd only look out the window if I heard a car idling. I can't say I'd have paid much attention otherwise." She turned her attention back to the sidewalk before them and continued walking, with Tricia keeping pace.

It made sense that Susan wouldn't draw attention to herself and why her car had been found at the municipal lot. She simply had to walk around the village after dark to throw away her garbage. It was relatively safe to do so—unless one considered the number of murders that had occurred in Stoneham during the past six years. Tricia had been accused of bringing bad luck to the village—of being its resident jinx—but it was to be expected that a once-dying village would see an uptick in crime when prosperity made its return big-time.

But Tricia also remembered that Chief Baker had said members of the police force had prodded Susan to leave the municipal parking lot before nightfall. Did they sometimes cut her slack, or was the fact that the department had only a few officers the reason they didn't waste manpower harassing Susan? And where did Susan go when the cops told her to leave the lot? Did she stealth camp on side streets or on the outskirts of town? Tricia would probably never know.

The women reached the municipal lot. "Have a great day at work," Tricia said.

"You, too."

Marie veered off into the lot, and Tricia continued to the

corner where, despite the lack of traffic, she waited for the village's only light to turn green so she could cross the road to resume her walk on the other side, heading south. No one popped out of any of the doorways, so when she came to the end of the block, she crossed the street once again and headed back north, encountering no one until she neared the municipal parking lot once more. Terry McDonald, the owner of the All Heroes comic-book store, came charging around the corner, nearly barreling into her.

"Tricia! I'm so sorry. I didn't see you there."

"Don't worry about it. Do you have a minute?"

"Oh, sure. I don't open the shop until ten. I came in early because I've got a shipment of DC and Marvel comics in for a sale I'm having this weekend. I've got to stick them in plastic bags and get 'em priced and in the racks. What's up?"

"I'm sure you must have heard about Susan Morris being found in my dumpster last week, right?"

"Hasn't everybody?" Terry asked.

"It sure seems like it. Anyway, I know you stay open late a couple of nights every week. I wondered if you ever saw her walking in the alley behind your store."

"Walking, yeah—when she wasn't running away from me." Tricia brightened.

"At first I thought she was digging through my trash, but then I realized she was burying something in it."

"What was it?" Tricia asked innocently.

"I dunno. But she obviously didn't want me to know she was doing it. I guess it all makes sense now that we know she lived in her car."

"Yes," Tricia agreed. "Did you get a chance to talk to her?"

"Not really. Just to yell 'Get outta here!' and then she ran." He gave a stifled laugh. "Well, maybe not ran—sort of walked fast. She was kind of old."

Older than him, that was for sure.

"Hey, what do you think about Russ Smith quitting as Chamber president?" Terry asked.

"That we're going to have to call an election."

"I voted for you last time, Tricia. I'd do it again. Russ

sure has left one hell of a mess to clean up, but I'm sure you can handle it."

"Thanks for the kind words, Terry, but I'm not sure I want to run again."

"It would be a shame if you didn't. If you're half the president your sister was, the Chamber would be back in shape in no time."

"I'm flattered you think so."

"I'd better get to my store. Those comics aren't going to jump into the bags themselves." He quickened his pace and charged off.

"Have a great day," Tricia called, and gave Terry a wave as he turned back to acknowledge her good wishes.

Speaking to Marie and Terry was a good start. All Tricia needed now were a few more corroborating stories and she'd go to Chief Baker to tell him her theory—and hope he didn't throw her out of his office.

She was about to start off again when she saw a familiar corroded pickup pull into the municipal lot. She walked slowly down the sidewalk and paused while its owner parked and got out of the vehicle. "Hey, Russ!" she called, and waved.

Russ Smith glared at Tricia as she rushed to intercept him when he got to the sidewalk.

"I hear congratulations are in order," she said brightly.

"What for?"

"Selling your newspaper."

He shrugged. "Oh, that. Yeah. I'm glad it went fast. I'm sure your *boyfriend*"—he emphasized the word so it sounded like an insult—"will do a great job." He started off with long strides, and Tricia had a hard time keeping up with him.

"I don't doubt it," Tricia said.

"As soon as the lawyers draw up the papers, I'm shaking the dust of this crummy little town off my shoes."

"Village," Tricia corrected automatically. She decided to push him. "It must have broken your heart when Nikki came and took little Russell back with her to California the other day."

"Eh, not so much," Russ said flatly, paused at the corner to look both ways, and crossed against the light, with Tricia right on his heels.

"What do you mean?" she asked innocently.

"C'mon, Trish. You always knew I wasn't interested in being a parent—just like you."

"I don't think we ever addressed the subject."

"Maybe not, but you let it be known you were a career woman."

"At one time I thought Nikki felt the same."

"Once upon a time," Russ said bitterly. "And now she's apparently returned to that stance."

Tricia didn't want to continue that conversation and changed tack. "Where will you go?"

"I dunno. I was thinking about the West Coast. The idea of living without snow and ice appeals to me."

That statement sent a chill through Tricia. After Russ had dumped her more than five years before, he had a change of heart and decided he'd take Tricia back. (As if!) When she rebuffed his attentions, Russ stalked her. Did he intend to travel to Los Angeles to stalk his almost ex-wife, too?

"I . . . I wondered if you ever met Susan Morris?"

"No," Russ said flatly.

"I understand she had a habit of dumping her trash in the dumpsters in the alleys behind Main Street late at night."

"So? How would I know about that? I close my shop at five every day, and I haven't worked a Saturday here in months."

"So I heard."

He stopped short, his expression conveying his annoyance. "From who?"

"You. You sent out an email to every Chamber member about its revised hours."

The taut muscles in his face relaxed. "Oh, yeah. I forgot about that."

They crossed Hickory Street, still heading north.

"What are you going to do about the Chamber?" Tricia asked.

"Resign. Ha! Now's your chance to get to run it *your* way."

"I don't know that I want the responsibility right now."

"You'd be a shoo-in," he assured her, without breaking stride.

"Maybe."

They reached the offices of the *Stoneham Weekly News*, and Russ reached into his jeans pocket to retrieve a set of keys. "I'd love to stand here and chat with you all day," he said with a sarcastic lilt to his voice, "but I've got a lot of stuff to clear up before I can hand the business over to Cambridge."

"Sure thing. I guess I'll see you at the next Chamber meeting."

"I guess," he said, and unlocked the door, went inside, and shut the door behind him without even a good-bye.

"Jerk," she muttered. Tricia wasted no time and turned to head back down the sidewalk. She had a feeling no one in the village would be sad to see the last of Russ Smith.

TWENTY-FOUR

Tricia made several more circuits up and down Stoneham's main drag, but no one she encountered had seen anything suspicious when it came to the dumpsters or garbage totes in the alleys behind Main Street. Maybe her theory was ridiculous. So far, not many people she'd come across had even known Susan, and those who'd run into her didn't seem to think she had any enemies. It was entirely possible that she was a victim chosen at random. Tricia remembered a news story concerning a man who walked into the Mall of America bent on killing someone—anyone—and had chosen a small boy to throw over a third-floor balcony. She remembered seeing pictures of the tow-headed tyke and considered the terror his mother must have felt when she witnessed that terrible crime. The boy lived but endured many long months of surgeries and rehabilitation. Was Susan's death just a random killing by some thrill-seeking degenerate? The idea repelled her.

Reentering Haven't Got a Clue, Tricia hung up her jacket and looked around her store. She could make a fresh pot of coffee, but it would be nearly an hour before Pixie arrived for work, and possibly longer until their first customers of the day arrived. She was about to head down to her basement office when the store's vintage phone rang. Sometimes customers called early just to learn the store's hours or ask if an order had arrived. She usually let the calls go to voice mail but instead decided to pick up the receiver.

"Haven't Got a Clue; this is Tricia. How can I help you?"

"Hi, Tricia."

"Mary, is that you?" Mary was Mary Fairchild from the By Hook or By Book craft-oriented shop just down the street.

"Yes. I just heard that Russ Smith is calling it quits as Chamber president."

"That's right."

"Then let me be the first to encourage you to take the job. You should have won last year. I still haven't gotten over my guilt for not voting for you in the first place."

"You had your reasons," Tricia reminded her.

"This has been a horrible year with Russ as the Chamber head. Even your cat could have done a better job."

Tricia wasn't sure if she should be flattered or insulted by that remark.

"Please consider it," Mary said with what sounded like heartfelt sincerity. "Stoneham's business community has suffered a terrible blow because of Russ's bad decisions. In my eyes, you're the perfect candidate."

"Thanks for your vote of confidence. It's a big decision. I'll definitely give it some serious consideration."

"Thanks, Tricia. By the way, I wanted to compliment you on that wonderful interview you did with the cable company a couple of weeks ago. I had no idea your collection of valuable vintage mysteries was so extensive. And it was terrific PR for the whole village as well."

"I learned a lot from the way Angelica promoted Stoneham as Booktown."

"See? You would make a wonderful Chamber president!"

Maybe she would at that. "Thank you again for saying so."

"Well, we both have businesses to run. I'd better let you go."

"Thanks, Mary. We'll talk again soon." Tricia hung up the phone. As she set down the receiver, she wondered if it would be better to have her conversation with Baker via the phone than in person. For one thing, it was less likely to be overheard.

She dialed his personal number and was rewarded with him responding in only two rings.

"Tricia, to what do I owe the pleasure?" Wow. He actually sounded affable. Tricia had grown to be wary of his moods.

"First of all, I wanted to ask your opinion on a theory I have about Susan Morris's death."

"Aw, come on," he said, as though put upon. So much for his good disposition.

"I've been right in the past," she reminded him.

"Lucky," he corrected. "You've been lucky."

"Luck, skill, deductive reasoning . . . would you at least do me the courtesy of listening to what I have to say?"

He sighed. "All right. Go ahead."

"Okay, this is going to sound far-fetched—"

"Doesn't it always," he muttered under his breath.

"—but I don't believe Susan Morris's death was premeditated."

"Why do you say that?" Did he actually sound interested?

"She was a nice woman. People liked her. She appears to have had just one bad habit."

"And what was that?"

"Throwing her trash in the dumpsters of the businesses along Main Street."

Baker was silent for a long moment. "Is that it?" he asked, his voice flat.

"Yes."

Another long silence ensued.

"Aren't you going to ask me if there's more?" Tricia said.

"Is there more?" Now Baker sounded really bored.

"It wasn't just the usual garbage she was throwing away." She waited and, when he didn't press her for more, spoke again. "She was throwing away the contents of her slop bucket."

Eventually, Baker let out a heavy sigh. "And you know this because?"

"Because I asked around. Shawn at the Dog-Eared Page chased her off, as did Terry at the comic-book store."

"What other evidence do you have?"

"Well . . . that's about it," Tricia admitted. "I did speak with a few others who live and work on Main Street, but most of the businesses are closed after five or six o'clock. Susan made her clandestine garbage runs late in the evening."

"And you think someone killed her because she was throwing away her . . . crap . . . in their garbage?"

"I didn't say it was a logical reaction, but what if somebody just snapped?"

Again Baker sighed. "I just don't see that happening."

If she was honest, Tricia didn't really think he would.

"Will you at least consider it as a possible motive for her murder?"

"Uh . . . well, it's on the table" was apparently going to be his best reply. "Anything else?"

"I understand you arrested Joe King yesterday morning."

"I did. One of my officers and I went out to talk to him, and he got a little upset at my line of questioning—so much so that he took a swing at me."

"Did you provoke him?" Tricia asked.

"Of course I didn't," Baker said, sounding affronted.

"Just asking," Tricia said diffidently. "What was his explanation for lying about how he obtained Susan's earring—especially since Susan's daughter didn't think she'd ever pick up a male hitchhiker?"

"He swears she did pick him up and take him to McDonald's. They sat inside and ate Big Macs, fries, and Cokes. Afterward, she offered to drive him back to the camp. That's when he said he found the earring. He picked it up off the passenger-side floor and stuffed it in his pocket. It had no intrinsic value."

Did Baker feel as apathetic about the ring he'd given to Diana or did he consider that collateral damage?

"King didn't want to get nailed for such a petty theft," Baker continued. "You said yourself, you had to dig to get the other earring out of the glove box, which means Ms. Morris probably had no idea where it was."

"Yes, but ask yourself this: Why would a man who was dishonorably discharged want to celebrate his time in the Navy?"

"Who knows why people do the stuff they do?"

"And you aren't just the least bit interested?" Tricia challenged.

"I don't think King killed Susan Morris. Is the guy a creep and a thief? Yeah, but that earring had no real value."

Maybe not to Joe King, but it meant the world to Susan Morris.

"So, where is he now?" Tricia asked.

"I asked Kimberly Herbert if she wanted to press charges. She just wanted the earring back. King came up with it, and I let him go."

"That doesn't answer my question."

Baker shrugged. "He left the station on foot."

"And you have no idea where he went?"

"No. Is that all?" Baker asked, sounding bored once again.

"No. Yesterday morning, after you arrested and hauled King away, a pickup towing a Bobcat arrived at the homeless camp. They destroyed it and chased off everyone who'd been living there."

"And?"

"Were you responsible for that?" Tricia demanded.

"No," he said wearily. "But I did know it was going to happen."

"And you didn't warn the men living there? The people who did that—"

"Own the land they were squatting on," Baker pointed out patiently. "They had every right to demand they leave."

"Those men had little more than the shirts on their backs. They were run off with nowhere to go and nothing to their names."

"Why do you care so much?" Baker asked.

"Because I've got more than an ounce of compassion in me," Tricia declared.

"Yes," Baker admitted. "You've always had a big heart and fought for those who have no voice."

Tricia blinked, taken aback by his admission. So he *had* noticed.

"I was lucky enough to find temporary homes for two of the men, but what of the other ten or so?" she demanded.

"They'll just have to make do. Isn't that what we've both done when life handed us lemons?"

"Except that we have money and better life skills to deal with those kinds of situations."

"You're right," he said affably. "You're absolutely right."

He was agreeing with her? This was a new side of him. No, not new . . . a side she'd known but hadn't seen for quite a while. The man had always been a little too cynical, no doubt because of his line of work. And yet she'd seen flashes of kindness from him. She'd thought it was long gone, but now . . .

But she wasn't finished. "Did Joe King know there was no encampment to go back to?"

"It may have come up in conversation."

Tricia shook her head. Where would King go? Would he hang around the village? Baker didn't tolerate panhandlers, and Stoneham had no homeless shelter. Would he have hitched a ride to Nashua or maybe Concord to find a place, or maybe crash with friends? Tricia hadn't been impressed by the man, but she did feel sorry for his circumstances. And she wondered if she should express sympathy for another situation.

"I heard that your wedding was called off."

"*I* called it off," Baker admitted, sounding just a little sheepish.

"And why was that?"

"Because . . ." He was silent for a long moment. "Because I knew that in the end it wasn't going to work out. I wanted it to work, but I came to the realization that Diana and I just didn't mesh like . . ."

Like who? Like he and his ex-wife had meshed, or like he and Tricia had? She'd called it quits when she thought he was unable to make a commitment, and now he'd proven it once again by abandoning the latest woman in his life.

"Well, I'm sorry you couldn't make it work," Tricia said contritely.

"You have no idea what it took for me to admit it. But calling it quits in a year or two would have been a whole lot harder."

Tricia didn't doubt that for a moment. She shook her head, unwilling to pursue that topic further. "Will you at least consider my theory about Susan Morris's death?"

"I don't know how I'd be able to prove it."

"Talk to the people on Main Street. At least two of them had similar stories. Maybe more would, too."

"Okay," he said, his tone resigned.

"Thank you."

"You're welcome."

Now, how could Tricia end the conversation?

"I'd better let you go. You or your men have a lot of questions to ask the business owners along Main Street."

"So we do."

"I'll talk to you later," Tricia said, realizing just how lame that statement sounded.

"I'm sure," Baker said quietly.

"Good-bye."

"Bye," Baker said, and ended the call.

Tricia set the heavy receiver back down and frowned. Why had her conversation with a man who'd once been her lover leave her feeling so discombobulated?

She wasn't sure . . . and for some reason it really bothered her.

TWENTY-FIVE

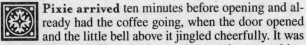**Pixie arrived** ten minutes before opening and already had the coffee going, when the door opened and the little bell above it jingled cheerfully. It was Mr. Everett's day off, so Tricia wasn't expecting to see him. Yet, right on time, he walked through the door to Haven't Got a Clue.

"Did you forget what day it is?" Tricia asked, giving the old man a smile.

Mr. Everett shook his head. "I've just come from your sister's. Sarge and I had a lovely walk. It's a beautiful morning. It's supposed to hit eighty degrees later this afternoon."

"I didn't have a chance to check the weather report, but that sounds fine to me." Especially after the last few days filled with rain and gloom.

"I'll second that," Pixie agreed. "Got time for a cup of joe, Mr. E?"

"I was hoping you'd ask."

Pixie nodded and selected mugs for all three of them from the shelf below the beverage station while Tricia led the way to the reader's nook, with Mr. Everett following. They took their usual seats, and Mr. Everett unbuttoned his cardigan sweater before sitting down. "I doubt I'll be needing this in an hour or so."

Tricia wondered if she should turn on the store's air-conditioning. If so, she wouldn't bother to change her pink sweater set.

Pixie served the coffee and sat down, too. "So you just dropped in to say hello?" she asked.

"That and to deliver a message."

"From whom?" Tricia asked.

"Grace. She asked me to tell you that Ms. Morris *had* contacted our foundation for financial assistance."

"When was this?"

"Only a week before her death. We have so many applicants that it hadn't been addressed before she died," he said sadly.

"What did she ask for?" Pixie asked.

"First and last month's rent for an apartment in a complex on the outskirts of town near the highway. I believe it was the same place where your husband lived before your marriage," he told Pixie.

"Oh, yeah, I remember that dump," she groused, and took a sip from her cup.

Tricia, too, remembered the cluster of shabby buildings, as she'd visited it once the summer before. "So she wasn't all that happy about living in her car after all?"

"There was no mention of that in her application. But she did say that she had a job and was sure she would be able to make the monthly payments. She just needed a little help with the up-front costs."

"How sad," Tricia said, and shook her head. "Would Grace and the foundation board have approved her request?"

"Undoubtedly. It was, after all, one of the more modest appeals we receive."

"I don't think Susan mentioned that to her daughter," Tricia said. "It might have given Kimberly some peace of mind."

"Maybe she didn't want her daughter to get her hopes up in case it didn't happen," Pixie guessed.

Tricia realized that Susan's memorial service was set for

the following day, and her sadness over the situation increased that much more.

"Grace invites you to call her if you want more information," Mr. Everett said. "Of course, she doesn't usually talk publicly about the applications the foundation receives, but she knew you two had a special interest in Ms. Morris—or Radnor—due to the circumstances of her body being discovered behind your store." Mr. Everett shook his head. "So many terrible things have happened in our village these last few years."

"That's true," Tricia agreed, "but there have been many good things, too."

"Yes. Many people have jobs—"

"Like us," Pixie agreed.

"—and the booksellers brought in tourists and encouraged reading at a time when far too many people are more focused on their cell phones," Mr. Everett noted.

"And, thanks to Nigela Ricita Associates, the whole village looks fresh and sweet," Pixie pointed out.

"Yes," Tricia agreed. "We may yet win the title of Prettiest Village in New Hampshire."

A customer came through the door, and Pixie shot to her feet to wait on her.

Mr. Everett sipped his coffee. "I may be back later, as I've promised your sister I would take dear little Sarge out for another walk after lunch with Grace. We're going to the Brookview Inn."

"For a celebration?" Tricia asked.

A rosy blush moved up Mr. Everett's neck to color his cheeks. "Every day with Grace is a celebration," he admitted shyly.

Tricia smiled. "I don't doubt that."

Mr. Everett drained his cup and stood. "I'd best be going and let you two ladies take care of our customers. And I do hope this wonderful weather brings them out in droves."

Tricia laughed. "So do I. Here, let me take your cup."

"Oh, no. I can wash it myself."

"Today you're not an employee; you're our guest," Tricia told him.

Mr. Everett nodded and relinquished his mug. "Thank you. I'll see you later."

"I'll look forward to it."

Tricia watched him go and carried his cup and her own to the washroom. As she swabbed the mugs with the Haven't Got a Clue logo on them with soap and a paper towel, Tricia wondered if she should give Grace a call. But then, what else could she possibly tell her that Mr. Everett hadn't already conveyed? And, honestly, nothing on the application could have anything to do with Susan Morris's death.

Perhaps it was time to stop asking questions about the woman and do as Angelica had suggested: let the Stoneham Police Department handle the investigation. Tricia had done what she could to bring what she knew to light. It was up to the cops to figure out what happened to Susan . . . if they bothered. Susan wasn't a resident of the village—in fact, she was considered a transient—but she'd apparently wanted to be a part of village life. Getting a job and then asking for help to find her a place to live nearby was proof of that. And someone had taken all that away from her. Someone who could still be in the village.

The thought made Tricia feel uneasy—very uneasy.

It was nearly noon, and Tricia was ringing up a customer's purchases, with another person waiting in line, when Pixie tapped her on the shoulder. "I can take over."

"Not to worry. I'm okay," Tricia assured her.

"Sure, but you're supposed to meet Ginny for lunch in about a minute."

"Oh, my goodness! I lost track of time," Tricia said as she made change for her customer and then thanked her for shopping at Haven't Got a Clue.

Pixie grasped Tricia by the shoulders and pushed her away from the cash register. "See you in an hour—if not sooner."

Tricia grabbed her purse and phone, then scooted around

the cash desk and out the door, heading for Booked for Lunch for her usual Thursday lunch with Ginny.

Of course, as usual, Ginny was late, and when she entered Booked for Lunch, Tricia noticed she'd lost the usual bounce in her step. She slid onto the bench seat across from Tricia, looking like she'd lost her best friend.

"Are you okay?" Tricia asked.

"Yeah, I'm just fine," she said sourly. "And pregnant."

"So I heard," Tricia said. "I'm sorry it had to happen at an inconvenient time."

"Yeah, well, Angelica has a lot of ideas on how to make it work."

"And how do you feel about that?"

"Grateful," Ginny said sincerely. "I've heard terrible stories about nasty mothers-in-law, but Angelica couldn't have been more supportive. She made me feel like we could actually make this work."

"I'm glad to hear that," Tricia said, proud of her sister.

Ginny ducked her head. "And I'm sorry I bit your head off on Sunday at our family dinner. I was just feeling . . ."

"Overwhelmed at the prospect of having another baby?"

"Yeah. Your heart was in the right place when you wanted to find a loving home for little Russell."

"Well, you don't have to worry about it now. Nikki came back to Stoneham, picked him up, and took him to California to be with her."

Ginny let out what could only be taken as a sigh of relief. "I'm glad to hear that. You know, for a long time I got the feeling that Nikki was jealous of me. I had a great job and a loving, supportive husband, and she was saddled with debt and a child her rat of a husband didn't want while struggling to keep her bakery afloat. But then she won that baking contest and seems to be on top of the world, and now I find myself envying her."

"Why?" Tricia asked.

"She's got her business—unless she decides to sell it. She's in California, where it will be warm all winter, and if the rumors are true, she's going to be a famous TV chef."

"Fame can't buy happiness," Tricia said.

"You don't think she's happy?"

Tricia shook her head. "She talks a good game, but now she's juggling even bigger problems. Okay, maybe that's just my opinion, but when we spoke the other day, she seemed pretty bitter to me."

Ginny nodded, looking thoughtful. "I guess I need an attitude adjustment."

"You'll get there," Tricia said, hoping she sounded encouraging.

"Yeah. I know I'll love this baby just as much as I love Sofia. It's just . . ."

"The timing," Tricia supplied.

"Yeah."

The café's door opened, and Tricia noticed Patti Perkins enter and make her way to an empty seat at the counter. Patti saw her and gave a rather enthusiastic wave before sitting down on one of the red Naugahyde-covered stools.

Molly, the waitress, stopped by their table. "What can I get you girls today?" she asked brightly.

"I'm afraid I can't stay," Ginny said apologetically. "I'm working on an important proposal for the firm that has the potential to make Stoneham *the* tourist attraction of southern New Hampshire next summer. I'm going to have to ask for my order to go."

"Oh, I'm sorry to hear that," Tricia said.

"We've still got at least five or ten minutes to talk," Ginny offered.

Tricia forced a smile. "Well, we'll just have to make the most of it."

Ginny ordered a club sandwich, and Tricia ordered her old standby, a tuna plate—also to go. If she was going to have to eat her lunch by herself, she would rather do it in her own home, especially since she hadn't brought along a book to read. Besides, she'd never felt comfortable eating alone in a restaurant.

Once Molly had retreated, Tricia said, "Tell me about the changes you and Antonio are going to make to your home."

Ginny immediately brightened. "I love my little cottage in the woods, but it's way too small for a family of four. I had some thoughts about how to expand it, but Angelica must have been thinking about it for quite a while, because everything she suggested just rang a bell with me. I admit it, I'm not as much of a homebody as I could be, but she's definitely got a vision of what we could do that actually makes me excited for the future."

"I'm so glad to hear that," Tricia said sincerely.

Ginny launched into the changes they were considering. It would be a big renovation, which would add a gourmet kitchen on the ground floor and a master suite above. The changes would be so great that the family would probably have to vacate the property for several months to make it happen, but Ginny didn't seem to be deterred by the possibility and looked forward to choosing the fixtures, appliances, and finishes.

Molly arrived with their lunches packed in environmentally safe packaging and, as usual, there was no bill for them to pay. Angelica was their benevolent benefactor.

Ginny got up first. "I'm so glad we got to talk today, Tricia. I really needed to clear the air and now I feel so much better."

Tricia rose and gave her former assistant and now niece by marriage a heartfelt hug. "It'll work out. I know it will."

Ginny held on tightly, and when she pulled away, there were tears in her eyes. In what seemed like an impulsive gesture, she gave Tricia a quick kiss on the cheek, grabbed her to-go box, fled with a "See you on Sunday," and was gone.

Tricia watched Ginny leave before she left a tip for Molly and picked up her order. On the way out, she stopped at the counter. "Hey, Patti, how's it going?"

Patti turned a broad smile toward her. "Much better since I found out I'll get to keep my job. Was it you who convinced Mr. Cambridge to keep us on?"

"From what I understand, it was *you* who sold him on keeping the paper's staff."

Patti laughed. "Staff? Yeah. Well, I guess you could call

us that. Did I mention that I'm the designated toilet cleaner—and it isn't me and Ginger who mess it up."

Meow!

"I'm excited about the future," Patti exclaimed, and grinned. "I haven't felt that way in quite a while."

"What do you mean?"

"It feels like we've been surviving on a wing and prayer for way too long. And, to employ another cliché, Mr. Cambridge appears to be a breath of fresh air."

"In what way?"

"Let's just say that I haven't always agreed with how things have been run at the paper."

"Oh?" Tricia asked, wide-eyed.

Patti lowered her voice. "Sometimes it seems like . . ." But then she didn't elaborate. "I have a feeling that in the near future I'm going to once again look forward to going to work," she said hopefully, her eyes shining.

What was it Patti wasn't saying about having Russ as a boss?

Molly arrived with a salad plate and what looked like Thousand Island dressing in a little paper cup on the side and plunked it down in front of Patti. "Eat hearty."

Patti gave her a smile and picked up her fork.

"Have a good lunch," Tricia wished her, and headed for the door.

It looked like a future without Russ Smith in it was going to be a pleasure for many people in Stoneham. Did it make Tricia a bad person to find herself included in those ranks?

TWENTY-SIX

The balmy breezes seemed to have brought out mystery readers in droves. Tricia and Pixie waited on a rush of customers until late in the afternoon. As always, such an influx of customers put them in high spirits.

"Can you believe it?" Pixie asked, grinning. "We didn't see this many warm bodies in one afternoon during the height of summer."

"This week's bottom line will be amazing," Tricia agreed.

The door opened and the little bell rang once again, heralding yet another person. Tricia never tired of hearing that sweet sound.

The brunette woman who entered was a stunner dressed in a navy business suit with a white blouse and stilettos that might one day put her in line for the same bunion surgery Angelica had recently undergone. She was at least a decade younger than Tricia and held a dark briefcase. Everything about her shouted *Power!* She eyed Pixie, seemed to dismiss her, and then zeroed in on Tricia, walking with purpose toward her.

"Hi. Welcome to Haven't Got a Clue. I'm the owner, Tricia Miles. How can I help you?"

The woman stopped, standing just a little too close to Tricia. "I'm Diana Porter."

"Nice to meet you."

The woman eyed her critically. "Is it?"

Tricia wasn't sure how to answer that question. "Uh, what kind of mysteries do you like to read?"

"None at all. But I am interested in solving one particular mystery," the woman continued.

Something about this person seemed off. It took a moment for the woman's name to register, and when it did, Tricia's stomach did a somersault "Oh, you're—"

"Grant Baker's *former* fiancée."

Tricia wasn't sure how she was supposed to react to that pronouncement. And for some reason a sense of guilt washed over her. "I'm . . . I'm so sorry to hear that your wedding has been postponed."

"It wasn't postponed. It was canceled," Diana said, her stare pointed.

"Again, I'm so . . . so sorry."

"And you should be."

Tricia took a step back. "I beg your pardon."

Diana's eyes blazed. "It's because of *you* I've been jilted."

"What gave you that idea?" Tricia asked, confused.

"Grant told me so. Apparently, he carries a torch for you."

Tricia felt like she'd been punched in the gut. And then she laughed. "You've got to be kidding."

But Diana's expression only hardened. "No, I'm not."

"I don't know if Grant mentioned it to you, but I happen to be in a stable relationship." Okay, maybe *stable* was the wrong word, but Tricia definitely had more feelings for Marshall than she did for Baker.

Didn't she?

"He did tell me that, but I wanted to hear it from you," Diana stated.

Tricia noticed Pixie had moved aside but was back to her old habit of eavesdropping. Caught, Pixie looked away and retreated behind one of the store's taller bookshelves.

Tricia folded her arms across her chest. "Grant and I split

up because he was unwilling to make a serious commitment to me. It sounds like he's making me the scapegoat for refusing to make such a commitment to you, too. I'm only sorry that you were so far into your wedding plans before he spoke to you honestly," she said rather defiantly.

Diana seemed to ponder Tricia's explanation. Then she shook her head. "'Doth thou protest too much?'" she asked, misquoting Shakespeare.

"No!" Tricia protested. "Believe me, the last person I want to be with is Grant Baker."

"So you say. But he made it clear to me that he has more affection for you than for me."

"Aye, there's the rub," Tricia commented. "Affection—not love. And I don't love him."

"But he says *he* loves *you*."

"Well, if he does, he sure hasn't shown it." Tricia let out an exasperated breath. "Look, I'm sorry you're going through this, but since I broke up with Grant, I haven't encouraged his attention. For heaven's sake, when we speak, he's usually rude to me, and I have no desire to deal with that in any kind of a relationship." Not when she had a good old dependable (if somewhat boring) connection with Marshall.

Again Tricia's insides wobbled. Good grief, *was* she still attracted to Grant Baker?

No. No. No. No. No!

Diana's hard glare was still upon Tricia.

"I'm sorry Grant broke your heart, but I had nothing to do with it."

Diana seemed to deflate, and suddenly she didn't seem like the hardened, high-powered attorney who'd walked in the door just minutes before. "I had the perfect dress and everything," she muttered.

"You must be devastated," Tricia said kindly.

"Yeah, well . . . I'll get over it. There are other fish in the sea."

"There you go," Tricia encouraged.

Diana studied Tricia in what seemed like minute detail. "I don't see the appeal," she said at last.

"Appeal?"

"Why he'd prefer you to me."

"Do you ever fight?"

Diana smirked. "With boxing gloves?"

Tricia glowered at her.

"No," Diana answered. "We've never had an argument or even much of a disagreement." She looked thoughtful. Was it Tricia's feistiness he'd admired and found lacking in the beautiful Diana?

"He's been rude to you?" she asked.

"Off and on ever since the day we met five years ago." The fact that he'd suspected her of murder on more than one occasion had never helped cement their relationship, either.

Diana shook her head. "I came in here ready to do battle with you over Grant, but now . . ." She sighed. "I'd better get going. I wish I could say it was nice to meet you, but I can't. In fact, I wish I'd never heard your name." And with that, she turned and headed for the door.

Tricia moved to the store's big display window and watched Diana stalk off up the street toward the municipal parking lot. A movement to Tricia's right signaled that Pixie had joined her.

"Wow."

Yeah. Wow.

Angelica stood at her kitchen's breakfast bar with her knee planted on her little scooter, stirring a fresh pitcher of martinis. "You mean she actually confronted you?"

Tricia nodded, eyeing the empty glasses, eager to take the first sip of her drink. After the day she'd had, she deserved it. "I have to admit, I felt sorry for her. The fact that they never had a disagreement spelled doom for their relationship. If there's one thing Grant Baker loves to do, it's spar with an opponent."

"Is that how you saw your relationship with him?"

"Let's just say the make-up sex was rather spectacular," Tricia said and winked, smiling.

Angelica positively grinned. "Why, you naughty girl, you."

Tricia's smile soon faded. "Yes, well, unfortunately, our discussion has me seriously questioning my relationship with Marshall."

Angelica's mouth drooped. "Oh, don't tell me you're going to dump him over this."

"I have no plans to drop him. But I wonder if we had a little more conflict between us if it would make our time together just a little more interesting."

"Be careful what you wish for," Angelica warned. She placed the pitcher on a tray along with the glasses and a pot full of salsa and a bowl of taco chips.

"Is that spicy sauce?" Tricia asked.

"Medium. I felt like cooking tonight, so I had Tommy bring over everything we need for chicken quesadillas."

"Is this the first time you've cooked since your surgery?"

"Other than microwaving something, yes. I should have been using my little scooter more. It's really very handy. I just wish it didn't look so dorky."

"I think it looks cute," Tricia said.

"Yes, well, since our adventures yesterday and then being stuck here all day, I've decided I've got to get out more, and if I have to look like a dork to do so, then so be it." She shoved the tray in Tricia's direction. "It's such a lovely evening: Why don't we go sit on the balcony? I've missed it during the past few days."

"Lead the way," Tricia said, and picked up the tray to follow.

Once they'd taken their usual positions outside, with Sarge sitting on the concrete floor between them, Angelica poured the drinks and they clinked glasses. "To this Diana person finding a better man."

"I'll drink to that," Tricia said. She took a sip, and the taste of the gin on her tongue was an effective—and instantaneous—muscle relaxant.

"What are you going to do about Grant?" Angelica asked.

Tricia focused on her sister's face. "What do you mean?"

"You have to confront him."

Tricia shrugged, raising her hands in a gesture of dismay. "Why?"

"Because he's professed his love for you. Don't you think you should do something about it?"

"Like what? He hasn't talked to me about his feelings."

"But according to Diana he felt strongly enough to call off their wedding."

"So what."

"Well, because," Angelica insisted, exasperated.

"No. That's not a conversation I want to have with him. Not now. Not ever. He blew his chance years ago. We're done."

"But why not at least talk to him?" Angelica persisted.

"Because he's like a little kid. He wants something while he wants it. Then, when he gets it, he tosses it aside."

"Like Sofia playing with the box instead of the toy that came in it?"

"Exactly," Tricia agreed.

They sipped their drinks in silence for a long moment. Angelica took in a deep breath and then exhaled. "Isn't this weather heavenly?"

Tricia was happy she'd dropped the previous subject. "I wonder how many more days like this we'll have," she said.

"Global warming is terrible in the long run, but on a day like this . . ." Angelica said wistfully.

"I dread the winter," Tricia said with despair.

"Why?"

"Because we have long days with no customers and high heating bills. It costs a lot to have two employees, too."

"But you wouldn't get rid of either of them, would you?" Angelica asked sharply.

"Of course not, although I'm sure Mr. Everett would come in for free. He doesn't need the money, but he loves the store, the customers, and feeling useful."

"There's a lot to say for feeling useful."

"Speaking of which, did Antonio call to say how Hank Curtis made out on his first day at the inn?"

"Yes, he did. And he spoke of him in glowing terms. Already Hank has been delving into the way things are done at the Brookview and has made some very good suggestions. If he can run things more efficiently and cost-effectively, I'm in. But I don't want to lose personnel. If his changes give our people time on their hands, then he'll need to find things for them to do to fill it."

"And Antonio is okay with all that?"

"Okay? He's over the moon. One thing I can say about my boy is that he has no ego. Whatever is best for the business he's in favor of. And, of course, he's been looking forward to expanding in other directions. If Hank works out, he can do whatever he wants with our brand. The sky's the limit."

"I'm glad to hear that." Tricia sipped her martini. "I had lunch with Ginny today, and she loved all of your suggestions on how to renovate their home."

"I'm so glad. I had more than one really evil mother-in-law, and I always told myself that I would never be that woman."

"I don't think you have to worry. From what I've observed, Ginny considers you her second mom."

Angelica's mouth trembled, and her eyes filled with tears. "You can't imagine how happy you just made me."

Tricia grinned. "Glad to oblige." But then her smile faded. "This afternoon, between customers, I started thinking about it and I've decided to give up looking into Susan Morris's death."

"Why's that?" Angelica asked.

"It doesn't seem to be going anywhere. I'm truly convinced that her death was just some kind of random act."

"What about your theory?" Angelica asked.

"I suppose it *is* rather far-fetched."

"Yes, I suppose it is," Angelica acknowledged. "But it's not like you to give up."

"It might also be that I'm tired of being dismissed by Chief Baker. You were right. I should just let him try to figure out who's responsible for Susan's death."

Angelica nodded. "I can't say I blame you."

"And yet . . ." Tricia began. She wasn't sure exactly how she felt about abandoning her own search for the truth. She had not known the dead woman—she'd never even laid eyes on her—but the fact that Susan had been discarded in her dumpster like so much refuse ate at Tricia's soul. Nobody deserved that kind of treatment, in life or in death.

"Yet what?"

"Nothing."

"If you say so." Angelica picked up one of the chips and plunged it into the salsa, spilling a little on the table. "Oh, dear. We forgot napkins."

"I'll go get some," Tricia volunteered and got up from her chair.

"Bring Sarge a biscuit, too, will you?" Angelica called.

"Will do."

Tricia went in through the sliding glass door and into the kitchen.

Was Grant really mooning over her? If so, was he likely to give her theory on Susan's murder another chance or would he just dismiss her again?

She'd lost count of how many times he'd rejected her ideas and looked at her with downright suspicion. That was no basis for a relationship and another reason why she'd called theirs off in the first place.

No. She was not going to give the man another chance.

Not now, not ever.

And yet . . .

TWENTY-SEVEN

 Tricia ended up staying far longer at Angelica's place than she usually did. The evening was so balmy, after dinner they went back outside, sat on the balcony, and looked at the stars, discussing Ginny's renovation and a host of other topics. It was almost eleven when Tricia returned home and received a thorough scolding from her cat, whom she fed before picking up her cell phone and then leading the way to her third-floor suite. The air in the bedroom felt stuffy, so Tricia put the phone on her nightstand and opened the window that overlooked the alley to let in some fresh air. After getting ready for bed, she sat up for an hour to read. But when she turned out the light, she didn't feel at all sleepy. She had too much on her mind.

One person, actually.

Was she still attracted to Grant Baker? She didn't think so. Did they have unfinished business? Not really. She'd made her feelings quite clear to him when they'd broken up. He'd done likewise.

Tricia rearranged the pillow behind her neck, then gave it a punch.

How dare Baker use her as an excuse to dump his fiancée! He probably didn't have any feelings for Tricia at all—except for contempt when she shared her ideas about Susan

Morris's death. It was just an excuse for his usual problem when it came to relationships: failure to launch.

Tricia tried thinking of other things, counting proverbial sheep, and listing her favorite mysteries in alphabetical order by author, and ended up tossing and turning for more than half an hour. Maybe she should get up and get a mug of warm milk. Sometimes that did the trick.

A draft made her shiver. It was then that Tricia remembered that she'd left the bedroom window open. The air had cooled, and she wondered if she should shut it, when she heard a loud rattling noise. She'd heard it only a couple of times before, so it took her a few moments to identify it: the sound of the metal fire escape ladder being released. Someone was trying for a third time to break into her store—only . . . the store was on the first floor, not the second or third floor. Someone was about to try to enter her home!

Tricia threw back the covers and leapt out of bed, grabbing her cell phone. Why hadn't the security system kicked off? She stabbed the screen to awaken it to call 911, but it remained dark. Rats! She'd forgotten to charge it before going to bed. She tossed it aside and raced to the window to look out and saw the would-be intruder standing on her balcony below, trying to see through the sliding glass doors to the living room. He wore a hoodie that was tied around his chin.

"Hey!" Tricia hollered.

The thief looked up—an instinctual move—and Tricia recognized the face that peered up at her.

"Joe King! The cops are on their way."

He didn't seem to hear her and grabbed the door's handle, trying to rock it open. But Tricia's contractor had given her an additional—and cheap—security measure by painting a leftover piece of molding that she could place in the channel that allowed the door to open, wedging it shut. That said, she wasn't sure it would be enough of a deterrent.

"Open up!" King yelled.

Instead, Tricia slammed the window shut. King still had access to the metal ladder to the third floor. He grabbed one of the ceramic flowerpots from the balcony and began to climb.

The building's landline was located only in the shop and the basement. Tricia ran for the door and down the stairs to the second floor but paused when she heard the sound of breaking glass. King must have broken the bedroom window! He still had a screen to contend with, but Tricia knew she couldn't stop him from getting in.

She ran into the shop and picked up the vintage phone's heavy receiver, but it, too, was dead.

The sound of running footsteps on the stairs above stopped, and she ran around the big glass display case—the only place of concealment—grabbing the phone and pulling it down, and was grateful it had a long cord. If she had to, she could use the receiver as a weapon to try to knock him out—but was well aware that if he wrestled it from her, he could use it against her, too.

Crashes from the living room above seemed to rattle the entire building. What was he doing up there? What was he looking for?

"Where is it?" he hollered loud enough for Tricia to hear him.

She bit her lip and considered her options. She could unlock the door and run into the street, but she was wearing only her pajamas and was barefoot. And what would she do then? She could run next door, but her keys hung from a little rack in the kitchen above. Angelica's unhealed foot would keep her from getting down the stairs to open the Cookery's door for her. She could run to Marshall's, but he slept like the proverbial log. Would he even hear her ringing his doorbell? Lastly, she could run to the police station, which was a long three blocks away, but at this time of night would anyone be there to open the door for her?

The crashes from above had halted, but now there was another sound—of breaking glass. King had to be trashing the climate-controlled case that housed all Tricia's vintage mysteries, including the prize of her collection, *Graham's Magazine*, which contained Edgar Allan Poe's story "The

Murders in the Rue Morgue," considered to be the first modern detective story.

Tricia reached for the front window's blind cord and pulled it, letting in light from the streetlamps. The shops and offices along Main Street were all dark—except for one. Should she make a run for it?

Go! something inside her ordered, and she whipped around the display case straight for the door, fumbling with the lock to open it. The security system should have gone off—but it didn't, and Tricia took off, knowing that King might be only seconds behind her. She ran up the street, hoping no glass or stones littered the sidewalk, keeping close to the buildings until she hit the cross street. The village's only traffic light blinked yellow on Main Street and red for the cross street, and the road was devoid of any moving cars. She crossed it, heading for the lighted building and cursing her luck. It was the *Stoneham Weekly News*. Russ had told her he never worked late. Had he left the lights on before leaving the office that afternoon? She prayed that wasn't so and kept running.

"Hey!" came a voice from half a block away. It was King! He held what looked like a cloth sack—maybe a pillowcase—filled with something and was chasing her!

Despite the stitch in her side, Tricia made it to the newspaper office and pounded on the heavy plate glass door. "Russ! Let me in. Russ! There's a maniac after me."

The police station was still another two blocks away, and Tricia wasn't sure she could make it there before King caught up with her.

"Russ!" she practically howled.

Russ emerged from his office and hurried to open the door.

"Tricia—what's wrong?" he asked, pulling her into the reception room and slamming the door shut and locking it behind her. "Why are you running around the village in your pajamas?"

"There's a . . . robber . . . one of the homeless vets. He

broke into my apartment. He must have been after my vintage mysteries."

Russ nodded in understanding. "I saw that interview you did on TV. Not a smart move, letting thieves know where you hide your goodies."

"But I didn't say they were in my apartment."

And then Tricia remembered what Mr. Everett had told her days before: that a man had come into the store, bought nothing, and spent a long time looking the place over. His only descriptor was that the man was wearing a sweat jacket.

"Call the police, will you please?" Tricia begged.

"Why didn't *you* call?" he asked, his tone a tad accusatory.

"I couldn't. My cell phone's dead, and King must have cut the phone and security system lines to my store."

Russ went to the window and peered through the glass. "I don't see anybody out on the street."

"He was after me, I tell you. Wearing a gray hoodie."

Russ shook his head. "There's nobody there."

Tricia fought the urge to smack him.

"I'm not in the habit of running around the village after midnight in night attire. I'm telling you that guy was chasing me. And for all I know, he was probably the one who killed Susan Morris."

"Really? What makes you say that?"

"He stole something from her just a day or so before she died."

"What was that?"

"An earring."

"I hadn't heard that."

"Well, I'm telling you about it now."

Tricia finally seemed to catch her breath and glanced around the reception area. "What are you doing here so late? I thought you told me you never worked late."

"I'm purging my paper files before I turn the operation over to your *boyfriend*." He did it again—referring to Marshall in a snide fashion.

"Do you have to say it like that?"

He shrugged. "Would you prefer I called him your *lover*? That sounds even more tawdry."

She scowled. "You didn't think it was tawdry when *you* were sleeping with me."

"Ah, those were the good old days. You were—and probably still are—a very good lover, Tricia."

A shiver ran up Tricia's spine. This was not a conversation she wanted to be having when her home had been invaded and robbed and the freak who had done it was probably hanging round in the shadows, waiting to come after her.

"Call the police!" she implored, but Russ just stood there. "Russ!" she tried again.

The sound of a siren cut the night, and Tricia rushed to look out the door. The car pulled to a halt, and an officer jumped out of it and started running—presumably after King.

"See, there was no need to call the cops. And I'm sure your other ex-boyfriend will show up any minute now to comfort you."

"What is your problem with me?" she asked, noticing how cold she felt—and it wasn't just because of her bare feet and skimpy night attire. Her gaze traveled to Russ's office, where she saw several big black bags, knotted at the top and ready for the trash.

"I don't have a problem at all," Russ said mildly. "Well, that's not true. All my problems stem from you—your rejection of me."

"Let's not go over that territory again," she said, and backed away from him. She'd never really noticed just how creepy the man was.

"Why not? I've got nothing but time. Well," he said, and gave a laugh, "that's not exactly true. I'll be leaving the village as soon as the ink is dry on the contract for the sale of the paper, but we've still got time."

"Time for what?"

"To be together."

"I'm in a relationship," Tricia said fiercely.

Russ shrugged. "Eh, you don't love Marshall. You didn't love Baker. And you certainly didn't love me," he said accusingly. "But that doesn't mean we can't have some fun."

Tricia's hackles rose, and again she spied the big bags of trash in his office and realized their significance. Had Russ been working late shredding papers, gone into the alley to toss the bags away, and run into Susan?

"You killed her," she whispered.

"Killed who?" Russ asked, turned his head to see what she was looking at.

"Never mind," Tricia said, realizing that if he *had* killed Susan, what was to stop him from attempting to kill her? But Russ wasn't about to ignore the statement.

"What did you mean just now?"

"That . . . that with your attitude, you must've killed Nikki's love for you," Tricia hedged.

Russ's expression hardened. "I don't think so."

"Then to what do you attribute her leaving?"

"Nikki and I are done. And that's not what you meant when you accused me of a crime just now."

"You must have misunderstood," Tricia said, and edged backward, smacking into the closed, locked door. Her eyes darted left and right, but there wasn't anything nearby but a short metal rack that held copies of the current edition of the *Stoneham Weekly News*.

The gumball lights of another police cruiser caught Tricia's attention to her right, rolling past slowly as Russ stepped closer. "I didn't misunderstand. You think I killed Susan Morris. You think I caught her out back messing around."

"Why would she do that?" Tricia asked, wide-eyed, but it was more with growing fear than innocence.

"You always thought of me as a hack, but I'm first and foremost a reporter—and a damn good one. You didn't think people would talk about you nosing around and asking questions about that bitch's habits."

"No, I didn't," she said, adding more conviction to her voice than she actually felt.

"I talked to Shawn at the pub the same night you did."

Damn.

"Really?" she bluffed.

"Then I ran into Terry at the All Heroes comic-book store. The people in this village love to gossip. And you like to stir up trouble." Tricia glanced to her left. "The officers have probably caught up with Joe King. I think it's safe for me to go on home."

Russ stepped so close, Tricia could feel his breath on her face. She turned her head aside and moved her hand closer to the metal rack.

"You're not going anywhere," Russ said, his voice low and menacing.

Tricia grabbed the rack and flung it at Russ, smacking him sharply in the head. He went down on the floor, but she had no time to assess the damage she'd caused as she turned and fumbled with the lock. But Russ wasn't as injured as he might have been and crawled to his knees, making a grab for Tricia as she opened the door, frigid air rushing in. Russ managed to grab her by the ankle before she could run outside, yanking and causing her to fall onto the cold concrete sidewalk. She bucked and kicked, flipping onto her back, her right foot connecting with Russ's jaw, sending him backward with a wail of pain.

Tricia rolled over, scrambling to her feet, and began to run south, not daring to look behind her. Someone stood on the sidewalk up ahead, and the beam of a powerful flashlight swept up her body and blinded her. She ground to a halt and raised a hand in front of her eyes.

"Tricia?" Baker asked.

"He's right behind me."

The light moved.

"There's no one there," Baker said.

Tricia threw a glance over her shoulder to make sure. "What are you doing here?" she asked, breathless.

"Angelica's dog heard your window break and he started to bark. She called nine one one. Henderson caught King with a sack full of old books. I assume they're yours."

"Yes, they are! He broke into my apartment while I was there and I barely managed to escape!" Tricia looked behind her. The lights were still on at the *Stoneham Weekly News*. She turned back to Baker. "Russ Smith killed Susan Morris."

Baker sighed. "And you came to this conclusion because?" he asked wearily.

"He also caught her dumping her waste behind his office."

Baker looked around Tricia. "Here he comes now."

Tricia turned. Russ walked slowly toward them, his left hand plastered against the side of his face. He stopped, and Tricia ducked behind the police chief, peeking over his shoulder. "Baker, arrest that woman," Russ said thickly. "She attacked me—broke my jaw."

"Well, if I did, it was your own fault. You were going to kill me, too!"

"Not only is she homicidal, she's delusional as well," Russ muttered angrily.

Baker turned to study Tricia's face. She'd seen that look before. The no longer friend—possibly not even acquaintance—was about to blow off her fear and concerns once again. Why did she even bother speaking with the man when he always seemed more inclined to believe the worst of her?

Baker turned back to Russ. "Let's walk back to my car, and I'll call for the EMTs to come and have a look at you," he said reasonably.

"Fine. Just let me lock my office. I wouldn't want a thief to get in and trash everything." He laughed. "But since I've just sold the joint, why should I care?"

Russ turned and headed back to his office.

Baker faced Tricia, studying her face.

"The guy's a jerk, but your theory stinks."

"That's what they told Darwin and Einstein, too."

Baker nodded. "What did you do to him?"

"Uh, I kind of hit him with a metal rack, and when he tripped me, I kicked him in the face, but I don't think I broke his jaw."

Again Baker nodded. He eyed her attire. "Cute jammies."

Tricia felt a blush rise up her neck to warm her cheeks. "Can I go back to my store?" she pleaded. "My feet are freezing."

"Wait until he comes back. I don't want you wandering the streets alone."

"Thank you for your concern," Tricia grated. She turned to leave, but Baker grabbed her by the arm, pulling her around to face him once again.

"I'll talk to him. I'll talk to his employees. I'll talk to his neighbors. But I don't want *you* talking to him. If what you say is true, it won't be easy or quick to build a case against him."

"What if you can't prove he killed Susan? He'll get away with it." And then she remembered what cracked the case against the thief who'd stolen Dolly Dingle figurines from the Happy Domestic several years before. "Video surveillance! You could ask all the businesses along Main Street for—"

"You don't need to tell me how to do my job," Baker admonished her.

"I'm just trying to be helpful." And then Tricia realized what he'd said: he *would* try to build a case against Russ—but only if he thought it was viable. She knew Baker would never arrest a suspect unless he wholeheartedly believed in that person's guilt.

"In the meantime, I don't want you anywhere near Russ Smith," Baker positively growled. "Don't see him, don't talk to him, don't even look at him."

"Yes, sir," Tricia said sarcastically.

Russ approached them once again. He'd donned a jacket and still held his hand fixed against his cheek. Behind him, the lights in his office had been extinguished. The three of them started walking south down Main Street, with Tricia in the lead.

"So, Mr. Smith," Baker began conversationally, "just what

were you doing working at your office so late in the evening?"

Tricia couldn't hear Russ's muffled reply.

Was Baker just placating her, or would he go through with his promise to test her theory?

Only time would tell.

TWENTY-EIGHT

During the next four days Tricia stuck close to home. She and Angelica had lunches and dinners at Angelica's apartment. Instead of taking walks through the village, Tricia employed her treadmill to get in her daily three-mile walk, and her only social encounters occurred when she took Angelica for her physical therapy appointment and their weekly Sunday family dinner. Once again Marshall begged off attending said dinner, but he called a couple of times during Tricia's hibernation. Called—not visited.

Baker kept a low profile, too, with no updates on how his investigation into Susan Morris's death was going.

As time dragged on, Tricia began to experience the same degree of cabin fever that Angelica complained about.

On Monday afternoon Baker tracked Tricia down at Angelica's home, where they were having yet another Booked for Lunch catered meal. June called from the Cookery and was told to "send him up." Of course, first Tricia made sure Sarge was relegated to his bed. He was friendly with just about everyone on the planet—but, for some reason, not Baker.

The chief knocked, and Tricia opened the door for him. "Hello, Grant. Come on in."

Baker nodded and followed her back to the kitchen island, where her tuna plate awaited.

"Angelica," Baker said, nodded in her direction, and took off his hat, holding it in both hands and looking just a little sheepish.

Baker's demeanor came as a bit of a surprise as he admitted, "You were right, Tricia. Video from the Have A Heart bookstore's surveillance cameras plainly showed Russ Smith's truck head down the alley toward Haven't Got a Clue about midnight on the night of Susan Morris's death. Once we could place him at the scene of the crime and tampering with physical evidence, he broke down. He admitted he confronted her, and when he saw what she was burying in his trash tote, he just snapped. Apparently it was the last straw, what with his wife leaving him and the emotional and financial strain he'd been under. My guess is he'll plead temporary insanity."

Tricia shook her head. "Poor Russ."

"You feel sorry for the jerk?" Baker asked.

"Part of me does. But I feel more pity for Susan Morris. What she did wasn't right, but it wasn't worth being killed for, either. What happens now?"

"We've booked him for manslaughter. It'll be up to the district attorney to decide if they'll bring any other charges against him."

"At least he'll be off the streets and not a threat to anyone else," Angelica said.

"Not necessarily," Tricia said. "He might make bail."

"How?" Angelica asked.

"Don't forget, he's expecting a check from Marshall from the sale of the *Stoneham Weekly News*."

Baker shook his head. "From what we've gathered, he was planning to leave the state as soon as the check cleared. It's likely he'll be considered a flight risk and have to stay in jail until the trial."

"You don't think he'll try to make a deal?" Tricia asked.

Baker shrugged. "He may try."

Tricia shook her head and sighed, then looked up, gazing

into Baker's amazing green eyes. "Does this mean I'm off house arrest?"

He frowned. "What do you mean?"

"You told me to lay low."

"And, brother, did she take you at your word," Angelica complained. "We've been cooped up for days."

"You're free to go where you want and do as you please," Baker said, but for some reason he didn't look all that happy about it.

"Thanks for delivering the news in person."

"Yes," Angelica put in. "And now that we know how you nailed Russ, I think we should invest in a surveillance setup," she told Tricia. "We could have a couple of cameras installed between our stores so that if there's ever another break-in, we'd have a better shot at catching the crook or crooks."

"I agree," Baker said. "That video we obtained is the strongest piece of evidence we have against Smith. Without it, he literally might have gotten away with murder."

Tricia let that statement sink in for a moment before her cell phone's ringtone broke the quiet. Sarge gave a bark and stood up in his bed. Tricia snatched the phone from the island and glanced at the number. "It's Marshall. I'll call him back later. He probably just wants an update on the Russ situation."

"Hmm," Baker muttered, picked a tiny piece of lint from his hat, and stuck it into his pants pocket. "Well, I'd better get back to work," he said, giving Tricia a long last look.

"I'll see you out," she said.

"Don't bother. I know the way. Enjoy the rest of your lunch."

He turned, and Tricia followed him to the door, closing it behind him. She returned to her seat, picked up her fork, but then set it down again.

"Diana was right. That man is definitely carrying a torch for you," Angelica said.

"Don't be silly."

"I've seen that look before. He broke off his engagement because he's pining for you."

"Well, he can pine all he wants: he had his shot and he blew it." Tricia picked up her fork with a feeling of defiance, dug into her tuna salad, and shoved it in her mouth.

"You ought to check Marshall's message. Maybe it's important."

Tricia chewed and swallowed. "How can it be important? He hasn't even made the effort to see me during the past four days."

"But he *has* called," Angelica reminded her sister.

"Yes," Tricia conceded, although their conversations weren't all that memorable.

"Listen to the message," Angelica pressed.

"Oh, all right."

Tricia picked up her phone and pressed the icon to listen to voice mail.

"Hey, Tricia. It's Marshall. I heard that Russ Smith has been charged in the Morris murder. That must mean you'll be free for dinner tonight. Call me."

Tricia frowned and set her phone down.

"Well?" Angelica asked. "Will you have dinner with him?"

Tricia shrugged. "I guess so."

"Well, don't sound too thrilled."

Tricia sighed. "That's the problem. I'm not."

TWENTY-NINE

 The stars were out in numbers on that brisk September evening as Marshall drove his Mercedes along Route 101 heading back toward Stoneham. "Penny for your thoughts?" he asked Tricia.

"It was a lovely dinner . . ." she began.

"Why do I think the next word out of your mouth is going to be 'but'?"

Tricia smiled in the darkened car. "So now you can read my mind?"

"Probably more than you'll ever know."

Tricia shrugged. "I was just thinking how strange it is that such a high-end steak house is only a mile or two from the former homeless camp. I haven't had a chance to speak with Hank Curtis, but Antonio told us yesterday that Hank's been able to track down most of the guys who got booted out of there. Several of them have moved on, heading south before it gets too cold. Bobby, who went to the shelter in Nashua, got a grant from the Everett Foundation and will be starting a job retraining program next week."

"That's great. At least a couple of the guys will have better lives."

"Of course, Joe King is in the clink—and he's going to stay there for a while."

"Good. That'll keep him out of your hair."

"I suppose," Tricia said halfheartedly.

"How did a homeless guy learn about your valuable mysteries?"

"The same way everyone else did: by watching that silly TV interview I did. Apparently it played on a regular basis for two or three days anywhere in southern New Hampshire that had a TV or a computer. The grocery store, the library—you name it."

"You couldn't have known you'd be targeted."

"I won't make that mistake if I get a major PR opportunity again."

"I knew you were feeling down; that's why I invited you out to dinner tonight. I just wish I could say something to cheer you up."

"I don't need cheering up, it's just . . . so much has happened since we got back from Ireland. Sometimes it seems like it was just a dream."

"I thought you considered it a nightmare."

"Don't be silly," she chided him, but she didn't elaborate, either.

Marshall took a spin around Stoneham's main drag so he could drop Tricia off at her door. "Can I come in for a few minutes? There's something I want to talk to you about."

"We've been talking for over two hours. You couldn't squeeze it in then?"

He looked at her with puppy dog eyes.

Tricia sighed. "Oh, all right. Just for a moment."

Marshall got out of the car and opened the door for her. With keys in hand, Tricia stepped onto the sidewalk, noticing a figure making its way up the block on the other side of the street. Probably someone leaving the Dog-Eared Page. *Cheers,* she wished, and opened the door to her shop, entering and disabling the security system.

Marshall closed the door, and Tricia strode to the reader's nook, where she dropped her purse and began to unbutton her coat. "What did you want to talk about?"

Marshall removed his coat and slung it over the back of one of the upholstered seats. "Let's sit."

Tricia folded her coat and set it on the big square coffee table before sitting on the adjacent seat.

Marshall reached out, gently took hold of her hand, and got down on one knee, looking up at her with adoring eyes. Every muscle in Tricia's body tensed as she watched him reach into his pocket and withdraw an old-fashioned ring with five glittering diamonds. "Tricia, will you do me the honor of being my wife?"

Tricia's breath caught in her throat. This was not what she had anticipated. She squeezed his hand as her mouth trembled.

"I know you miss being married, and I know I sure as hell miss being with the woman I love. We've both lost our mates, but we don't have to spend the rest of our lives alone," Marshall said.

"I . . . I don't know what to say."

"Say yes."

Tricia's heart sank. "I can't. Not now—not so suddenly."

Marshall rose to stand again. "You don't have to, love. I know it would be a big change, but marriage would be only one part of our lives. We'd still have our businesses; you'll have your cat—I'd never ask you to change any of that."

"We've never spoken about this kind of change in our relationship. It's too soon."

"Not for me," Marshall said earnestly.

"I can't even make up my mind about whether I want to run for the Chamber presidency, let alone make an even bigger decision like the one you're asking of me."

"You don't have to answer today or even tomorrow. But I wanted you to know how I feel. Now I need to know how *you* feel."

How *did* she feel? Two weeks before, she had wondered if they were through forever; now he wanted to devote his life to her?

Tricia sighed. "I just don't know," she answered honestly. "I need time."

Marshall nodded and slipped the ring back into his pocket. He stepped closer and gave her a brief kiss. "Okay. I can wait."

"Thank you," she apologized and stood.

Tricia walked him to the door, where he gave her another kiss—this one long and satisfying.

"I'll talk to you tomorrow," he said, and reached for her hand, giving it a kiss as well.

"Okay."

"Sleep well," he said.

Fat chance of that.

Tricia closed and locked the door and watched as Marshall got into his car and pulled away from the curb, heading for the municipal parking lot.

Once he was out of sight, Tricia padded to the cash desk, picked up the receiver, and fumbled in the dim light to dial a number on the old rotary phone.

"Tricia?" Angelica asked.

"You'll never believe what just happened."

"Probably not."

"Marshall just asked me to marry him."

"He did?" Angelica practically squealed. "That's wonderful."

Tricia let silence fall between them.

"You said no, didn't you," Angelica stated, her words clipped.

"I didn't give him an answer. I couldn't."

"What did he say?"

"He more or less said I could have all the time I need to make a decision."

"That's good . . . kind of."

"He said he missed being married and so did I."

"Well, you have carried a torch for Christopher ever since he died."

"But I didn't want to marry him again. I just feel bad that his life was cut short."

"Don't we all?" Angelica lamented. After all, it was Christopher's last, selfless act that had saved Angelica's life. "What are you going to do now?"

"I don't know. But I know one thing for sure: I'm not going to get a wink of sleep tonight."

A loud knock on the door interrupted their conversation.

"Someone's at the door," Tricia said. "It's probably Marshall."

"Don't you dare open it without looking," Angelica cautioned.

Tricia put the receiver down and leaned forward to peek out the blinds that covered the big display window out front, her mouth dropping. She picked the phone up again. "It's Grant Baker."

"What does he want?" Angelica practically spat.

"I don't know. I'll call you back when I know."

"Okay."

Tricia hung up the phone and walked over to the door, opening it.

"Hey, you should never open the door without looking first," Baker barked.

"I peeked out the front window. What do you want, Grant?"

"Aren't you going to invite me in?"

Tricia stepped back, exasperated, and Baker barreled right into her shop. He was dressed in civilian clothes, which might have made him appear friendlier if he didn't have a scowl plastered across his features.

"What do you want?" she repeated.

"I wanted to thank you for all your help on the Susan Morris murder case."

Tricia blinked in surprise. Had he ever uttered those words to her during the entire time she'd known him? Usually he berated her for getting involved.

"You're welcome," she finally said. "But you could have picked a better time to tell me. Like during regular business hours."

"We can't talk privately during business hours."

"We've done it plenty of other times."

"I guess," he grumbled.

"What did you want to tell me? Has Russ been arraigned? He didn't get out of jail, did he?"

"No, nothing like that. It's just . . . well, I saw Cambridge leave here a few minutes ago."

A flash of anger coursed through her, and Tricia remembered the figure that had been walking along Main Street when she and Marshall returned from the restaurant. "Are you spying on me?" Tricia demanded.

"No. I was out for a walk and—"

"You don't even live near Main Street. Why are you walking around here at this time of night?"

"I needed to think, so I went for a walk. Is that so hard to believe?"

"Yeah," she said shortly. She crossed her arms over her chest. "What were you thinking about?"

"How wrong Diana was for me. How we never really connected."

"Then why did you ask her to marry you?"

"I didn't. She asked me."

"Then why on earth did you say yes?"

"Because . . . it was time. I was tired of being alone."

"Yeah, well, do what Angelica did. Get a dog."

"I don't want a dog. I want you."

"Don't be ridiculous," Tricia said.

"Marry me," Baker practically barked.

"What?"

"I said marry me."

Something inside her trembled. She looked into Grant Baker's mesmerizingly green eyes and felt something within her melt. Tricia always was a sucker for green eyes.

Then she opened her mouth and gave him her answer.

RECIPES

TRICIA'S LEMON CRACKLES

½ cup butter, softened
½ cup brown sugar, packed
¼ cup granulated sugar
1 large egg
2 tablespoons lemon juice
1 tablespoon grated lemon zest
1½ cups all–purpose flour
1 teaspoon baking powder
½ teaspoon baking soda
¼ cup granulated sugar

Preheat the oven to 350°F (180°C, Gas Mark 4). In a large bowl, cream the butter, brown sugar, and first amount of granulated sugar. Add the egg and beat well. Add the lemon juice and zest. Beat until smooth. In another bowl, combine the flour, baking powder, and baking soda. Add to the butter mixture in two additions, mixing well after each addition. Roll the dough into 1-inch balls. Roll each ball in the additional ¼ cup of granulated sugar in a small bowl until each is coated. Arrange the dough balls approximately 2 inches apart. Bake for 10 to 15 minutes or until golden brown. Let the cookies stand on the baking sheets for 5 minutes before removing them to wire racks to fully cool.

Yield: 48 cookies

OLD-FASHIONED APPLESAUCE CAKE

> ¼ pound (1 stick) butter or ½ cup vegetable
>   shortening
> 1½ cups granulated sugar
> 1 cup applesauce
> 2 large eggs
> 2 cups all-purpose flour
> 1½ teaspoons baking soda
> ½ teaspoon salt
> 2 teaspoons ground cinnamon
> ½ teaspoon ground nutmeg
> 1 teaspoon ground ginger (optional)
> ½ cup raisins
> 1 cup chopped walnuts

Preheat the oven to 350°F (180°C, Gas Mark 4). Butter and lightly flour two 8-inch round cake pans or one 9 x 13-inch cake pan. Cream the butter or shortening; gradually add the sugar and beat well. Add the applesauce and blend. Beat in the eggs and mix thoroughly. In a separate bowl, combine the flour, baking soda, salt, cinnamon, nutmeg, and ginger (if using), add to the first mixture, and beat just until mixed. Fold in the raisins and nuts. Spread in the pans or pan and bake, 25 to 30 minutes for the layers, 35 to 40 minutes for the rectangle pan. Test to see if a toothpick comes out clean. Cool in the pans for 5 minutes before turning out onto racks to cool completely. Maple buttercream or cream cheese frosting goes well with this cake, or dust with confectioners' sugar before serving.

Yield: 6 to 8 slices

TOMMY'S EASY GUACAMOLE

> 3 medium ripe avocados, peeled and cubed
> 1 garlic clove, minced
> ¼ to ½ teaspoon salt
> 2 medium tomatoes, seeded and chopped, optional
> 1 small onion, finely chopped
> ¼ cup mayonnaise, optional
> 1 to 2 tablespoons lime juice
> 1 tablespoon minced fresh cilantro
> Crackers, tortilla chips, or French bread slices

Mash the avocados with the garlic and salt. Stir in the remaining ingredients. Serve with the crackers, chips, or bread.

Yield: 2 cups

TOMMY'S CHEESY CORN DIP

> 4 ounces (1 cup) cream cheese, softened
> 1 cup frozen corn, thawed
> ¾ cup spicy chipotle ranch dressing
> 1 cup shredded Mexican-blend cheese
> Tortilla chips

Preheat the oven to 375°F (190°C, Gas Mark 5). In a medium bowl with an electric mixer on medium, beat the cream cheese, corn, dressing, and ½ cup of the Mexican-blend cheese. Transfer to a 2-cup ovenproof baking dish and top with ½ cup Mexican-blend cheese. Bake for 10 minutes or until bubbling. Serve with the tortilla chips.

Yield: 1½ cups

Turn the page for a preview of the next
Booktown Mystery
by Lorna Barrett

A Deadly Deletion

Available in hardcover from Berkley Prime
Crime in July 2021!

Are you out of your mind?" Tricia Miles said, raising her voice. She had good reason to do so, too.

Stoneham Police Chief Grant Baker stood before her in stunned silence. His marriage proposal had been the second Tricia had received within ten minutes—and she hadn't expected either of them.

Tricia's relationship with Marshall Cambridge had pretty much been "friends with benefits." She enjoyed his company, he encouraged her independence, but there had been a distinct lack of passion. She hadn't given him an answer, but she had an answer for Chief Baker.

"Absolutely not!"

"Why won't you marry me?" he asked, sounding like a petulant child.

Tricia kept her jaw from dropping in shock, but only just. "You couldn't commit to me when we were together, and now you've jilted your fiancée weeks before that wedding to ask me to marry you. What are the odds you'll have cold feet again?"

"Zero," he asserted.

"Yeah, and I've got a bridge for sale in Brooklyn," she said sarcastically. She pointed toward the door. "Go."

"Tricia, can't we talk this over?"

"There's nothing to talk about. Go!" she repeated. When he didn't move, she stalked off in the direction of the door, threw it open, and gestured for him to leave.

Just as Baker reached the threshold, the roar of a powerful engine thundered somewhere on Main Street. At first, Tricia wasn't sure which direction it was coming from, but as it grew louder, she realized it was heading north. Baker pushed her aside and darted onto the sidewalk outside Tricia's store, Haven't Got a Clue, just as a big white pickup truck—with lights out—veered toward the sidewalk and Baker. Tricia grabbed him by the back of the shirt pulling him back into her store as the truck swerved back into the street. Before either of them could react, they heard someone yell and the terrible sound of a thud before the truck disappeared down the darkened street.

Baker was the first to recover and dashed up the sidewalk with Tricia in hot pursuit.

Up ahead in the middle of the street lay a crumpled form. As Tricia approached, she recognized just who it was.

"Marshall!" she cried.

Baker fell to his knees in front of the supine figure, searching for a pulse, first at the man's wrist, and then reached for his throat.

"Do something!" Tricia cried as tears welled in her eyes.

Baker rose to his feet, his expression one of shock.

"I'm sorry, Tricia. He's dead."

The blue-and-red emergency lights still flashed out on Main Street more than an hour after the accident.

But was it an accident?

Of course, it was. It had to be.

"Did you say something, Tricia, dear?" Tricia's sister, Angelica, asked, sounding worried.

The rotating colors from the flashing light bars on the

police SUVs below came through the second-floor windows, looking gaudy against the living room's pastel green walls.

Tricia held a glass filled with whiskey, ice, and soda—her second. For some reason, she found the cold condensation beneath her clenched fingers to be of comfort. Well, not comfort, but it proved to her that she could feel something besides the terrible numbness that had encircled her soul.

Marshall. Dead.

"I can't believe it. I . . . I just can't believe it," she murmured.

"I'm here to listen," Angelica said softly from the adjacent chair. "That is if you're up to talking."

Tricia looked up to take in her sister's worried gaze.

"He asked me to marry him." The echo of that proposal kept rattling around in her brain.

"And you were going to say no."

"I was," Tricia said. "But that didn't mean I didn't have feelings for the man. If nothing else, he was my friend." And lover.

Tricia absently petted the soft fur atop Angelica's dog's head. Every so often, the Bichon Frise raised his head, looked up at her with soulful brown eyes, and whimpered. He knew when one of his human friends was in pain.

"He had so many plans," Tricia lamented.

"What will happen with the sale of the *Stoneham Weekly News*?" Angelica asked. "Did Marshall sign the final paperwork?"

Tricia shrugged and took a sip of her by-now watery whiskey. "I don't know. Why do you ask?"

Angelica suddenly stiffened in her chair. "Uh, no reason," she said, but for some reason, her voice had risen in pitch.

Tricia shook her head. What would happen to the women at the little weekly newspaper? They'd been nervous when its owner had put it up for sale—and was now destined for jail. Surely nobody else would be interested in buying the horrible little rag. Marshall had planned to resurrect the dying enterprise. Earlier that evening, over dinner, he'd outlined the plans he'd devised for the paper. Tricia now wished she'd paid more attention to that conversation.

Suddenly, she had a lot of regrets.

"Are you sure I can't get you something to eat?" Angelica asked. Offering food was her way of showing concern. She put such care into the dishes she prepared for others—and, of course, herself.

Tricia shook her head. "We had a lovely dinner at the country club outside of Nashua." She frowned. Marshall's last dinner. And then she'd gone and spoiled his evening by refusing to give him an answer to his proposal. But then, maybe he'd died with his heart full of hope.

Like her ex-husband Christopher?

Yeah, she'd promised him moments before he died that she'd again wear the engagement ring he'd given her years before. And she had, but only for a few months and mostly on a chain around her neck. She wouldn't get the chance to do the same with the ring Marshall had offered.

"I suppose Chief Baker will want you to make a formal statement," Angelica said.

"It'll be brief, that's for sure. I didn't see much of anything. Just that white pickup careening down the block." She shuddered at the memory, slopping the last of her drink onto poor Sarge, who didn't seem to notice. Another wave of anguish assaulted her. Tricia hadn't taken the time to do more than drag a comb through her hair and freshen her makeup for her (last) date with Marshall.

Her mouth trembled.

"Why don't you stay here tonight?" Angelica suggested and reached to place a hand on her sister's arm.

Tricia looked down at the boot her sister still wore on her right foot—part of her recovery from bunion surgery. Although Angelica was getting around better, she was in no position to host a guest. And if Tricia was going to have to change sheets, she'd rather do it on her own bed—and certainly not that night.

"It's good of you to offer, but I think I'll just go home."

"What if the chief wants to get hold of you?"

"I'll text him to let him know I'm going back to my apartment, but first I'll take Sarge out for a tinkle break before I leave."

"Oh, you're so good to both of us," Angelica clucked.

Tricia got up, taking her now-empty glass to the kitchen and placing it in the dishwasher. Then she headed for the door, slipped on her jacket, and reached for the dog's leash. He knew that sound and came bounding across the room like a gazelle. "We'll be back in a few minutes," Tricia called.

"I'll be here."

Tricia reached down and picked up the dog, carrying him down the stairs. Not that he couldn't handle them, but he sometimes tended to try to trip whoever was at the end of his tether.

Tricia disabled the security system and exited the Cookery's back door, still carrying Sarge, finally setting him down when she reached a patch of grass on the other side of the alley.

Knowing this was his last foray outside for the night, Sarge took his time sniffing for the perfect spot to christen. "Speed it up, Sarge. It's chilly out," Tricia chided him, but Sarge was not to be hurried.

Tricia gazed up and down the alley. It was illegal to park vehicles after hours behind the businesses that lined Stoneham's Main Street. And yet . . .

Tricia squinted. Could it be a white pickup truck parked at the south end of the alley?

After what happened to Marshall, Tricia wasn't about to investigate.

She yanked on Sarge's leash. "Ready or not, it's time to go in," she told him.

Sarge dug in his heels.

"Sarge!"

The vehicle's headlights suddenly flashed to life—instantly switching to the powerful high beams—and the truck was immediately on the move, heading straight up the alley.

Tricia bent down, grabbed Sarge, tucking him under her arm like a football, and made it across the asphalt and up the concrete steps behind the Cookery just before the truck would have hit her.

It roared past, heading for Hickory Street. Surely Stoneham's best would catch the driver and arrest him—or her.

Breathing hard, and with shaking hands, Tricia reentered the Cookery. She set Sarge down and fumbled for her phone, quickly texting Chief Baker.

The same truck that hit Marshall just came after me in the alley behind the Cookery!

Seconds later, Baker answered. *Stay put.*

The sound of a siren broke the night as Tricia turned on every light in the Cookery and planted herself by the store's entrance, peering out the door's plate glass window to watch for Baker. He was there in seconds. Tricia fumbled to unlock the door.

"Did your men get him?"

"It's too soon to tell," Baker said as Sarge, who was no fan of Stoneham's top cop, began to growl. "Are you sure the truck was aiming for you?"

"There was nobody else in the alley."

Small though he was, Sarge had sharp teeth, which he bared, looking like he might pounce at any second.

"Can you put that damn dog away?" Baker barked.

"This is his home," Tricia remarked, "and he's protecting it. It's what dogs do."

Baker's lip curled, but he took a step back just the same.

Tricia picked up Sarge who launched into full-throated barking. "I'll take him upstairs. Then, if you'd be so kind, would you walk me home?" It was only a few steps down the sidewalk, but Tricia felt rattled.

Baker's eyes lit up. "Of course," he readily agreed. "I'll check in with my team and be back in a minute."

"Thanks."

Tricia turned the lock on the door and, still holding onto Sarge, headed for the door that led to Angelica's apartment. She had a feeling her evening was about to get a whole lot longer.

ABOUT THE AUTHOR

LORNA BARRETT is the *New York Times* bestselling author of the Booktown Mysteries, including *A Killer Edition*, *Poisoned Pages*, and *A Just Clause*. She lives in Rochester, New York.

CONNECT ONLINE

LornaBarrett.com
LornaBarrett.Author
LornaBarrett

Ready to find
your next great read?

Let us help.

Visit prh.com/nextread

Penguin
Random
House